THE GIRL I WAS

THE GIRL I WAS

A Novel

JENEVA ROSE

CORNER STAR PRESS

CORNER STAR PRESS ✸

Print ISBN 978-1-7378637-0-0

This is a work of fiction. Names, characters, places, and incidents either are the product of the author's imagination or are used fictitiously, and any resemblance to actual persons, living or dead, is entirely coincidental.

To the girl I was.
Without you,
I wouldn't be me.

*"Sometimes I wish life was written pencil
so we could erase it and write it all over again."*

—Thisuri Wanniarachchi

ONE

AN EMAIL WITH the subject line "Please come to HR" pops up on my computer just as I'm about to log out for the day.

I groan audibly. It's 4:25 p.m.—I can sneak out and say I didn't see the email.

I tap my fingertips against my desk, contemplating. They don't make the cute nail click sound, though; I'm prone to chewing them off. I have tried to stop biting them many times throughout my thirty-some-odd years, but it's no use—they always find their way back to my teeth. Old habits don't die.

The sound of drawers opening and closing in the other cubicles, shuffling feet, and laughter fills the office. Everyone else is packing up for the day.

I push out my desk chair and grab my purse and jacket. Fine, I'll stop in to see what HR wants. I've been a contract employee at the company for a year, working in social media marketing. Perhaps they're finally wising up and hiring me permanently.

Outside of HR, I knock twice.

"Come in," Janet calls out.

Opening the door, I find her sitting behind her desk. She's plump, with dark eyes and a permanent scowl. Must come with the job.

"Hi, I got an email saying I was supposed to come here," I say.

She clears her throat and shuffles around a few file folders on her desk, then gestures for me to sit.

"Yes. Alexis Spencer."

"The one and only," I say, taking a seat. I push my hair behind my ear and force a casual smile. I've never been promoted before, so I'm not sure how to act in these situations. Good things rarely happen to me, but I could get used to this giddy feeling—like a swarm of butterflies fluttering around my belly. It makes me sit up a little taller.

"You've been a contractor here for one year."

I nod. Is that a question or a statement? My tight smile eases into a real grin as I realize this is it: I'm finally getting hired on. I don't even care what the pay is. I just want those glorious bennies! Paid time off. Dental. That 401k thing Andrew's always talking about.

And the coveted health insurance. Last year, when I broke my arm falling down a flight of stairs at a bar, I just had to hope the bone would fuse together properly over time or however broken bones mend. When I got into a car accident—okay, *two* car accidents—I refused an ambulance and called an Uber to take me home both times. Sure, I had to pay a cleaning fee, but I didn't die, so it was fine. Without health insurance, I was living every day dangerously. And I'll finally get one of those yearly checkups; it's been ten years since my last one. "Doc, I'll have the works" is what I'd tell them. "Check every nook and cranny."

Janet hesitates, looking down at a file folder and then finally back at me. She folds her lips in before she speaks. "I'm sorry to say this, Alexis, but we're going to have to let you go."

"Wh-what?" I stammer. "Why? You guys said you were hiring me on full time."

She shakes her head. "I'm afraid not. The company has decided to outsource our contractor work."

"It's already outsourced. To *me*." My eyes widen in disbelief.

"And they're going to outsource it further. I'm sorry, but budgets were slashed again, and the company had to cut somewhere." Janet glances over my shoulder, her eyes like a pendulum, thanks to that damn clock behind me. She wants to just start her weekend already.

"Okay," I say. "Is there any severance?" I'm actually not even sure what that is. I heard it mentioned on an episode of "The Office."

"No," Janet says slowly, as if speaking to a child. "You're a contract employee, so there are no benefits." She clears her throat and starts to stand. "We'll need you to clean out your desk, and I'll need to collect your employee badge." She holds out her hand.

I look down at the badge clipped to my shirt. It's red, not like the employees' green badges. "Alexis Spencer" is written in bold black letters; in the photo, I have a big smile.

"Can't I keep it?" I rub the hard plastic. "As a keepsake."

"No, I'm sorry. For security reasons, you can't keep it."

I let out a sigh and unclip the badge, handing it over. My fingers clamp down, holding it for an extra second or two before Janet rips it away.

"I'll walk you to your cubicle now." She pulls out a cardboard box from behind her desk.

Begrudgingly, I take it from her, raising my chin. "I don't need to be walked to my desk," I say, but my voice cracks, betraying my bravado.

Janet gives me a stern look. "It's policy, Alexis."

Defeated, I follow her out of the office, down the hallway,

and back to my dark, tiny cubicle. She glances back at me several times, like I'm some sort of criminal she needs to keep an eye on.

Janet stops just outside my cubicle, crossing her arms in front of her chest and saying, "I'll be right here."

On my desk, everything but the plant Andrew bought for me when I got the job belongs to the company. It's a little brown at the tips of the fleshy leaves. It's a succulent, and I didn't really know how to care for it, so I just brought it a Dixie cup of water on Fridays. The plant and I have a lot in common, both a little rough around the edges with the inability to properly care for ourselves.

"Well, I guess I didn't really need the box," I say, picking up the plant, but I accidentally knock it over instead, dirt flying all over my former desk. "I stand corrected."

Janet waves me off as I walk out onto the busy streets of Chicago, holding the box that's far too large for such a tiny plant. People pour out of high-rise buildings, hurrying to beat traffic and get home to start their weekend. Without a job, what is a weekend now? Just an end? Because I have nothing to do during the week. I let out a sigh and then take a deep breath of that crisp city air—which is a combination of bus diesel, meaty hotdogs, and rotting garbage. Car horns and sirens blare in the distance, a staple of any major metropolis. It's mid-October and rather chilly here in Chicago, so I set my box down and slip on my jacket. The plant rolls around as I pick it back up. It's surely not going to survive this. Not sure I am either.

My phone buzzes, and I pull it from my purse. It's Andrew.

"Hello," I say in my cheeriest voice.

"Alexis? What's wrong?" he asks.

We've known each other for seventeen years, so he knows

I'm not a cheery person. We were friends before we were partners, but we've been dating for seven of those years, and yes, that's a long time. But I'm what you call "not the easiest person to love." My words, not his.

"Nothing. Just walking home." I try to be as nonchalant as possible. A jogger bumps into me but quickly apologizes. I give a tight smile back.

"Oh, okay. Great. Don't forget: we have dinner reservations at Alinea."

My shoulders drop, but I stop myself before audibly groaning. I completely forgot about dinner.

"I didn't," I lie.

"I'm leaving the office early, so I should be home soon. I love you," he says.

I can practically hear him smiling, and I wish I could match his enthusiasm. But that's just not me. It never has been. Even the "*Girl, Take a Bath*" chick couldn't help me, because I put the "toxic" in toxic positivity. Also, there's no positivity. I've tried to have that upbeat outlook on life with excitement and all that jazz, but it's impossible. Actually, it's biology. I looked it up once. It's an old defense mechanism that we as humans see the worst in things in order to protect us from potential danger. Sure, there's been evolution and whatnot, but I didn't seem to evolve like Andrew did.

"Love you too." I end the call, slipping my phone back into my bag. I already know dinner isn't going to happen, and I know this because I know me.

TWO

I HEAR THE front door open and close as I lie in bed, wearing plaid pajamas and munching on a bag of SkinnyPop popcorn. I'm not even sure why I buy this brand. Yes, it's low in calories, but I end up eating the whole bag anyway. I toss another handful in my mouth. My hair is tied up in a high ponytail, and I have a half a bottle of wine in my belly. The other half is waiting for me in the kitchen.

"Alexis, I'm home. Are you almost ready?" Andrew calls out.

I swallow hard and stare at the large television screen sitting on the long dresser across from our king-sized bed. "The Bachelor" is on. Andrew's footsteps echo through the apartment, and moments later, the bedroom door opens.

"Alexis, what are you doing? We have to leave in thirty minutes." His eyes are wide, and his voice is full of disappointment. He's dressed in a suit and tie with cap-toe Oxford shoes, a pair of tortoiseshell glasses perched on the bridge of his nose.

"I'm not feeling well." I sip my wine before returning my attention to the television. Why are all the women so pretty and thin on this show? Where're the average-looking chicks? Or the plus-sized women? Is TV love only for attractive people?

Andrew furrows his brow and drags a hand through his

hair. It's mocha brown and stands at attention, thanks to the overpriced clay he rubs into it every morning.

"If you're not feeling well, why are you drinking wine?"

"It calms me."

"What's going on, Alexis?" He sits next to me. Pushing a few pieces of hair out of my face, he looks into my eyes, but I don't look back. If I do, I might fall apart.

"I know something's up. Just tell me so we can talk about it."

"It's nothing," I say, scooting out of bed and making my way to the kitchen. The Chicago skyline is lit up through the floor-to-ceiling windows in the living room: a million bright lights set against the black night. When Andrew and I first moved in, I was in awe of the sight, and I told myself I'd never take it for granted. But you can get used to anything, I've learned. Even the most spectacular things.

Andrew follows behind. He's not going to let this go, and neither am I.

"I've known you too long, so you're not fooling me," he presses.

"I just don't feel like going out to dinner." I grab the open bottle of wine from the island countertop and pour the rest of it into the glass. It's nearly to the rim. The perfect pour.

"I made these reservations months ago."

"So I made up my mind an hour ago that I'm not going." I gulp my wine. Immediately, my core feels warm, and I'm more relaxed.

"Seriously, what's wrong?" Andrew's voice is calm but now edged with frustration. He's not like me in that sense—I am, without fail, emotional and impulsive in almost every situation. We're actually different in every way. Where my hair is blonde, his is dark. Where my eyes are light green, his are a deep chocolate brown. Where my stature is petite, his is towering. Where my outlook on life is pessimistic, his is optimistic. Opposites attract, I guess.

"Nothing, I just don't want to go." I shrug. I have a very peculiar conflict style, the only thing for which I credit my communications degree: avoidance meets quick-to-anger rashness. I also learned it's not healthy, but that was where the education stopped. I've defined it and identified it, and I've learned to live with it.

"Are you serious? We've been wanting to go to this place forever."

"I haven't. You have."

"That's just not true, Alexis. Please, for me." His eyes plead with mine.

Self-destruction, begin activation, a tiny voice inside my head says. I gulp my wine again, fuel for the little whisper. "Just go by yourself if it means that much to you. Or better yet, take another girl." I narrow my eyes.

"What?" Andrew looks at me like I'm crazy. "Where the hell did that come from?"

"Go ahead," I dare him. "Take someone else. It's better that way." I scowl into my wine.

Andrew closes his eyes, rubbing his forehead. "Fine. I'll cancel the reservations, if that's what you want." He undoes the cuffs of his white button-down and rolls up the sleeves. Tugging at his tie, he loosens it and leans against the counter. Folding his brawny arms in front of his chest, he exhales and crosses one foot over another.

"That's exactly what I want." I raise my chin.

"Okay." Andrew stares at me. "Well, what do you want to do tonight then?"

"Nothing."

His eyes scan the kitchen island, landing on the cardboard box.

Shit. I forgot to toss that. This is the last thing I want to talk about. I'm not a person who works through things. I work around them.

He picks up my decrepit succulent. My mind suddenly flashes on a memory of Andrew giving me the little plant.

"Congrats on your new job, my love. It's a succulent, which sounds like 'success,' and I know you're going to have so much of it. I'm beyond proud of you." Andrew beamed as he handed it to me. He came home early from work when he heard I'd finally landed a job after almost a year of searching. I looked at that fleshy little plant and thought quite a few things.

1. It was the sweetest thing anyone had ever gotten for me.

2. I couldn't believe he entrusted a living thing to me.

3. That succulent connected me to success, a job, and Andrew, and as long as I could keep it alive, I would have all three.

The memory fades away quickly as I remember that Sucky the Succulent most likely didn't survive the trip home today. And yes, the name I gave it should tell you all you will ever need to know about me.

"Hey, this is the plant I got you. What happened to it?" Andrew looks at me. "Did you lose your job?"

My cheeks redden to the shade of the merlot I'm drinking. "It's none of your business." I narrow my eyes again as I meet Andrew's incredulous gaze.

"Alexis, we live together, and we've been together for seven years. It *is* my business. What happened?"

"What always happens. The universe shits all over me. You know how my life is . . . it's shit. Always has been, always will be."

"Not again," he groans.

Self-destruction activated, the tiny voice says.

"Oh, screw you!" I yell, marching toward the bedroom and flipping my wispy hair. Yep, always one for the dramatics, I am. Had there been a small end table or standing fan in my path, I would have certainly knocked it to the ground to punctuate my anger even more.

Andrew stomps after me. "You know what, Alexis?"

"What, Andrew?" I spin around. The wine glass is already at my lips, right where it belongs.

His shit-brown eyes widen. "You need to grow up!" Typically, when I wasn't mad at him, I'd say his eyes were like milk chocolate or like some other brown-colored, pleasant thing. But, not now. Right now, his eyes are shit.

I lower the glass. The crimson-colored wine leaves its mark on my sharp tongue.

"I'm in my thirties. I'm as grown as I've ever been."

"Alexis, look at you." He points at me, as if I don't know who I am. "You just lost your job. You have a horseshit attitude about everything, and you're so stuck in the past you can barely exist in the present. Your life isn't what it is because you're unlucky. It's what it is because you never took responsibility for it, for any of it." He draws in a long, deep breath.

I've never seen him this angry before. Our fights were usually like the flame of a candle: small and quickly extinguished. But this one is epic in comparison.

His turd eyes burn with dejection, staring so deep into mine that I have to look away for a second. It's as if he's preparing for a showdown: the bull and the matador.

We lock eyes again, and I tip the wine glass back, pouring copious amounts of liquid courage/regret down my throat. It gives me a small amount of time to think of something clever or mean to say. I haven't decided which route I'll take. A few drops slither out from my lips, dribbling onto my pajama top. I wipe the drops away with my other hand and silently curse the stained fabric.

Yes, I do always blame my shortcomings on a lack of luck or on my shitty past, and Andrew knows me better than I know myself—although I would never tell him that. We were friends long before we started dating, because we just didn't get the timing right. I also had issues with commitment. The more people you have in your life, the more you can lose. And then there were periods that we were on and off, but we always found our way back to one another, and we've been going strong for seven years—minus this fight, of course. Since Andrew's been in my life for so long, he had the "pleasure" of knowing my college party-girl self, who did what she wanted and didn't give a damn about anyone. I blame her for my current life.

See, eighteen-year-old me lived by a number of "inspirational" quotes, except she used them to rationalize her failures, her laziness, her shortcomings, and essentially everything that went wrong in her life. Some of those words she lived by included:

"Everything happens for a reason."

"It will all work out in the end."

"If it's meant to be, it will be."

"Things go wrong so you can appreciate them when they're right."

"Everything is okay in the end. If it's not okay, then it's not the end."

"Whatever will be, will be" (and when she was feeling festive, "Que sera, sera").

As it turns out, inspirational quotes can be quite discouraging and uninspiring when taken out of context and placed in the wrong hands. Those "words to live by" were my "words to hold responsible." It was just so much easier to blame the universe rather than myself for my problems, and I still tend to do that, but not to the degree my former self did. I'm like a jigsaw puzzle that someone got bored with and decided not to finish putting together.

Shit. Andrew's still staring at me, and I'm now sucking at an empty wine glass. Jeez, how long have I been standing here drinking air?

"Well, are you going to say something?" His patience with me has clearly worn thin.

I set the glass on the bedside table and retake my position in front of him, poker-faced. "Yeah, I'm going to say something."

Silence fills the room. I don't know what to say because, well, wine. But I'm not going to lose this battle. *Think. Think!* I probably should apologize and drop the whole thing, but that's not really my style. I enjoy getting the last word in, even if the last word is completely wrong, entirely moronic, and wholly untruthful.

"Then say it, Alexis." He tightens his jaw.

I try to stand a bit taller, faking self-assurance. "If that's what you think of me, then we shouldn't be together. Clearly, this isn't working."

"Is that what you really think?" he presses.

"Yes, Andrew. You want to stand here and judge me like I'm such an awful person? Well, *you're* the one dating me, so what does that say about you? Or maybe I am the way I am because you make me so damn miserable."

Okay, that's a lie. The truth is Andrew doesn't make me miserable. He's actually the best thing in my life. He's the reason I'm slightly less intolerable now than how I used to be.

Without him, I'd be worse off, if that's even possible. After all, I am unemployed and broke. But in heated moments where getting the upper hand is at stake, you have to say awful things you don't really mean. That's just how relationships work.

"Thank you." He stands up straight, turns away from me, and heads out of the bedroom.

"For what?" I had never gotten a response like that before. I follow behind, calling his name and hoping he was thanking me for pointing out something insightful and that his gratefulness isn't sarcasm.

Andrew turns back to me, his coat slung over his arm. "For stopping me from making the biggest mistake of my life." He slides a small blue box from his coat pocket, and not just any blue—Tiffany blue, the most beautiful blue in the whole world. He opens the box, revealing a diamond ring that puts the Christmas lights hanging from our balcony—which I have yet to take down, and yes, I know it's the middle of October—to shame. It's closer to Christmastime now, so it really doesn't make sense to take them down.

Before I can say "Yes," he snaps the box closed. The box makes that noise, that beautiful clap with an echo, like in *Pretty Woman*, but unlike Richard Gere, Andrew's not kidding.

I look up at him. "You were going to propose?" My lip quivers. I try to stop it, but I've hit that level of unstoppable sadness. First, it's the lips you can't control. Then, your breaths come fast and deep, almost like strained, raspy hiccups—so embarrassing. Next, your face crumples up like a piece of cheap aluminum foil, regardless of the amount of Botox you've had injected. That sadness is deeper than paralysis.

Tears fill his eyes as he tries to hold back his disappointment. "I was."

I reach my hand out, but he doesn't grab for it. I let it fall back down to my side.

Shit. What did I do? I always mess everything up. I could be taking helfies (hand photos) of my gorgeous ring right now and uploading them to every social media platform available, showing the world I'm not a loser, that someone out there likes it enough to put a ring on it, and that I'm worth something. But no—instead, I'm standing here watching my whole relationship disappear faster than the wine bottle I just put away.

"I love you, Alexis," Andrew says with complete and utter sincerity.

"I love you, too." I say it quickly before he can get in a "but," a "however," or some other dumbass conjunction that will clash with his affection for me.

"But . . ." he says.

Damn it. There it is.

"Loving you isn't enough anymore. It's just not. I love you with all my heart, all my being, and all of my existence, but it's not enough. How can I plan a future with you when you're so stuck in the past?" He drops his head a bit, looking down.

I'm not sure if the question is rhetorical, but I need to answer it. The tears are escaping from my eyes faster than I can wipe them away. "Andrew, I . . ." I try to get the words out, but they're lodged in my throat.

"Don't." He puts on his coat and slips the box back into his breast pocket. "I love you, but I'm leaving."

Oh my God! What did I do? Andrew is my everything. What? This can't be it. We can't be done. I thought this was just another stupid battle, but it was the war.

I grab his arm as he turns to reach for the door handle. Dropping to my knees, I plead and beg for the first time in my life. "Please. Don't do this, Andrew. I love you so much it hurts," I sob through the words. I hold on to him as he twists the door handle. But without another word, he leaves, and as my hands slip from his arm, I fall to the ground.

And there it is: I've officially hit rock bottom.

THREE

SOMEHOW, AFTER WHAT seems like a lifetime of ugly crying, I pick myself off the floor and stumble into the kitchen to grab another bottle of wine. I pop the cork and drink straight from the bottle because that's what you do in these situations. If I had any ice cream, I'd surely be packing my face with that right now too.

I wander aimlessly around the apartment, just me and my bottle, ending up in the walk-in closet off the second bedroom. It's a mess of papers and jumbled boxes—all mine.

"Everything happens for a reason," I repeat to myself through gasping sobs. "In the end, everything will be all right. If it's not, then it's not the end."

I reach for a large cardboard box on the top shelf labeled "College Memories" in permanent black marker. The box falls to the ground, spilling out its contents like vomit all over the floor: photo albums, shot glasses, CDs, T-shirts, and journals. I plop down in the middle of the mess, hugging the wine bottle to my chest.

Flipping through the albums, I try to recall my own memory of each photo but fail to do so because every one was taken when I was drunk. I barely recognize the girl in the photos, the girl I was: an eighteen-year-old size four dressed in skintight, barely there party-girl outfits, sporting heavy eye makeup and long blonde extensions that extended past the small breasts she prayed every day would grow. Just a young, naïve, stupid girl without a clue.

Now in my thirties, I dress somewhat appropriately. I'm now a size ten-ish, but sometimes I lie about that, claiming to be an eight or a six if I'm dehydrated. I've traded the extensions for a more sensible lob. My makeup is subtle. My clothes are modest, with room for my organs to expand and move around. My breasts have grown several cup sizes, thanks to Dr. Kerson. Apparently, God doesn't listen to prayers for larger breasts. Thoughts and prayers, my ass.

I take another swig of wine.

In one picture, I'm on my knees—taking a beer bong. In another, a couple of blotto frat guys hold me up by my legs while my hands grip the sides of a beer keg. I'm wearing a denim miniskirt—*classy*. In yet another photo, I'm clutching a shot glass and posing with a group of fellow college kids I no longer recognize. They were probably my best friends that evening, as all people you meet during a drunken escapade are.

Taking a deep drink, I consider the few recollections I have of college. I always wished that my college memories would outlast my student loan payments, but with $22,000 in debt left, I don't think that's going to happen.

A few photos later, I recognize the group of three girls I'm standing shoulder-to-shoulder with, all huddled in front of a beer pong table. I'm in the middle, wearing a crop top I cut up myself and tight low-rise jeans that are two sizes too small. I'm not actually drunk in this picture. Buzzed, yes. Soon to be drunk, yes. But not drunk yet. I'm smiling, my long blonde hair has perfect ringlets, my makeup looks freshly applied, and my eyes aren't glazed over. Wow, quite a rarity; the Mona Lisa among my photo collection.

Katie stands beside me in the photo, several inches taller. Her shoulder-length, no-nonsense haircut fits her; she was the mom of our group. Despite her average looks, she was an above-average friend, always there to hold my hair back and make sure I didn't die of alcohol poisoning or asphyxiate on my own vomit. Without her, I wouldn't have made it past twenty years old. She got me through a lot of dark and difficult times—times that are partly to blame for why I am the way I am. She and I grew apart, as most people do after college. According to Facebook, she married and became an emergency room doctor at a hospital in Chicago. I, on the other hand, got temp job after temp job, most of which didn't require a college degree, and never married, as earlier events this evening show.

I moved to Chicago too, but not for some fancy career. Andrew got accepted to the University of Chicago's Booth School of Business, and after graduating with his MBA, he was recruited by Baird's Chicago office for something to do with banking. I'm not really sure what all his job entails, but he makes a lot of pretty PowerPoint decks.

I know what you're thinking—he's quite the catch. How did someone like me keep someone like him around for so long? The hundred-hour work week makes the heart grow fonder, but my guess is he thought I was a diamond in the rough that needed time to develop. Turns out, I was actually just a dirty rock.

I empty the last few drops of wine into my mouth, toss the bottle aside, and peer at the face of my former self. "Damn you," I slur.

My eyes scan to the right of the photograph, and I smile, seeing Nikki beside me in a fit of laughter, her mouth open. Nikki and I were best friends, roommates, and partners in crime (meaning we always partied together). We're still friends to this day, and by that, I mean Facebook friends that occasionally like each other's posts and never miss out on writing "Happy birthday!" on each other's walls. She's married now with kids. Having a family of her own was what she had always wanted, and she got it.

I examine the last person in the photo: Claire. She's standing, perfectly poised. Her deep brown hair is full of thin caramel highlights, ending just below her large, natural breasts. Claire was average in everything except her looks. She had it all: big lips, perfectly shaped eyebrows, high cheekbones, an hourglass shape, and large emerald eyes. She even made the girls drool.

Claire was in college for one thing—her M.R.S. degree. But not just any M.R.S. degree—the trophy wife degree. I received a save-the-date in the mail a few weeks ago from her. Written in black flowing cursive letters on a piece of thick and expensive-looking paper were the words "Save the Date for the Wedding of Dr. Jon Ashford and Claire Denton." Ha! Only Claire would include the title of Dr. in her save-the-date.

I had bumped into her a few months ago (which is maybe the only reason I received a save-the-date). She told me everything: she had met Dr. Jon Ashford while waitressing at a high-end restaurant. In a stroke of serendipity, a week later, she was rushed to the hospital after being struck by a car while out for a jog. Who ended up being her doctor? None other than Dr. Jon Ashford. What are the odds?

Well, for any normal person, one in a billion—but for Claire, one in one-and-a-half. I'm pretty sure she purposely got hit by a car in front of his hospital. I definitely wouldn't put it past her. One broken leg, a minor head injury, and a fractured rib for the chance to marry a doctor? The Claire I knew would make that trade any day.

I look at the faces of my friends, realizing they each got everything they wanted in life: a husband, a family, a successful career, and trophy-wife status. It all just worked out for them. And then there's me, well, her. I glare at myself and flick the photo away so I don't end up ripping it apart.

That selfish bitch took everything from me: Andrew, my future, my career, everything. Eighteen-year-old me only cared about herself in the present. She had no regard for me, well, the me I am now. I wish she would have taken things more seriously, tried harder, studied more, partied less, and given my future a chance. Things would have been different if she would have taken responsibility for her own life, because now it's mine, and let me tell you, it sucks.

I was so stupid and ignorant, and yet I thought I knew it all. I honestly thought it would all work out in the end, that one day things would be exactly how I had always pictured they'd be. I thought this perfect ending I dreamed of would require little to no effort from me, because life is just supposed to work out. Right?

I don't realize I'm crying again until a teardrop splashes onto the pile of photos. I reach for an old rolled-up college T-shirt. As I pull it toward me, it unravels to reveal a full bottle of cheap Russian vodka. My friends had bought it for me at a flea market from a Ukrainian woman after my mo—

No. I won't think about that now. Today's been hard enough, and I don't need yet another reminder of how shitty my life has become.

The vodka label is mostly peeled off, minus a graphic of a circle with four black dots equally spaced around the perimeter. Each dot has a line connecting to a fifth black dot in the middle of the circle. A Post-It note taped just below the label reads, "*Dear Lexi, we love you. We always will. The woman told us to drink this in case of emergency. 'Drink to forget. Drink to repeat,' she said, whatever that means. We're not entirely sure; it was hard to understand her. Love, Katie, Nikki, and Claire.*"

I wipe my face with the T-shirt, getting a whiff of stale Miller Lite beer in the process. I grab the bottle of vodka and a shot glass from the box, unscrew the rusty cap, and pour a shot.

I raise my glass to the stack of photos. "Here's to you, you dumb bitch. I wish that I could fix you, that I could go back in time and fix every mistake I ever made. I wish you had a fricking clue. I wish I could take back every stupid thing you ever did." I toss back the shot. And then another.

And then another.

And then another . . . .

FOUR

I LIFT MY head from a lumpy pillow that's definitely not mine. My head is throbbing, my body is achy, and my eyes are covered in a thick coat of mascara and gunk. The yellowed sheets I'm wrapped in smell of sweat and beer. I groan, sitting up in the small twin-sized bed in a room I don't recognize at all. Wiping at my face, I attempt to focus.

Where the hell am I? Whose bed is this? Shit, what the hell did I do last night?

I pull the sheets off and let out a huge sigh of relief that I'm still wearing my clothes, but not ones I remember putting on: straight leg Abercrombie jeans and a white long-sleeve top with several wine and beer stains on the chest. My hair is a tangled mess, and my clothing is somewhat disheveled from a heavy, drunk sleep (I hope).

Where's my purse? Or my shoes, for that matter?

Looking under the bed, I pull out a pair of women's underwear that isn't mine, an open box of condoms, and dirty socks and boxers. The walls are splattered with posters of half-naked women, Tara Reid in a bikini, Christina Aguilera in a still-shot from her "Dirrty" music video, and Sarah Michelle Gellar in a red leather get-up. Pretty outdated, if you ask me. My bare feet slap against the scuffed-up hardwood floor as I pace the room.

Andrew is going to be so pissed at me. Wait, does he even have a right to be mad? He's the one who broke up with me, so it's really none of his business! And since we're broken up, it's not cheating, right? Oh God, I sound like Ross from "Friends." I'm the *we were on a break* person. Ugh.

But wait—did I even cheat? I'm fully dressed. I woke up alone, granted in someone else's room, a guy's room, for that matter. Oh, whatever. I'm young-ish, wild, and free. And apparently that translates into I have no shoes, no purse, and no recollection of last night.

Loud yells and grunts coming from downstairs startle me. Okay—I'm not alone.

Quickly checking a hanging mirror, I try my best to smear last night's makeup back into its place and finger-comb my hair. I hike up jeans a little higher and pull my breasts up into their store-bought position. I still look like a bag of trash, but it'll have to do.

I need to get home, find Andrew, and make things right—before he leaves me for good. I feel like a cat in our relationship, nine lives, baby. Although, I might not have any left. But first things first, I have to figure out where the hell I am.

Sliding my hand against the stucco wall to steady my hungover self, I tiptoe down an old wooden staircase to the first floor. The stairs creak slightly with each step. As I reach the landing, I see a group of college-aged guys huddled around an old tube television in the corner of the living room. Two are playing a video game while the others watch. Empty beer cans and red Solo cups litter the room, which smells like a combination of pizza, weed, beer, and vomit.

Well, if I did sleep with any of them, at least they're all hot (always a silver lining). The guys are shirtless, wearing somewhat baggy sweatpants. I can't help but notice how young they all look. Maybe eighteen, nineteen, twenty . . .

Oh, God! Am I a cougar?

And what's with those frosted tips? All the guys look like members of NSYNC. Who wears their hair like that these days anyway? I mean, aside from Guy Fieri. But that's one of his privileges for being the mayor of Flavortown.

I suddenly stumble, crashing to the floor. The guys all turn around and look at me.

"ALEXIS!" the guy with the frostiest tips yells out.

I quickly get to my feet, brush myself off, and put my hand up, quietly saying, "Hi."

"Damn, girl, you went hard last night," says the guy that looks like a GQ model. It's like he's walking around with an Instagram filter on.

"I couldn't even keep up with you," a pale guy with a large tribal tattoo covering his arm says.

"Ummm," I say as a flush of red creeps up my face.

Jesus, did I sleep with all of them? I'm such a slut. I went hard. They couldn't keep up with me. Andrew is never going to marry me now. I'm the sluttiest slut I know. I may as well just go and get my slut award and die.

"Get down here, girl."

As soon as I cross into the living room, one of the guys hugs me, picking me up nearly a foot off the ground. My hands make contact with muscular shoulders and bloated biceps. If it weren't for Andrew, I'd be in love with this gorgeous man (boy?) right now.

I force a half-smile, not knowing what to say or even who any of these boys are, including the guy currently holding me in the air like we're reenacting *Dirty Dancing*. He sets me back down, and they all crowd around me, holding up their hands.

"Don't leave us hanging," says frostiest tips boy.

Oh, I know this. I high-five each of them, and they high-five each other and exchange words like "Sweet" and "Awesome." Then they retake their positions in front of the TV.

There's no way I slept with these guys. They're like children with abs and muscles and hot bods and facial hair and frosted tips—and did I mention muscles?

I take another small step toward the group. "Have you guys seen my purse?" I ask.

Without looking back, the GQ model replies, "You didn't bring one."

"Okay, what about my shoes?"

"You weren't wearing any."

"What?" I ask.

The guy who just picked me up turns his head my way. "You wandered in off the street drunk as all hell with no shoes and no ID. At first, we thought you'd been robbed or something, but then you started singing, 'Shots, shots, shots, shots, shots, everybody!' Sweet lyrics, by the way. I mean, no one knew who you were, but hell, girl, you can party, and as president of Alpha Sigma Sigma, I hereby declare that you're welcome here anytime."

Wait, Alpha Sigma Sigma, like ASS? That can't be right. Am I dreaming? I close my eyes tight and then reopen them, thinking it'll wake me up. Nope, I'm still here.

"What was your name again?" I ask.

"Mark. No need to call me president. We're way past formalities." He looks me up and down, gives me a wink, and then refocuses his attention back on the TV screen.

Before I can get a word in, the tattooed guy asks, "Did you come up with that yourself?"

"Come up with what?

"That song." Then they all join in, singing, "Shots, shots, shots, shots, shots, shots, everybody!"

"If you ain't getting drunk, then get the hell out the club," Mark belts out.

What rock have these guys been living under? "Ha, no. It's an old LMFAO song."

They all look at each other quizzically. The GQ model says, "Huh, never heard of it."

"Are we going to play or not?" a guy holding a controller impatiently interrupts.

From what I can gather, it looks like they're playing a Madden football game on the grainy screen. The guy un-pauses the game, and frosty and tattoo boy begin to rapidly smash at the buttons on their controllers.

"What are you all playing?" I ask, not knowing what else to say.

"Madden '03," Mark replies.

"Aren't they up to, like, Madden '20 now?" I'm proud that I even know anything about football or video games. My older brother, Justin, is big into football, so that's where that knowledge comes from. Andrew's also a team owner of the Green Bay Packers, as many Wisconsinites are. He owns .0000000000000000000000000000000000000000001%— but you'd assume he was a majority stake owner with how he completely overreacts to their losses or wins.

"No," the guys respond in unison, laughing a bit. "Girls really don't know anything about football," the GQ model says. They all laugh and high-five one another.

I slowly edge toward the front door. "Well, I'm going to get going, guys. I have to find my shoes and iPhone."

"iPhone? What the hell is an iPhone?"

"Damn, girl. You still drunk?" Mark asks.

I honestly might be, but I know what an iPhone is. These guys are hot but apparently really dumb too.

"Okay, see you around," I say, reaching for the door handle.

Before they can finish their goodbyes, hoots, and hollers, I'm already out on the front porch.

It's cold out—like, really cold—but the bright sun shows me a charming neighborhood, with large old houses lining the street. There isn't really any traffic—odd for Chicago. The birds are chirping, and there's a good amount of green everywhere: trees, bushes, and grass.

Wait a minute.

Downtown Chicago doesn't have nature. And where are all the sirens? I must be in one of the subdivisions. Why the hell would I come way out here? There's no way I'm finding a cab. Damn, and I had a plan all worked out. I could take a cab to my street, and when it's time for me to pay, I'd run away as fast as my bare feet would take me. No money, no cellphone, and no shoes needed for that plan.

I'll just have to get ahold of Andrew somehow and beg him to come and rescue me. I'll leave out the whole frat guy house thing and tell him I was robbed or something.

I see large buildings that seem about a mile away. Maybe I'm not as far away from the apartment as I thought. But Chicago looks really small from here. Like, *really* small. I must still be a bit drunk—a dizzy, headachy feeling hits me. I hold my head and try to focus my eyes. Those buildings definitely don't look as tall or as big as they should, but perhaps I'm not seeing things correctly. I rub my arms with my hands, trying to warm myself up as I walk.

A car full of girls stops at the light beside me, windows down, blaring R. Kelly's "Ignition." They're all laughing and singing along to it without a care in the world. I used to love that song, but that was before that R. Kelly sex cult documentary came out. His music was never the same to me after that. The light turns green, and the car speeds off.

Up ahead, two girls with matching messy buns and large sunglasses walk toward me. The brunette is wearing a navy-blue Juicy Couture tracksuit, and the blonde is wearing a pink one. They still make those? Now that's tacky. I mean, not to judge or anything.

"Hey, ladies," I say as they come within a few feet of me.

They both stop dead in their tracks and look at me from head to toe. Oh great, now they're judging *me*.

"Can I use one of your cellphones? It's an emergency," I tell them. "I was robbed." Sympathy always makes people more willing to help.

"Oh no, you poor thing," the blonde says.

Is she being sarcastic, or is she generally concerned about my well-being? I honestly can't tell.

"We don't have cellphones, sorry," the brunette says.

Okay, she *was* being sarcastic. Who in this day and age doesn't have a cellphone? My grandpa has a cellphone, and he's ninety-two. The little girl across the hall in our apartment building has a cellphone, and she's seven. What the hell?

"But there's a payphone on campus." The blonde points behind her. "It's two blocks that way."

"Seriously?" I say with a bit of attitude.

"Yeah," the brunette replies innocently. "Right at the edge of campus."

"Here's a quarter for the call." The blonde takes a coin from her Dooney & Burke crayon heart bag and places it in my hand. "Good luck." And they're on their way once more.

A payphone? Are you fricking kidding me? "Bitches," I mutter as I pocket the quarter and keep walking.

Oddly, I recognize these houses and buildings. Maybe this

is the University of Chicago. I went there once, but I was really drunk, so that's probably why this all looks so familiar. I pick up the pace and am now in a full sprint until I reach the payphone.

Picking up the receiver, I stuff the quarter into the slot that says twenty-five cents and dial Andrew's number—the one number I've memorized besides my own. He's had it since he was eighteen. It rings.

Wow, I'll be damned. This thing works.

"Hello?" Andrew answers with a big yawn.

"Andrew, it's me. I'm so sorry about last night. It was all my fault. I want to get back together, and I want to marry you. I love you more than anything. You know that, right?" I say all in one breath.

Silence.

"Who is this?" he asks.

"Andrew, it's me, Alexis! I need your help. I don't know where I am, and I was robbed last night." There's panic in my voice.

"I think you have the wrong number."

"Really? You're really going to play that game? Are you fucking kidding me?" Pressing the receiver firmly against my ear, I wait for him to speak.

A woman's voice calls out in the background. "Baby, who is that?"

"It's no one, Melissa. Go back to bed," he whispers away from the phone.

"Are you fucking kidding me?" I repeat shrilly, my blood boiling. "You proposed to me last night—well, were going to propose to me—and now you're screwing your ex? How could you do this to me? We've been together for seven years and you're back with her, the girl who cheated on you and gave you chlamydia, after one night? What the hell, Andrew?"

All I can hear is my heavy breathing.

"Are you cheating on me?" Andrew asks.

"No, but you're cheating on me, you asshole!" I yell into the phone.

Melissa's voice is muffled. "Why would you ask me that? Of course not."

What? What the hell is going on? I can hear them talking back and forth in the background. Then that asshole puts his phone down.

"I would never cheat on you," Melissa says, a little more clearly this time.

"Yeah, right, you lying, cheating homewrecker!" I yell.

The phone clicks. He hung up on me! Cheating is bad, but hanging up on me? That's unforgivable. I slam the receiver back in its holder.

Fine. I don't need him. I'll find my own way home. I'm a grown woman. I can figure this whole thing out. It's his loss.

I take a deep breath of the cool, brisk air. It's all going to be okay, I tell myself. Things go wrong so they can go right.

FIVE

I FEEL LIKE I know this place, but I can't put my finger on it. That three-story brick building straight ahead? I feel like I've been in there at least a dozen times. Strange—maybe my blackout memories are coming back to me. I mean, how else would I remember a campus building from the University of Chicago, a school I've never actually attended? Maybe I've discovered some sort of scientific thingy in which drinking large amounts of alcohol eventually brings back memories previously lost from drinking large amounts of alcohol.

Wow. That's Nobel Science Prize-worthy.

I swing open the door of the brick building as if I'd done it many times before. The plain long hallway is lined with wooden doors and frosted windows. I creep down the hallway, peeking into open doorways. The rooms are filled with seated students looking straight ahead at the front of the classroom, listening to professors lecturing on and on.

At one such classroom, I take a good look at the octogenarian teacher, glasses lingering at the end of his nose and a voice so monotone it would put insomniacs to sleep. Mr. Bernard? That's Mr. Bernard! He was my Math 101 professor my freshman year of college. Man, did he hate me. Partly because I was awful at math, but mostly because I seldom attended his classes. Wow, he hasn't aged a bit.

Wait a minute—he should be dead by now, right? How the hell is he still alive, and teaching to boot?

"Lexi Spencer," Mr. Bernard announces, glancing at the paper on his clipboard and then around the classroom. "Is Lexi Spencer here?" He pauses, then says, "Absent again." He lets out a little sigh and makes a mark on his paper.

Oh my God, that's me! That's my name—well, Alexis, but that's me. I haven't gone by Lexi in years. I fail to resist the urge to burst into the classroom, exclaiming that it's me.

"I'm here! I'm Lexi Spencer," I say from the doorway before I can stop myself.

Mr. Bernard looks directly at me, frowning.

"Mr. Bernard, it's me, Lexi Spencer, er, Alexis now. I haven't seen you in so long. How have you been? You look so young—well, young for being so old," I ramble nervously, not really knowing what I'm saying. "What's your secret?"

Mr. Bernard rubs his forehead, scowls, and looks down at his clipboard again. I can see he's scratching out my name.

It's like he's looking right through me, like I'm not even here.

"Oh, fuck! Am I dreaming? No, wait. Am I dead? I'm here." I start waving my hands in front of him. "Hello, can you see me?"

He doesn't react to my presence at all.

"Shit! Did I die last night? Is this hell? Honestly, the universe got this one right. Sitting in Mr. Bernard's class for the rest of my life would be my own personal hell. Can't say I didn't see this coming," I ponder out loud.

"Excuse me, miss!" Mr. Bernard says sternly.

"Holy shit, you can see me!" I exclaim. "I'm alive! I'm alive!" I jump up and down, extending my arms out like I'm at the top of a human pyramid. Wow—I really thought that maybe I was a ghost for a second there.

"Miss, I need you to leave my classroom immediately."
Mr. Bernard points his long crooked finger at the door.

The classroom erupts in laughter, and I hear whispers:
"She's crazy."

"What a drunk."

"All aboard the Hot Mess Express!"

"Okay, sorry," I respond in utter embarrassment, turning to exit.

As I leave, I can hear Mr. Bernard say, "And for goodness sake, tell Lexi to stop sending her friends to her classes to get attendance points. This is the third time she's done this. Next time it happens, I'm failing her."

I leave the classroom, embarrassed and confused. Lexi sending friends to her classes just to get attendance points? Wait, I used to do that. Did he just recognize me and embarrass me in front of his class to get back at me for the semesters (yes, I took his class more than once) of hell I put him through?

Sitting on the floor at the end of the hallway, I let my head fall into my hands. What the hell is going on? Something isn't right. The frat. The campus. Mr. Bernard. What am I missing?

I pick my head up and consider banging it into the wall behind me when I notice a bulletin board hanging on the wall across from me, crammed with dozens of announcements. My eyes scan the board, picking out the words in the boldest and largest fonts.

"Spring Break 2003."

"Tryouts for the '03 Cheerleading Squad this Friday."

"Marcus Cinemas: Now Showing *Spider Man*, *Sweet Home Alabama*, *Signs*, and *The Ring*."

What?

I run to the bulletin board to get a better look. I open

my eyes as wide as I can, then blink several times. Am I seeing clearly? I rip the papers off the board and read them out loud. "'Find the Science Club on Myspace.' 'Have you tried iTunes?' 'Don't forget to sign up for Winterium 2002 classes.'"

Taking a few steps back, I'm out of breath, in shock, and entirely jumbled. *What year is it?* I'm suspended into a whirl of disbelief. It feels as though the walls are moving in on me. The world is spinning. My head is pounding. My eyes can't focus. My legs give out. I fall to the ground. Deep breath in. Deep breath out. Deep breath in. Deep breath out. I've been drunk, but never this drunk.

Suddenly, it hits me: the frat guys, who had FROSTED TIPS, had no idea who LMFAO is. They were playing Madden '03 and thought I was stupid for suggesting that there are several newer versions of the game. They also didn't know what an iPhone is.

Those two girls without freaking cellphones were wearing Juicy Couture tracksuits.

That car of girls was jamming out to R. Kelly. Like ewww, he pissed on a child and is the leader of a sex cult. No one jams to that anymore.

A payphone exists, and it works.

Mr. Bernard is still alive. He referred to me as Lexi, something I haven't gone by in over a decade.

"Holy shit!" I yell out loud. "It's 2002?"

SIX

N o, this can't be right.

I must be dreaming. That's the only reasonable explanation. I drank so much last night that I probably blacked out for at least three days. This is just a really long, admittedly *very* realistic, messed-up dream. I'll probably wake up any minute now.

I get to my feet. "Wake up, wake up, wake up," I say over and over again, slapping the palm of my hand against my head. I pinch the back of my arm and squeal involuntarily. Okay, that didn't work.

I raise my left leg high and stomp on my right foot as hard as I can. "Oww!" I yell as I hop around on my left foot, clenching my hands around my throbbing one.

I try to stand up straight, but that same weird disorientation I felt back at the frat rushes my brain—dizziness, the throbbing headache, the unfocused vision. The spinning world. It feels like I just got off the Tilt-a-Whirl. I steady myself against the wall, trying to get my balance, my focus, and my thoughts back.

Maybe it's all a cruel joke someone's playing on me. I don't know how. But it's possible. Right?

I stumble outside. The large buildings I saw in the distance earlier are dorms. Students are everywhere, walking to and from classes, many wearing black and yellow shirts emblazoned with the word "Titans." The main road is lined with maple trees covered in yellow and orange covered leaves that fall to the ground intermittently.

My jaw drops—I'm at my old college campus, the University of Wisconsin Oshkosh, home of the Titans.

I shade my eyes from the glaring sun with my hand and approach a girl walking briskly toward the dorms. Her hair is blonde on top and black on the bottom—so out of style.

"Hey, what's today's date?" I ask.

"November 1st," she says, keeping her pace.

I follow behind as quickly as my painful bare feet will take me. "No, what year?"

She gives me a weird look. "2002."

"Damn it!"

Stopping abruptly, the girl turns to face me, and I nearly run into her. She looks me up and down, concern spreading across her face. "Are you okay?"

"Umm, I don't know . . . . I have no idea what's going on. I don't know what year it is. I'm not sure how I even got here," I say, almost crying.

"Maybe I should call the police."

"No, don't." The police will throw me in a mental ward for sure.

"Has someone hurt you?" Her voice is calm.

"Only Andrew," I answer, not realizing what she meant.

"Did he hit you?"

"Oh, no, no, no," I say. "He broke up with me."

"Ohhhhhh, now, that makes sense," she says and takes a deep breath. "Well, it's not the end of the world. I've been there. Last year, when my boyfriend broke up with me, I forgot who I was, where I was, and what day it was. All I could do was cry, sleep, and eat ice cream for weeks, nearly months." She puts her hand on my arm. "It gets better."

I nod slightly.

She cocks her head. "Do you go here? I don't think I've seen you around."

"I used to." Or if it's 2002, I *do* go here. "I'm Alexis, by the way," I say quickly.

"Veronica." She looks at my bare feet. "Do you need anything? Looks like you're having a rough day."

"No. I'm fine."

"You sure?"

I nod.

"Okay. I hate to leave you like this, but I've gotta run back to my apartment before work. I work at Kelly's Bar, right by the Scott Halls." Veronica pats my shoulder. "Stop in sometime, and we can chat."

"Thanks," is all I can manage as she walks off.

I stumble over to a wooden bench and sit immediately. Leaning forward, head in my hands, I rock back and forth, barely realizing what I'm doing. Students pass, walking to and from class. Some give me odd looks; others don't notice me at all.

I need to make sense of all this. I've gone back in time seventeen years. But how? Things like that don't just happen, do they?

I pick my head up and look around. Two tall buildings at the edge of campus catch my eye. I know them: North Scott and South Scott. They're dorm buildings. I lived in North Scott on the eighth floor. If it's 2002, then that's where I'm supposed to be. My old friends will be there, my roommate, my dorm mates—they'll all be there.

Maybe I got my wish. Maybe I was sent here to fix the past in order to fix the future. This might be my second chance—my do-over! The universe has *finally* heard my pleas. I can do it all over again—study hard, stop partying, avoid making all those huge mistakes, and somehow that'll change the outcome of my life. Future me will have a chance! So, with a few tweaks and changes, I should end up with an incredible career and married to Andrew.

Okay, I can do this. I've seen the movies—this'll be cake.

"Everything is okay in the end," I say aloud. "If it's not okay, then it's not the end."

I nod and stand, marching toward my old dorm.

SEVEN

I SLIP IN with another student at the side door of North Scott. He gives me an odd look, like he's going to call me out, but he doesn't say anything, maybe because I look so cold and barefoot—and pathetic.

I make a quick stop at the bathroom because I haven't peed since 2019, and I should probably get myself cleaned up a bit. I splash some water on my face and take a good look in the mirror above the sink. My pale, dull face, surrounded by strands of greasy blonde hair, stares back at me. The crow's feet at the corners of my eyes and the smile lines surrounding the crooks of my mouth jump out at me. Jesus! I'm supposed to be eighteen, right?

I press and pull at my face, trying to smooth out the wrinkles. I look younger than my age—always have. A combination of genetics, a babyface, and the Botox I started getting in my late twenties helps, but I definitely couldn't pass for eighteen. I look down at my 36D breasts. I didn't have these at eighteen, either. I press them hard against my body, trying to make them smaller. And then there's my nose. It's not the same as when I was eighteen. A little softer with a slight slope. I trace the curvature of it and look at my profile in the mirror. A deviated septum got this baby fixed—or at least that's what I tell everyone.

Great. I'm stuck in 2002 as a thirty-something-year-old woman. Well, universe, you really screwed the pooch on this one. There's no way in hell I'm going to fit in with my friends. It will be just like the good ole days, except I look nothing like myself in the old days. Or maybe my friends can overlook my deteriorated appearance. Stranger things have happened.

I stare deeply at my reflection. "You can do this," I say to myself out loud. "You'll fix you, make all the right decisions, and, in seventeen years, you'll be married and successful. Just be confident, and no one will ask any questions."

A toilet flushes. I scramble out of the bathroom before anyone sees me talking to myself like a crazy person.

Up on the eighth floor, the door to my dorm room is unlocked, thank God. I open it slowly, praying Nikki isn't there, and stick my head in.

The desk on the right side of the room is covered in piles of clothes; on the left, the other desk is clean and tidy. Obviously, mine is the messy one. The large pink shag carpet came courtesy of Nikki. I spy our mini fridge at the other end of the room, topped with boxes of granola bars and a basket of fruit. The bed on the left is tidily made, and the other—

I gasp. Holy shit!

A girl with heavy, smeared makeup and long blonde hair sprawls across the bed on the right, tummy down, in a dead sleep. She has one black five-inch heel on. Her mouth hangs open, her minidress is hiked up above her hips, and her ass is almost completely exposed, save for a skinny red thong.

That's *me*! What? *How?*

I close the door behind me and move closer to get a better look. Oh my God, did I always look that disgusting? Drool is dripping from my gaping mouth, I'm snoring, and my hair looks like it belongs on the business end of a mop handle.

Shit. So I'm here *and* she's here.

Mid-snore, she jerks, eyes fluttering open into a pained

squint. She sits up, groaning the whole way, and wipes at those gunky eyes. It takes her a moment to register that there's another person in the room. But I can see when her brain clicks, because her mouth opens to let out a piercing scream.

"Shhhh, be quiet!" I hiss.

"Who the hell are you?" she yells.

I take a deep breath, trying to decide how to go about this. Do I lie? Do I tell her the truth? Do I kill her and take over her life? Wait, wouldn't that kill me too? Like, if I smother her with a pillow, would I instantly die?

"Umm . . . well, I'm . . . you, I guess. I'm Alexis," I say, really just piecing it all together myself in this moment.

She stands up, backing away from me, trying to cover herself with a pillow. Panic sets in on her face as she glances wildly around the room. Oh God—she's looking for things to hit me with. She spies her other stiletto on the floor.

"Don't you dare think about throwing that shoe at me," I warn, putting my finger up.

"I wasn't thinking that," she lies.

"Just listen to me." I take the smallest of steps toward her, but she flinches, so I stop.

She puts her hand against her forehead like she's checking for a fever. "Am I still drunk?"

"Probably, but that's not the point. Look, I'm you, but in the future." I slap a smile on my face, hoping it'll be convincing. I'm sure it's coming off as creepy instead, because she looks even more confused and maybe even a little scared. "I don't know why I'm here, but I need to get back to my time."

She shimmies her dress down and drops the pillow, kicking off her lone heel. "Did I do drugs last night?"

"I'm serious. I'm Alexis. I'm you."

"It's Lexi," she retorts, putting her hand up.

"Oh yeah, I forgot I went by Lexi. I guess I thought it made me sound sexier."

"I *am* sexier," Lexi challenges dumbly, putting her hands on her hips. "I don't know who you are, but you need to leave now." She points at the door. "Get out of my room."

"Please, I have nowhere to go," I plead. "I need your help. I need to find a way back." I'm starting to ramble. "I don't know how it happened, but if I can reverse it—or maybe, I don't know, if you don't do all the stupid shit I did in college, if you go to class and don't drink, maybe things will become right and I can go back?" Yeah, that sounded right—or, at least, that's how it works in the movies.

I slap my hand against my head. Of course! I was sent here to change my younger self so my life doesn't go so off the rails and I end up happily married to Andrew. That's the only way to get out of 2002.

"You're crazy. Get out of my room or I'm calling security." She raises an eyebrow.

Dammit. I should have thought this through. Of course she doesn't believe me.

"Security!" she yells.

"Okay, okay." I start backing toward the door.

Wait, what? We don't have random security that comes when called. Does she think I'm an idiot?

I stop and stand up a little taller, widening my stance, raising my chin, and puffing out my chest.

"Why are you standing like that? It's weird. Stop doing that," she says.

I deflate, attempting to stand normally. What am I doing? Let's think. If I was Lexi . . . I shudder, remembering I was Lexi at one point in my life. If I was Lexi, how would I convince myself that future me *was* really her? Oh, I got it.

"Lexi, I'm really you . . . and I can prove it."

She pops her hip out to show she has attitude. "Okay. If you're really me, tell me what I did last Friday night." She smirks.

I tap my head, as if doing so will loosen some brain cells to give me the right answer. "Um, wait. *You* don't even remember what you did last Friday."

Her smirk vanishes. "Touché. Then tell me something about myself that no one else knows."

"You drink a lot."

"I said that *no one else* knows." She taps her foot on the ground impatiently. From her dresser, she pulls out a pair of sweatpants and a T-shirt, still eyeing me warily.

"A-ha!" I almost shout. "You wear those bra inserts to make your boobs look bigger."

"I do not!" Lexi retorts as she slides two inserts from her bra into a drawer and closes it.

Yeah, I wouldn't admit to that one either.

"You crashed your car last year," I say triumphantly.

"Everyone knows that." Lexi begins to undress. She's clearly having fun with me, merely entertaining me. She must still be intoxicated too, since she's undressing in front of a total stranger. Only I'm not—I'm her.

I look away for a second, then look back. Hey, it's my body too. I can look if I want. Wow, I was much thinner back then, and look at how tan I was! I haven't tanned in years, well, ever since all the cancer reports started coming out. I'm toned, tight, and tan; no wonder Andrew fell in love with me. But I haven't looked like that in years. Why did he stay in love with me?

And look at my lower back—no tramp stamp! She hasn't

gotten it yet. Great! I can convince her not to get it because it's awful, and I've regretted it ever since.

"See something you like?" Lexi turns toward me in her bra and panties. She bites at her lower lip seductively.

"What the hell is wrong with you? That's, like, incest, you perv."

"Well, actually, if you're really me, then it's more like masturbation. A very weird form of masturbation."

I shake my head. "Just put some clothes on." Then I snap my fingers. "Oh! You're a virgin."

"I've told people that, but no one believes me. No idea why." She shrugs.

"Probably because of the way you dress?"

"Yeah, maybe. But why would I lie about that?"

"That's just it. You're not lying. You really are a virgin." Maybe she'll believe me now.

"Just because you believe me doesn't mean you *are* me."

"True." I scratch my chin for a moment. "You originally didn't get into this school because you failed the second semester of chemistry and had to retake it your senior year."

"Yeah, that was pretty embarrassing. I just don't get science."

"Me neither," I say, shaking my head.

"But that doesn't prove that you're me. Any of my high school friends could've told you that." She looks down at her bare wrist as if she's checking the time. "All right, I've had enough. Now that I'm sobering up, this is just weird, and I'm starting to fear for my own safety because I think you might be insane. You need to leave."

"Wait, wait! Let me think," I plead.

"Get out of my room." Lexi pushes me. "Get out!"

Despite my protests, she pushes me until I'm outside the

room. I have to think of something. This would be so much easier if she didn't reveal practically everything about herself to other people.

I turn back around, looking at my former self. Without saying another word, she slams the door in my face.

It's exactly the greeting I expected from her.

EIGHT

D EFEATED, I WALK off campus toward the bars. The shower shoes I stole from the dorm bathroom slap against the sidewalk. My home in 2002 is that dorm room I was just thrown out of. I can't go to Andrew. He doesn't even know who I am yet! My old friends would think I'm crazy, just like Lexi did.

Why did I think I could just waltz into Lexi's trash life and get her on board right away? Perhaps a drink will help me figure out my next move. I could use a little hair of the dog anyway—my head feels like it's been split in half. And I'm not sure if it's from being hungover or the time travel. I spot Kelly's Bar and decide to venture in. I have no money, no ID, no phone, and I'm not even wearing real shoes, but it's the only place with a friendly face: Veronica.

At four in the afternoon, the bar's nearly empty. Avril Lavigne's "Complicated" plays softly from a jukebox while I take in the long bar top, several round tables, and a couple gambling machines in the corner. Complicated is right. Even seventeen years later, Avril gets me. Heavy smoke lingers in the air; two men at the end of the bar puffing on cigars are the source. Gross. Well, that was 2002 for you.

Veronica pops her head up from behind the bar. Her face lights up when she sees me. "Hey, didn't think I'd see you in here so soon," she says, wiping down and rearranging some bottles.

I take a seat at the bar. "Didn't think I'd be in here so soon."

She chuckles. "Funny how life is. That's why I never make plans. Nothing to be disappointed in if you don't make plans or have any expectations."

I think that's exactly why I'm in the position I'm in right now: no plans, no follow-through. I just nod.

"What can I get you? It's on me," Veronica says.

I knew this was the right place to go. "Vodka soda."

"You got it."

She pours a strong drink, using Ketel One instead of some rail liquor, and sets it in front of me. "Feeling any better?"

"Things are harder than I thought they'd be." I take a long drink.

"They always are," she says, wiping the bar top down and topping off other patrons' beers.

I sip my drink, considering my options. I could just leave this town, go back to Chicago, and hopefully time will eventually catch up to me. I'm not entirely sure how time works. I don't even understand time zones or Daylight Saving Time. How is it four p.m. here and, like, eight p.m. in New York? What *is* time? And that's not even a philosophical question. I literally can't comprehend it. This time travel thing couldn't have happened to a worse person.

I could get blackout drunk and hope that I wake up in the future, which is how I got here. Maybe there's something to that.

But if Lexi is here too, then it must mean that *she's* the answer to my shitty situation. I mean, the girl is a mess—no wonder I ended up with such a pathetic life. I can feel it in my gut: it's her fault that my life didn't pan out. But maybe if she stops drinking, starts studying, and stops being such a screwup, I can finally go home. That's it—*she* needs to change, like, *now*. I'm here to fix her-me, not me-me. I'm the solution, and she's the problem. But I have a better chance of ending poverty or enacting world peace than fixing her. I mean, she's impossible.

The vodka soda warms me from the inside out, just like it always does. "Hey, Veronica?" I call out.

She leans back from the bar. "What's up?"

"If you wanted to get someone to trust you, how would you go about that?"

She makes her way over to me. "Well, trust is earned."

"Okay, not trust, then. How would you convince someone to take your help who absolutely refuses?"

"Does this have to do with that ex of yours?"

"In a way." I take another sip of my drink. Technically, it does. If Lexi doesn't let me help her, then I can't get back to Andrew and fix our relationship before he moves on to some skeeza. Being away from him makes me realize how good he was to me. He would be the voice of reason in this situation. He'd tell me to slow down, take deep breaths, and relax before I became completely overwhelmed. I need him now more than ever.

"You can't help someone who won't help themselves, but I guess just don't take no for an answer. People eventually give up or they hit their rock bottom, and then they have to turn to help." She shrugs.

I drink the rest of my vodka soda in one big drink. She's right: I can't take no for an answer. I'm going to *make* Lexi accept my help.

"Want another?" Veronica picks up the glass.

"No, but thanks. I'm taking your advice, and I'm going to make Lexi hit rock bottom." I jump off my stool.

Veronica gives me a puzzled look. "That wasn't—"

"Thanks for the drink!" I yell over my shoulder as I run out of the bar.

About ten minutes later, I pound on Lexi's door so hard my hand immediately begins throbbing. I try to internalize my mantra: *Don't take no for an answer. Force her to let you in. Make her hit rock bottom.*

Lexi opens the door, narrowing her eyes. "You again?"

"Yes, me . . . well, you." I make my eyes even narrower than hers. "I'm not taking no for an answer. You're going to accept that I'm you. You're going to accept my guidance and help like I'm your goddamned fairy godmother, and you're going to let me stay with you."

"You're crazy," she says, trying to shut the door.

I put my foot in front of it and shove it open with so much force she falls backward onto the floor.

"What the hell?! Hellllp!!!" she yells.

"Stop it." I quickly close the door behind me and crouch down beside her, putting my hand over her mouth to stop her from screaming. Her eyes grow wide, and she tries to shake me off.

"Just listen to me, Lexi! I *am* you. I am stuck here, and I am not leaving unless you help me. Wherever you go, I will be there. Class—well, you don't actually go there—but parties, to the bathroom, to eat, when you're hanging out with your friends. I'm your shadow now."

She opens her mouth as wide as she can and bites down on my hand.

I scream, pulling away from her.

"Help! She's trying to kill me," Lexi yells.

"Stop!" I cover her mouth again, spreading my fingers so she can't bite me.

Lexi breathes dramatically through her nose, big inhales and exhales, before shaking my hand off her face and crawling backward.

"I'm not going to kill you, only because I'm pretty sure I'd die too," I say, wiping my hands against my jeans.

She doesn't scream this time. She just stares at me with wild, fleeting eyes. "What do you want from me?"

"I want you to believe me, to believe that I'm you. As soon as you do that, we can start trying to figure out how to get me back to my time."

"Fine, I believe you," she huffs.

"No, you don't. Don't lie to me." She's looking around the room. Oh great, she's planning another sneak attack. But then I remember something. "Oh, I've got it!"

"You've got what?"

I point my finger right at her and smirk. "You got your period at sixteen."

"First of all, gross, and second, that's not even true. I got it at fourteen." She stands up, crossing her arms in front of her chest defiantly.

I throw my head back, laughing. "You told everyone you got it at fourteen, but it was sixteen."

She stamps her foot, still adamant that I'm not her.

"You saw in one of Justin's—that's right, Justin, *our* brother—one of his porn magazines that hot girls shave down there"—here, I point at her genital area—"so you tried shaving down there and you ended up cutting yourself so bad that you used a couple of Mom's pads. Mom noticed that some of her pads were missing, and when she asked you about it, you told her you got your period. For the next two years, you had to pretend every month that you had your period. You'd fake having cramps, use it to get out of gym class, throw out the pads Mom bought you—but not before squirting ketchup on them, and you had to keep track of your fake period as if it were real." I'm laughing so hard, I'm out of breath.

Lexi gasps. "How did you know that?"

"Because I'm you, Lexi."

Her mouth falls open. "I've never told anyone that."

"Neither have I."

"Oh my God." Lexi shakes her head in disbelief.

"I know."

"How is this even possible?" She backs up until she involuntarily sits on her messy bed. Looking me up and down, she glances at herself in the mirror and then looks back at me, trying to make sense of it all. Comparing herself to me—as if she even compares.

"I don't know how it's possible. I can't believe it either, but here I am, and," I point to her, "here you are."

"Wait. There's no way you can be me! Your nose is different, and your boobs are way bigger than mine."

I tap my nose. "Nose job." I point to my bust. "Boob job."

"Really?" she asks admiringly. "I've always wanted breast implants."

"I know," I say, rolling my eyes.

"Can I touch them?"

"I guess, they're technically yours."

Lexi pokes at them, then pats the top of them, and then pushes them up from the bottom and drops them. "Wow, these look great," she says, pleased.

"Thanks."

"What's with the nose? Our nose is fine. Why did you change it?" She furrows her brow.

"I think all those Snapchat and Instagram filters screwed me up. One day, I just started hating it."

Lexi's face is blank.

"Never mind. Don't worry about that right now," I say.

She looks me up and down again. She's judging me. "But your hair—what did you do to my hair? It's awful." Lexi grabs at the ends, lifting up a few strands.

"What are you talking about?" I slap her hands away and smooth my hair down. "It looks professional. It's a lob, a long bob, and it's my hair, not yours."

"You're right. I would never take ownership of that atrocity." She steps back, looking at her figure in the mirror and running her hands down the sides of her body. "You're not as pretty as me or as skinny."

I roll my eyes. "Thanks."

"You could stand to lose, like, twenty pounds, and that's me being nice."

I glare at her. "Rude. I lost forty pounds like three years ago. I think I look pretty damn good."

Lexi whips around in shock. "Wait . . . I get fat? Seriously? This is such bullshit," she whines, stomping her foot like a child. She opens the fridge and starts pulling out items to read the nutritional labels.

"Oh, relax! I said you lost the weight."

"Which means you also gained it." She scowls at me. "Did you have a baby or something?"

"No. I just wasn't taking care of myself. Got a little depre—" I stop. "Actually, it's none of your business." I don't have to explain myself. It's my body. I can gain weight. I can lose it. I can do whatever the hell I want with it, because my body is exactly that: mine.

"It *is* my business. If you're me, then that's my body too." She tosses a carton of chocolate milk into the garbage.

"Enough about my body. I have to figure out exactly what I'm supposed to do here so I can get back to my time." No response from this awful eighteen-year-old. "What are you doing?"

"Throwing away anything with calories," Lexi says over her shoulder.

"Stop. You don't get fat for a while. Now focus."

I spot an old celebrity gossip magazine lying on her desk. The various problematic headlines are scattered in bold letters across the cover. *Paris Hilton, perfect at 100 lbs., Christina Aguilera Strips Down and Packs on the Pounds, Was Britney Spears Too Muscular for Justin?* Ugh! I slide the magazine into the trash. Lexi doesn't notice. Pop culture in the early 2000s really messed me up—probably all women, for that matter. Thank God for the body positivity movement.

"Maybe," she whips her head in my direction, "you were sent here to warn me that I get fat so I can stop it from happening." *Point proven.*

"Yeah, that's it. I traveled back in time to warn you of your impending pounds."

She stands, takes a large step forward, and begins a set of lunges. "You never know . . ."

"No, you idiot. I was sent here to fix you, obviously."

"Me? Why me?" Lexi lies down on the ground and starts a set of crunches.

"Because you're the reason I'm single, unemployed, and have done nothing with my life."

"Don't forget about your awful hair." She points to my head in the middle of a crunch. "And your big belly."

"What? My belly's not big." I look down at my stomach and hike up my jeans a little higher.

"Yes, it is. We used to have abs."

"You don't have abs right now."

"Well, we *will* this summer," she says, doing her crunches even faster. "Anyway, how can you blame me for you being such a loser? I had nothing to do with that." Lexi now stands and begins a set of jumping jacks.

"You're a drunk party girl who will lead me down a path of self-destruction." I grab a granola bar from the top of the fridge, unwrap it, and take a bite.

"I like to think of myself as carefree and fun-loving." Lexi lunges forward again.

"Stop doing that!" I yell.

"Doing what?"

"Exercising."

"Maybe you should do some of these too. I'd appreciate it if you'd tone up my ass." Lexi eyes my butt and cringes.

I put my hand in front of my butt, covering it from her view. "My ass is fine."

"Not from where I'm standing."

I set the half-eaten granola bar down on top of the fridge.

"Good girl. You don't need those carbs anyway." Lexi smiles at me.

I pick up the granola bar and cram the rest of it in my mouth. "Yum, carbs." I smile wider than Lexi.

"You tubs! Spit that out right now." Lexi grabs the garbage can and holds it up to my face.

"Too late. All gone," I swallow and open my mouth, showing a mixture of granola residue and saliva clinging to my tongue.

"Ew. You know that's all going to your ass," she says, disgusted. "Don't come crying to me when your mom jeans split."

"Big butts are in style, thanks to the Kardashians."

"What's a Kardashian?"

Wow, a world where no one knows what a Kardashian is. How refreshing.

"Okay, let's get back on track. Let me think. What was I doing before I showed up in 2002? I was drinking wine and vodka..."

"Whoa, whoa, whoa," Lexi interrupts. "Looks like the apple doesn't fall far from the tree."

"What? I'm not your parent, you half-wit."

"Speaking of apples," Lexi takes an apple from the fruit basket, "how many calories do they have?"

"I don't know... like a hundred?"

"Whoa. Not today, you tricksters in disguise." Lexi tosses all the apples into the trash.

"Will you focus?"

"I am focused." Lexi drops another apple in the trash.

I rub my forehead with both hands, trying to remember. "Okay, I was looking at old pictures of me—uh, you—and wishing I could go back and fix everything." I snap my fingers. "I'm here to fix you."

"I don't think so. I'm perfect the way I am." She flips her long, blonde, fake hair over her shoulder. But her cheeks blow up a bit. Surprise blooming across her face, she reaches for the garbage can and immediately vomits into it.

I pat her back as she heaves another splash of last night's vodka and, from the looks of it, pizza. "Yeah, you're the epitome of perfection."

NINE

I THINK WE'VE finally come to terms with what's happened to us, and I've explained to her that if she wants her life back the way it was, then she'll have to cooperate, because right now, I'm stuck here in 2002 with my greatest enemy: me at eighteen. I tidied up the utter mess on her side of the room while she slept off her hangover. As I expected, she hasn't been much help—just a pain in my "fat ass," as she likes to call it. She's awake now and just as useless as she was when she was asleep.

"I need to get some new clothes. These are all I have," I say, gesturing to my high-waisted jeans and wine-stained white top.

"You can borrow mine. They'll be way too small on you. Like a cabbage patch doll trying to fit into Barbie's clothes." She pats her knee, punctuating her laughter.

I scowl at her and place my hands firmly on my hips, like I was staring down a disobedient child, which she basically is.

"Fine. I'll get you some new clothes since you conveniently left your money in the future." Lexi grabs her purse off the desk chair. "On second thought, I'll just use credit to pay for your clothes. That way, you can pay for them in the future." She smirks.

"Right." I roll my eyes. "So, the plan is that I'm your older sister and I'm visiting you for a little while."

"Like anyone's going to believe I'm related to you," Lexi huffs.

"What? Lexi, we look exactly the same."

"Aside from the girthy ass, that hair atrocity, the nose you butchered, and those great tits that I can't wait to get, by the way," Lexi retorts.

"Lexi, look at me. I'm you. You're literally talking shit to yourself *about* yourself."

"Whatever, Alexis. You're just jealous of me." She raises her chin.

"You're right, I'm jealous of me."

"Ugh, this is excruciating." Lexi kicks her feet at the ground.

She's such a drama queen. I don't know how I'm going to survive her. I've been resisting the urge to smother her with a pillow since I got here.

"I have a great idea." Lexi stops kicking, and her face is practically glowing. "What are the winning lottery numbers for today?"

"I have no idea. Why would I remember that?"

"Well, do you remember any of the winning numbers from any day?"

"No."

"Useless. Fine. Just tell me something cool about the future."

"I'm not sure I should. What if I change it for the worse?"

"Like I'm going to remember . . . I can barely remember last night. Come on, tell me what it's like. Please."

"Okay. Honestly, it's not that much different from now, from what I've seen. Technology has advanced, obviously. We have iPhones, Siri, Facebook, Twitter, Snapchat, Instagram, YouTube, Netflix, and emojis, which is how most everyone communicates now. Oh, and Amazon has basically taken over the world."

Lexi just stares at me. "I have no idea what any of those words mean."

I pat her head. "You'll figure it out one day."

She waves her hands at me. "Forget all that. Is there anything bad that I can avoid? Like, does anything awful happen to me aside from you letting me get . . . ?" She motions to my body.

I groan. She's so shallow. But the memories I've tried to forget start to rush at me. I swallow hard, repressing the feelings they bring along with them. I want to tell her, but I can't bring myself to.

Before I lose control of my emotions, I answer calmly and firmly, "No, nothing bad happens to us."

The door opens, and I hold my breath, not knowing how I'm going to react to seeing Nikki. Do I get up and hug her? No, that would be weird, but I haven't seen her in forever. I'll just act normal. I'm Lexi's older sister. I grimace at the sound of that.

"Hi," Nikki says, coming home from class. She's so young and beautiful with long, thick brown hair, dark lashes, and dewy skin sprinkled with freckles.

"Hey, Nikki. This is my sister, Alexis." Lexi gestures to me.

I hold my hand out for a handshake. "Hi, it's so great to see—uh, meet you."

She shakes my hand, looking confused. "I thought you said you only had a brother," she says to Lexi.

"Yeah, that was when I was pissed off at Alexis," Lexi explains. "We're good now. So, I have a sister again."

Wow, she's good on her feet. I mean, I am. I forgot how quick-witted I was.

"Lexi . . . and Alexis?" Nikki points to each of us as she says it.

"Yep," I say.

"Your parents were pretty lazy with the names, huh?"

"Yeah, well, they never wanted another one. So, Lexi got stuck with a shorter version of my name. Not very original." Ha! I still have that quick wit. Old age hasn't gotten the better of me yet. But we really should have given me a different name.

Nikki shrugs, never one to question anything.

Lexi pulls a banana out of her basket of fruit, peels it, and starts eating.

Nikki licks her lips. "Can I try a bite?" she asks.

Lexi holds the banana out to her. "Yeah. Go right ahead."

Nikki takes a bite.

"Have another," Lexi says.

Nikki takes another bite.

Lexi grabs a granola bar. "Here, have this too."

Nikki takes it and starts munching away.

Oh God—not the "Get Nikki Fat" plan! I completely forgot about that.

See, Nikki did this thing where she always asked to try everyone else's food, no matter what they were eating. I can't even count the number of times she "tried" ramen noodles. As college students with no real income, we were fed up with constantly feeding Nikki. Even when you politely told her no, she would say, "Come on, just one bite," or "Don't be such a fatty." So, we decided she must be stopped, and the "Get Nikki Fat" plan was born: we all agreed to always say yes to Nikki when she asked to try our food and to then encourage her to have some more of it. We figured eventually she would get fat and have to gain some self-control. By the end of our first year of college, Nikki had put on the freshman fifteen . . . twice.

Yes, I was a terrible friend. But in my defense, she had her body and her confidence back by junior year. I put more effort into her weight loss than in my studies, mostly because I felt bad. If I had known how much weight she would gain, how many pairs of my jeans she would stretch out, and how many times I would have to tell her, "You're not fat," then I would have never participated in the plan. And knowing what I know now, I have to stop it.

"Lexi, stop that!" I yell.

"Stop what?"

"You know what you're doing." I narrow my eyes.

"I have no idea what you're talking about, Alexis." She throws her hands on her hips.

"You'll regret it," I tell her.

Lexi's eyes widen. She grabs the granola bar out of Nikki's hand and tosses it into her mouth.

"What the hell?" Nikki asks, incredulous. "You said I could have that."

"Changed my mind. I'm hungry." Granola flies from Lexi's mouth as she talks.

"Whatever." Nikki starts unpacking her books from her bag, stacking them neatly on her desk. "What are we doing tonight?"

"The usual. Drinking. Partying." Lexi plugs in a curling iron beside her mirror and turns her face this way and that, admiring herself. She glances at my reflection in the mirror and cringes. I close my eyes for a moment, wishing I was anywhere but here.

"Sweet. What are you wearing?" Nikki begins pulling

clothes out of her closet, mainly minidresses, miniskirts, ultra low-rise jeans, and low-cut tops.

"I was thinking my ripped denim jeans and a crop top." Lexi brushes out her hair and starts curling her extensions.

"Maybe you should wear something a little more conservative," I suggest.

Nikki raises an eyebrow. "That's no fun."

"Yeah, sis." Lexi smiles coyly at me.

I've been here a few hours, and she's already making plans to get drunk. This is going as smooth as a stucco wall.

"I'm going to get chasers from the vending machine. Need anything?" Nikki asks.

"Red Bull, please," Lexi calls out as Nikki leaves the room.

"You can't be serious." I stare at Lexi as she stares at herself in the mirror, carefully curling each section of her hair. Her fake hair sizzles as she wraps it around the hot rod.

"What?"

"Going out and getting drunk when I told you we need to get our lives together."

"If I don't do what I would usually do, won't that completely change the future? Like, maybe you'll end up even more single or more unemployed . . . ." Lexi changes into a low-cut crop top.

Her breasts look big. She's definitely wearing those inserts. When did she slip those in? I was always a ninja with those things.

"Well, maybe. But no, that would completely defeat the purpose of me being here," I try to rationalize.

She slides on a pair of super low-rise jeans that feature, like, a one-inch zipper. Those things better never make a comeback. I like that I can tuck my stomach into my jeans and not worry about my underwear showing.

"Honestly, I'm still not convinced I'm the problem." Lexi grabs a pad of paper from her desk and begins flipping through it. "I've written a list of things I think you should change." She points to each item on her list as she reads it out loud: "First your hair, then your ass. Third, your know-it-all attitude; fourth, your lack of a boyfriend. Five, your lack of drive; sixth, t—"

"Okay, stop," I interrupt. "First of all, lists are stupid, and second, if this were about *me* changing, then I wouldn't have to be here in this era with you. Right? I could have accomplished that in my time."

"I guess." Lexi shrugs. "But let's try it my way first, and if it doesn't work out, I'll do it your way."

"What's *your* way?" I give her a quizzical yet firm look.

"I haven't decided yet. I'll think it over more tonight. I do my best thinking while I'm drinking." She smirks as she admires herself in the mirror, looking over her shoulder at her back.

"Joy. Can't wait to hear what you come up with."

"I'm thinking about getting a tattoo right here," she says, pointing to her clean lower back.

"NO! Don't!" I react before I even think about reacting.

Lexi jumps a little. "Freak out a little more. I said I was *thinking* about it. I probably won't even get it."

Yeah, right. That "live, laugh, love" tattoo written in cursive with two hearts between the words on my lower back says otherwise. I have to stop her from getting that. It's the least I can do while I'm here.

I recall getting the tattoo at a janky parlor in downtown Oshkosh.

I stumbled in a little tipsy, not too tipsy so they'd turn me away for being intoxicated. They should have though. I slapped a piece of paper with the mock-up of my tattoo on the counter and said to the bearded gentleman. "I want this on my lower back because this tattoo is going to remind me to live and to laugh and to love every day."

The only reminder it's served is how much of an idiot I was.

Nikki comes back carrying three cans of Red Bull. She hands one to Lexi. "Here, I got you one too, Alexis," she says, handing it over.

I take the Red Bull. "Thanks." I'm exhausted, and I need the energy to keep up with Tweedledum, who's still staring at her lower back.

"So, you're coming out with us, right?" Nikki asks me. "I have to see where Lexi gets her crazy partying skills from."

"She definitely didn't get it from me."

"Actually, I think I got it directly from you." Lexi smiles.

"I'm just going to stay in. No drinking for me. It's been a really long day." There's no way in hell I'll be caught partying with a bunch of eighteen-year-olds. Besides, I need to come up with a way to get out of here.

"Suit yourself." Nikki shrugs and cracks open her can of Red Bull. "How long do you plan on visiting?"

"Hopefully not long at all," I say.

"You two must be really close." Nikki laughs as she makes Lexi and herself drinks, filling two glasses with half vodka and half Red Bull.

"We're practically the same person," Lexi says, laughing.

She hands one to Lexi and walks to her closet, fiddling around with accessories. When Nikki turns around, she's wearing a popcorn shirt, tattoo choker necklace, and a Von Dutch hat. "Is this too much?" She gestures to her outfit.

"Hike the scrunchie shirt up, and it's perfect!" Lexi beams, taking a gulp of her drink.

It literally couldn't be any tackier, but I keep my mouth shut and take a sip of my energy drink.

A few more vodka Red Bulls later, Nikki and Lexi drunkenly head out.

"Don't wait up." Lexi closes the door behind her with an evil smile.

If my memory serves me right, it won't be long before she returns. As much as I used to drink, I still had a low tolerance for alcohol. I had the bright idea of not eating right before a night of drinking so I would get drunk faster and would switch out my calories for alcohol instead of food. That plan rarely worked, since I'd get wasted way too quickly, and afterward, I would eat everything in sight to soak up the alcohol and try to avoid throwing up (which I rarely avoided). I remember eating a whole loaf of bread at a house party because I wanted to stop myself from puking. It didn't work, and I ended up throwing up sixteen pieces of bread.

I lie down on Lexi's bed and close my eyes for what seems like fifteen minutes, after which I'm jolted awake by the door being thrown open.

Katie and Nikki carry Lexi in, one of her arms around each of them. She's crying hysterically. Snot runs out of her nose. Her perfect curls that she spent over an hour doing now resemble a bird's nest. Black mascara is smeared underneath her bloodshot eyes.

"Lexi, it's going to be okay," Katie says to Lexi.

Katie's light-brown shoulder-length hair has a gloss to it, and not one strand is out of place. That's exactly what her hair looks like in her thirties as well. She's wearing a Rugby shirt with flare yoga pants. Katie was never one to try too hard, except when it came to her studies. She didn't care what others thought of her, and she always dressed for comfort, not for show. I think the only reason she ever came out drinking with us was to make sure that we made it home okay.

"You don't need him," Nikki says reassuringly to Lexi, patting her on the back. It comes out slurry. She looks as drunk as Lexi, minus the snot.

I scoot off the bed before Lexi collapses onto me.

"He broketh up with me," Lexi wails, kicking her feet and flailing her arms like a toddler. Her words are also slurred.

Oh, this is a breakup. Who was I dating at this time? It couldn't have been anyone too serious because I don't even recall this happening. Wait . . . .

"Greg? Big muscles, small brain, smaller penis? I haven't thought about him in forever. I think he works at a gas station now."

Nikki and Katie give me an odd look.

"How do you know what your sister's boyfriend's penis looks like?" Nikki scrunches up her face.

"Ummm, we have a similar dating history," I answer quickly.

"Okay . . . ." Nikki pushes Lexi's hair out of her face, but it tangles around her fingers, so she ends up having to use her other hand to free herself from the mess that is Lexi.

"He was my everything. I'm never going to love again," Lexi cries.

I don't even remember crying over him. He was definitely not her everything. Sure, he had a nice body, but nothing beyond that. I think most of our conversations were him telling me what muscles he worked out at the gym and how many egg whites he ate. I can't believe I thought I loved that guy. I can't believe I cried over that guy.

"I don't think I'm ever going to get over him!" Lexi sobs louder.

"Yes, you will. You don't need him." Nikki unsteadily helps Lexi pull off her heels.

Katie heads toward the door. "I'll be right back," she calls back as she leaves.

"No, you guys don't understand. I thought I was going to marry him." Lexi wipes her face with a Kleenex, smearing her mascara, blush, and bronzer into a swirl. She's a Picasso painting.

I laugh out loud, weathering the girls' dirty looks. Come on—I dated him for *maybe* a few months. I never once thought I was going to marry him. I can't tell if she's doing this for sympathy, or she's actually torn up about the whole thing, or she's just super drunk. At the time, it probably felt like the end of the world, but now it doesn't even register as a big moment in my life. It's odd that when we look back, the big moments are the little ones and the little moments are actually the big ones. I remember meeting Andrew for the first time, and it was nothing. It was just a little moment. But now, looking back, it was one of the biggest moments of my life.

"Lexi, seriously. Greg is a loser. You don't love him. You never did, and I guarantee you'll forget about him by the end of the week," I tell her, trying to stop this obnoxious blubbering and put things in perspective. Plus, I want to go to sleep.

She turns to me. "How would you know? You have no idea how I feel. I love him."

Really? Has she forgotten who I am? Did the alcohol already erase that memory? I can't work with this.

"Lexi. I know exactly how you feel," I say firmly.

She sniffles some more and then looks me right in the

eye. She tries to regain her composure, then bursts into tears again. "I can't help it."

Ugh, I was so weak. Not even I, who is she in seventeen years, can convince her that this breakup is not a big deal, that in the grand scheme of things, it has absolutely zero impact on her life.

Katie comes back with water and some Tylenol. She hands them both to Lexi and tells her to drink the whole glass before going to sleep. She was a doctor even before she was a doctor.

"Hi there, I'm Katie." She holds out her hand, and I shake it.

"I'm Alexis, Lexi's older sister."

"Nice to meet you," Katie says.

A sadness hits me. She was always such a good friend. It's a shame we fell out of touch. When I get back, I'm going to call her. There's no reason we shouldn't remain friends. Well, maybe there is. She was a better person than I was. She worked hard. She achieved her goals. She grew up.

"What happened to Claire?" Nikki asks.

I knew we were missing someone. Claire isn't here. My guess is she found a guy with "money potential," as she used to say.

"She met some guy with money potential, according to her," Katie answers.

Called it. Good old Claire.

"She went home with him?" Nikki asks.

"Yeah." Katie shrugs.

"He must have some serious 'money potential' for her to ditch us and go home with him." Nikki helps Lexi undress and put on pajamas.

"According to Claire. He's an art major, which means he's

majoring in unemployment. I tried explaining that to her, but her response was, 'Ever heard of Leonardo DiCaprio? Yeah, didn't think so,'" Katie says. "I think she meant Leonardo da Vinci though."

"Thank God she's pretty." Nikki laughs.

Nikki's purse starts buzzing. She pulls out a Nokia cellphone. I was always so jealous she had one. Her dad was a businessman who traveled a lot and felt guilty about never seeing her, so he got her a phone to keep in touch. He bought her a ton of other stuff too, which is why our dorm room is so cutely decorated.

"It's Claire," she says and begins to read a text message: "'I left that guy's house after seeing his art. There's no way he's going to make money off that garbage.'"

"Is she coming over?" Katie asks.

"Let me check." Nikki taps at the buttons on her phone. She pushes each button several times, and it takes her a little over a minute to type "Coming over?'"

Back then, if you wanted to text someone, you had to put in an effort. Just to type the letter "O" you had to press the number six, three times. The struggle. Plus, every text cost like 10 cents. For me and Katie, who paid our own way through college, a cellphone was just too expensive.

The phone buzzes again, and, looking at it, Nikki says, "No. She's going to sleep."

Lexi's snoring signals the end of the night. Katie leaves for her room two doors down. Nikki tosses me some extra pillows and a blanket so I can make a bed for myself on the floor, since there's no way I can move Lexi. She's like a pile of wet cement, snoring as loud as a concrete mixer. One day down, who knows how many to go.

TEN

NIKKI SLAMS HER hand against her blaring alarm clock, which reads 7:30 a.m. It goes off again a few minutes later, and she hits it, but I see that this time she slowly gets out of bed.

"Morning," I say, my voice cracking.

"Hey." Nikki grabs a towel and her shower tote.

"Does Lexi have class today?"

"Yeah, but I doubt she's going."

I sit up, rubbing my eyes. "What time is her class?"

"Eight-thirty," Nikki says over her shoulder as she exits the room.

Oh, she's definitely going to class today. She tried it her way last night, and she just ended up getting drunk and dumped. It's time to try things my way.

I nudge her motionless body. "Wake up, Lexi."

No response.

I wind my arm back, pillow in hand, and swing it at her body.

Still nothing.

"Lexi, wake up!" I yell.

Nada. How can she not hear me?

Tossing the pillow on the bed, I grab the half-full cup of water from her nightstand, the same one Katie told her to drink all of. I tip the glass, letting a stream of water fall right onto Lexi's head.

She jumps up, screaming. "What the hell is wrong with you?" She wipes her wet face with her blanket.

"Great, you're up."

"No, I'm not up." Lexi crashes back onto the bed.

I grab her feet and pull. Before she can scream again, Lexi lands on the floor with a thud. I dust my hands off: a job well done. It feels like I have a teenager of my own.

"You have class in an hour. Get ready and put on something respectable."

Lexi stands up slowly, only to sit on her bed, holding her head in her hands. "I'm not going to class today."

"Yes, you are." I throw a sweater and a pair of jeans at her face.

She swats them to the floor. "No, I'm not. I'm taking a mental health day. I went through a very traumatic experience last night, and I need time to process it."

I roll my eyes. "I don't care what you went through last night. You're going to class if I have to drag you there myself." I put my hands on my waist and stare her down, showing her I mean business. I'm bigger than her, older than her, and wiser than her. There's no way she's getting out of this.

She stares right back, narrowing her eyes. "There's no way in hell I'm going to class today."

An hour later, I'm pulling Lexi by her wrist across campus. She fights me the entire time, moaning and groaning, and struggling to get away.

"I'm not going!" she yells.

Necks crane in our direction as we pass fellow students.

"You're making a scene." I jerk her a little harder, trying to get her to fall in line with me, but she continues to fight back.

"I don't care. I need a mental health day," she pouts.

If I hadn't already gone through this time period, I'd be really embarrassed right now. I give her the benefit of the doubt and assume she's still drunk. I'm hoping her hangover hits her sooner rather than later so she'll feel weak, and I'll be able to move her around easier.

"Almost there," I say, pulling with all my might. I'm also carrying her book bag because she refused to.

We finally reach the classroom. It's a pit class full of a hundred-plus students—either a science or a math course. I don't know because—surprise, surprise—Lexi didn't know. I have no idea how she functions without me. She finally stops fighting me and takes a seat near the back. I sit beside her and pull out a notebook and pen, placing them in front of her.

"Take notes," I order her.

She pushes it back toward me. "I don't take notes." She points to her head. "This baby's a steel trap."

A middle-aged man in a sweater vest and black slacks walks in, setting his briefcase on the table in front of the whiteboard and turning the projector on.

"Hey, Lexi, what's your professor's name?"

"I don't know."

She is seriously worthless. It's only the tenth week of classes.

"All right, people, today we're going over chapter seven: 'The Periodic Table of Elements.' Please turn to page one hundred thirteen in your books," the professor instructs.

I rummage through Lexi's book bag, looking for a book. There's only a planner and a few notebooks, all blank—because of course they are.

"Where's your textbook?"

"I never bought it. It's a waste of money. Seventy-five dollars for a book? That's ridiculous. I can fill up a six-disc CD changer with that kind of money."

I let out a deep breath, willing myself not to smack her.

Lexi grabs a pen and a notebook. Wait—she's going to take notes. It's a miracle! Maybe she's teachable. It's just going to take time and patience—and lots of alcohol—for me to deal with her.

The professor begins lecturing about the periodic table, rambling on and on about elements and covalent bonds and science and stuff I neither understand nor care about. Lexi is right. This is a waste of money and time. In the last seventeen years of my life, not once did I have to refer to the periodic table or even talk about any element, aside from gold and silver, of course. Also, diamonds. Are diamonds elements?

I glance over at Lexi. She's not taking notes—she's written out "live, laugh, love" in cursive and placed small hearts between the words.

Dammit—she's drawing that stupid lower-back tattoo!

Without thinking, I push the notebook off her desk.

"What the hell?!" Lexi says loudly.

The class stops, and everyone looks at us. She scowls at me and bends to pick up her notebook.

"Is there a problem?" The professor aims his question at Lexi.

"No," she responds nonchalantly.

"What's your name?" He picks up his grade book.

"Lexi Spencer," she says, sitting up straight in her seat.

He scans his book and notes something down with a pen, then looks back at Lexi.

"Why don't you help us with the next question, Lexi? Can you tell us what yellow metal is an alloy of copper and zinc?"

Lexi glances at me with a "Help me" look.

"What is it?" she whispers to me.

"Say Tungsten?" I whisper to her, not sure myself. I don't even know if it's a real word, but it sounds science-y.

"Tungsten," Lexi answers proudly. She probably assumes I knew the answer, but you know what they say about assuming.

"That is a metal, but it's gray, not yellow. Try again," the professor says.

"Thanks a lot, asshole," Lexi whispers to me through her teeth.

"Oh, I got it," I whisper confidently. "Say sulfur."

"Sulfur," Lexi blurts out.

The professor frowns. "You got the color right, but sulfur is a nonmetal. This is a college course. Surely you know sulfur is a nonmetal?" He squints his eyes, waiting for Lexi to respond, but she says nothing. "The correct answer is brass. Please see me after class, Lexi," he says.

She glares at me and whispers, "A lot of good your precious degree did you."

"I never said I knew anything about science. I was a communications major. Don't blame me for not being able to answer an eighth-grade science question."

"You're partially responsible, you being me and all." She continues sketching out our regretful tattoo.

After class, I wait for Lexi outside the classroom. She tried to run out and not talk to the professor, but I led her to him and left the room. Lexi flings open the door, carrying a sheet of paper. Her brows are pulled together with a pout on her lips. She's pissed.

"So, how'd it go?" I ask.

"Bullshit." She pushes past me toward the exit.

I quicken my pace to keep up with her. "What's the paper for?"

"He wants me to see a tutor. It's information on the tutoring center." Lexi crumples the paper and tosses it in a nearby garbage can.

"It couldn't hurt. You should go."

"That's not really my thing. I'm not an idiot, and I don't need anyone's help." She pushes the doors open, jogging down the steps of the building.

She's really not an idiot. She's just a hindrance to herself and her own potential. The only thing that's ever gotten in her way is her. Lexi is not one to ask for help. She could be laying up in a hospital bed and would still refuse help from anyone, including the doctor.

"Where are we going?" I ask.

"To lunch. Katie, Claire, and Nikki are meeting us."

"Really? Wow, I haven't seen Claire in ages. You know, I'm going to her wedding in a month," I say.

Lexi stops dead in her tracks and looks at me, stunned.

I suddenly realize I shouldn't have said anything about the wedding.

"Her wedding? Is this her first marriage?"

I know what she's thinking. If it's Claire's first marriage, that means she doesn't get her M.R.S. degree for another seventeen years.

"Ummm . . . yeah," I say, hoping she'll drop the subject.

Lexi starts laughing. "That's hilarious. That's Claire's only goal in life, and it takes her that long to find a rich guy that'll marry her? I should just tell her to give up now."

I grab her shoulder, pulling her to a stop. "You can't tell

Claire. First, you'll sound insane, and second, you'll mess with her life. She can't know that."

"But it's *so* funny."

"Is it really that funny? What are *your* goals, Lexi?"

She gives me a blank stare.

"Exactly. You have no goals, and guess what? Seventeen years from now, you will have accomplished nothing. At least Claire is working toward something, even if it is vain and superficial."

Lexi stares at me for a few more seconds. Then her face lights up. "It will all work out in the end." She starts walking away.

"Nope, stop that. No, it won't," I say, following her.

She continues walking nonchalantly. "If it's meant to be, it will be."

"You're delusional."

"Things go wrong so you can appreciate them when they're right."

"Not true for you. They never go right because you never take responsibility for your own life."

"Everything is okay in the end. If it's not okay, then it's not the end."

"If you say one more inspirational quote, I'm going to hurt you," I warn.

Lexi laughs. "Que sera, sera."

I sprint toward her and tackle her to the ground. I swing my arms, trying to connect with her face, but she mirrors me, and instead of punching her, my arms bounce off of hers. With a frustrated yell, I grab a fistful of her hair just as my own head yanks back. She does the same goddamn thing to me. I can't win; she's in my head. People start to gather around us.

"Catfight!" some guy crows.

Another guy yells, "Get her!" and "Kick her ass!" Who is he cheering for?

"Stop pulling my hair!" Lexi yells.

"You stop pulling mine!"

She cocks her free hand back, forming it into a fist as I do the same. Like it's been choreographed, we thrust our fists into each other's faces, connecting with our respective right eyes. The hits are synchronized. I fall backward, and so does she. We hit the ground simultaneously.

We lie there on our backs, holding our throbbing eyes and trying to catch our breath. A few people try to help us up, but we just sprawl there. After the crowd dissipates, I sit up, perched on my elbows, and look at Lexi.

"Are you going to listen to me now?" I ask.

Lexi sits up. "Are you going to listen to me now?"

I sit up so I'm higher than she is. "What are you talking about? I just put you in your place. Have a little respect for your elder."

She does the same, copying my movements. "What are you talking about? I just put you in your place. Have a little respect for the better version of yourself."

"Are you just saying what I'm saying?"

"Are you just saying what I'm saying?" she repeats.

"For fuck's sake, Lexi. We can't go on like this. Look, I know neither of us likes the situation we're in. You don't want me here, and I don't want to be here, but being at odds isn't going to make that better. Let's say I do leave you alone and just take off. How does that play out? There's another version of you walking around the planet. You're okay with that? I don't think so. We don't have to be friends, but we do need to at least be civil."

She weighs my words. I think she might just tell me to fuck off and go live my life. Who cares if there's another version of her out in the world? Lexi moves her twisted lips side to side.

"So do we have a deal? A truce?" I extend my hand toward her.

Lexi eyes it with hesitation, like she doesn't trust me. After a few moments, she puts her hand in mine and shakes it.

"Fine," she says.

A small sense of relief comes over me. Finally, I'm getting her to agree to something, but I don't trust she'll actually follow through. It's a start, though.

ELEVEN

I GRAB A tray and get in line, my eyes laser-focused on all the goodies up ahead. Pizza. Burgers. Fries. Corndogs.

My eyes light up as I pick up the ooiest, gooiest piece of cheese pizza. Before I can place it on my tray, where it belongs, Lexi slaps my hand, knocking the slice back onto the pan.

"What the hell?" I say loudly.

"You don't need that," she says.

"I thought we weren't meddling anymore."

"This isn't meddling, because that," she points at my body, clearly disgusted, "is mine too, and you're failing to maintain it."

I let out a huff and slide down the line. She's the worst. I look pretty good for my age. Sure, I don't work out regularly, but when you get to a certain age and your metabolism dips, it's like, why fight it?

I pick up a golden-brown corndog, admiring it for a moment before setting it down on the tray.

Lexi flicks it off my plate. "You don't need that either," she says with a smirk.

I take a deep breath and slide quickly away from her down the line. Before she can get to me, I have a burger sitting on my tray, with all the toppings and extra cheese. It's perfect. When I look back, Lexi's not behind me anymore. Good.

Maybe she gave up. But when I look down at my tray again, the burger is gone.

NOOO!

Glancing around, I see Lexi carrying my beautiful burger to a trash can and promptly disposing of it. She looks at me with a devious smile. I'd like to take my tray and smack her in the head with it, but I won't because I'm the adult here.

Marching toward her, I narrow my eyes and raise my chin. "What am I supposed to eat then?"

"Ever heard of a vegetable?" she says with a laugh.

When we finally sit down at a table, all that's left on my tray is a salad, an apple, a bottle of water, and some steamed broccoli. My salad looked quite appetizing—until Lexi removed the croutons, shredded cheese, bacon, and ranch. Now, it's just a pile of wilted lettuce with tomatoes and cucumbers. There is a bit of ranch residue left since she wasn't able to scrape it all off.

"Great," I say. "I guess I'll just starve to death."

"Beauty is pain, Alexis," Lexi quips.

Katie sits down at our table and eyes my tray. "Are you on a diet, Alexis?"

"It would appear I just started one." I stab my fork into a sad-looking cucumber.

Lexi smiles at me as she picks the pizza off her plate and takes a big bite, the grease from the cheese and pepperoni dribbling down her chin.

"Are you sure you should be eating that?" I twist up my lips.

She chews happily and dabs her chin with a napkin. "It's my cheat day."

What a load of bullshit. I spear a cherry tomato and

begrudgingly pop it into my mouth. If this isn't motivation to travel back to my time, then I don't know what is.

"Hey, guys, sorry I'm late," Claire says, tossing her book bag on the ground. When she flips her long, sleek hair behind her shoulder, her caramel highlights practically shimmer in the light, looking as though she just came right out of a hair commercial. Her plump lips are impeccably glossed. I still remember her perfected three-step process: first, a pinkish lipstick; then a nude color in the center; and then a sheer shine on top. But it's not her lips or even her cleavage that draws you in. It's her eyes—like two large emeralds set perfectly into her face. It's as though she was put on this earth solely to mesmerize others. "My engineering class ran over," she explains as she sits.

"You're not in engineering," Katie says, biting off some of her ham-and-cheese sandwich.

"Well, not technically, but I'm learning a lot."

"Like what?" Lexi asks.

"Well, today I learned that Tom is single, and his dad's the CEO of a Fortune 500 company. Brent is here on a full-ride scholarship and will most likely go to an Ivy League school for his master's after graduating. Ryan's family has a lake house that he'll inherit someday, and Jake is failing engineering, so I'm not really interested in him anymore."

Katie rolls her eyes. "None of that information has anything to do with engineering."

"Did you not hear me say Jake is failing engineering? That has the word 'engineering' in it." Claire smirks, grabbing a few chips from Katie's tray.

Claire always put a ton of effort into her "degree": She joined the sailing club in hopes of meeting a guy with a boat; attended (but didn't enroll in) engineering, pre-med, and law classes to meet future rich men; and became a cheerleader to get close to the basketball and football players ("You never know, they could get drafted into the NBA or the NFL!"). Considering the fact our college was a Division III school, that was highly unlikely.

Claire glances at me and smiles. "Oh, hi. I'm Claire. Wow. You look just like Lexi."

"She looks nothing like me." Lexi scowls. "She's my super old sister, Alexis."

"I'm her older, wiser sister, Alexis," I say. "Nice to meet you."

"Seriously, Lexi. You two look identical. You'll probably look just like her in ten years," Claire says.

"More like twenty years," Lexi raises an eyebrow. "And her whole look isn't one I'd let happen to me."

"What's that supposed to mean?" I narrow my eyes at her as I bite my apple. It crunches between my teeth, spraying juice everywhere.

"You know exactly what that means." Lexi raises her chin, peeling off a pepperoni slice from her pizza and tossing it into her mouth.

Claire smiles tightly, clearly feeling awkward amid our jabs. "Anyway, how long are you in town for?"

"Not sure, but hopefully not too long." I sink my teeth into the apple again, ripping at its red flesh. It's not even good—I don't even know why I'm eating it, well, actually I do. I'm starving. Whoever named these things Red Delicious was a goddamn liar.

"Yeah," Lexi adds. "Hopefully not long at all."

"Sweet, you'll have to come out with us." Claire grabs a few more chips from Katie's tray.

"Yeah," I say, knowing I have no desire to ever go out

with them. Seeing Lexi drunk, disheveled, and blubbering last night was more than I cared to see. How does she not realize how embarrassing that is?

Claire changes the subject. "So, everyone," she says excitedly, "Jason asked me out on a third date. His family is super wealthy, and he's pre-med." She crunches on another potato chip, lost in thought. "I think he could be the one."

Lexi spits up some of her water in a fit of laughter. Oh no—she'd better not tell Claire what she knows.

"What, do you not like Jason? Did he tell you something? Does he not see me as marriage material?" Claire sounds a little panicked.

"Oh no. He's definitely the one. He's perfect. They're all perfect," Lexi says, still laughing.

I kick her in the shin under the table.

"Ouch!" she squeals, coughing a bit to mask her laughter.

Claire folds her arms in front of her chest. "Then what's so funny?"

"Nothing. I was just thinking of something else that happened earlier," Lexi lies.

"Well, okay. Anyway, like I was saying, I'm going out with him again, and I think if I put out, it'll seal the deal—you know, make him fall in love with me," Claire gushes.

"Don't," Lexi and I say in unison.

"What? Why?" Claire twirls her hair with her finger.

"Because you should make him wait," Lexi says. She and I nod repeatedly, like bobbleheads.

"Yeah, hold off for a while," I tell her. If Claire starts off with that mentality, she'll have slept with the whole town before she's thirty. I do recall telling her not to do this. Who in their right mind would think that having sex with a guy would make him love you and want to marry you? Well,

Claire, I guess. I suddenly remember Jason, who was a real douche. Claire and Jason dated for quite some time, but he cheated on her with several different women. He's actually the reason she developed serious trust issues.

"Fine, I guess I'll wait," Claire says, pouting slightly. "But if I don't get married for a really long time, I'm going to blame you guys."

"Looks like you'll be blaming us," Lexi quips.

I shoot her a glare.

Before Claire can catch on, Nikki interrupts, sitting down with a tray heaped with cafeteria food. "Ugh, I'm famished," she says as she takes a massive bite from her hamburger. She looks around at everyone else's food while she chews, stopping at mine. "Ooh, that looks healthy. Can I try your salad?" she asks.

Really, it's wilted iceberg lettuce with ranch residue on it. I honestly don't get it. I push the tray toward her. "Sure, knock yourself out."

Lexi blocks the tray. "You're not supposed to do that."

"It's fine. It's healthy," I insist, pushing a little harder. I just can't choke down any more lettuce. Lexi lets the tray slide to Nikki, who grabs her fork and finishes off my salad before attacking her own plate.

"What's the plan for tonight?" Nikki pauses her eating to ask.

"There's a party at Sigma Tau," Claire says while fiddling with her cellphone. I'm sure she's just playing snake because it's the only feature that phone has.

"The engineering frat? No, thank you." Nikki says, taking on her slice of pepperoni pizza.

"What's wrong with the engineering frat?" Claire asks.

"They're nerds."

Claire shoots Nikki a look. "They're the most brilliant guys at this school, with huge potential for major lifetime earnings."

"I'll go, but only for a little bit." Katie opens one of her books and begins highlighting sections of it. She was always one to use every spare second to study.

"I'm in," Lexi says. "But I'm bringing my math homework again. The last time I brought it along, some random guy did it, and I got an A."

That *was* a great system I had in place: while some guy did my homework, I'd play beer pong and take shots. I *should* scold her for this and tell her it's not right, but I probably wouldn't have passed chemistry otherwise.

Lexi looks at me, like she's waiting for me to chide her, but I say nothing.

"You're such a cheat," Nikki says to Lexi.

"The only cheating that's going on is you cheating on your diet," Lexi quips.

"Rude!" Nikki gasps.

"But so true," Claire adds.

Lexi and Claire laugh as Nikki pushes her tray away. Katie doesn't look up from her book.

"Fine, I'll restart the diet tomorrow," Nikki pouts.

"That's what you said yesterday," Lexi says.

"And the day before," Claire adds.

"And the day before," Lexi continues, laughing.

"Okay, stop!" Nikki huffs.

"We only give you shit because we love you." Lexi gets up and wraps her arms around Nikki's shoulders.

"Yeah, we're totally kidding," Claire says as she joins in on the hug.

"And *you're* the one who keeps saying you want to go on

a diet. If you need help sticking to it, I'll help you out. Just say the word," Lexi tells Nikki. "Come to the gym later with Alexis and me."

"It's not about the gym really. It's my eating . . . I . . ."

"Hold on," I interrupt Nikki. "I never said I was going to the gym."

"Yeah, I know. *I* said you were going to the gym. You need to get that ass in shape. It's not a good look for me . . . I mean, you."

"It's none of your business." I raise my chin, challenging her.

"Your business *is* my business." Lexi raises her chin higher than mine.

"Then your business is *my* business," I say, raising my chin even higher.

We both stare at one another, straining our necks.

"You two are weird," Claire says, shaking her head.

Katie nods in agreement.

Nikki is watching while eating popcorn, and I have no idea where the hell she got it from.

"Alexis," Lexi says, "I need you to work out. I can't look like that."

I throw my hands up and look down at my body. There's nothing wrong with it—it's age appropriate. Curves are totally in, and so is body positivity. I'm what they call mid-sized. Such a better label than the previous chunky, chubby, and thick. God, the early 2000s were so superficial! We lower our chins, but our eyes stay narrowed.

"I look fine," I say. "You're just a bitch."

Lexi leans forward, two inches from my face. "If I'm a bitch, then you're a bitch."

"Okay, this is getting really weird," Nikki pipes up.

I whip my head in her direction. "Stay out of it, Nikki."

"Yeah, just sit there and eat your popcorn," Lexi adds.

"Don't be rude to Nikki!" I yell at Lexi.

"You were rude first." Lexi is practically ready to leap across the table at me.

"Technically, you were rude first. You are younger, after all."

"That makes literally no sense," Katie adds.

"Yes, it does," Lexi and I say in unison.

Katie shoots us a confused look while Claire stays glued to her phone and Nikki keeps munching away.

"How about this? If you go to the gym today and let me train you, I will do something you want me to do. Deal?" Lexi extends her hand.

I hesitate, looking at her hand and then at her face, wondering if I can actually trust her. I wouldn't trust me at that age. Lexi only looks out for number one, and that's herself. But if she were lying, I'd be able to feel it, right?

"Fine." I shake her hand.

"What are you going to have me do?" she asks, raising an eyebrow.

I smile. "You'll see."

I'm not sure exactly what I'll use this negotiation for yet. Maybe she'll go to every class for a week, swear off alcohol and partying for a month, or I'll stop her from getting that damn tattoo. Maybe I'll be petty and not let her speak for a whole day.

I'll have to think this one over, though. I feel like I got another wish, and I don't want to waste it like I did the last one, getting sent back to 2002.

TWELVE

I GLANCE AT myself in the mirror hanging from Nikki and Lexi's door. I've stuffed myself into a pair of running shorts and a tank top courtesy of Lexi. They're at least two sizes too small. She was right. I do look like a cabbage patch doll trying to stuff itself into Barbie's clothes.

I turn to the side. Ugh. My legs look like sausages escaping their casing. The only thing that's working is the tank top. Thanks to its size, it's lifted my breasts further than Dr. Kerson's talented hands managed.

Lexi and I stopped at the computer lab after lunch to Yahoo "time travel." (Yeah, in 2002, Google was not the top search engine.) I found nothing that was of any help. Maybe I'm just the first person to experience it, or I'm literally insane. Yep—that's probably it.

I let out a deep breath, trying to mentally prepare myself for this gym session. Lexi said several times that this is going to be the hardest workout of my life and that I'll either get fit or die trying. I honestly think she's going to kill me.

Lexi strolls into the room wearing a sports bra with matching neon orange running shorts.

"You're working out in that?" I ask, incredulous.

"Yeah, obvi. What else would I wear? These are standard workout clothes." She turns side to side, posing like she's some sort of model, but the only thing she's modeling is delusion.

"Standard workout attire are sweatpants and a T-shirt. That is standard 'I'm going to the gym to get attention' attire."

Lexi turns her nose up at me. "You're just jealous." She looks me up and down. "Let's go, cabbage patch." Lexi opens the door, leaving me behind as she skips down the hallway.

I follow begrudgingly. As I turn the corner, the doors of the elevator begin to close with Lexi inside. She smirks. I run to the elevator and push the button vigorously.

"Take the stairs," Lexi calls out in a singsong voice as the doors of the elevator close.

Ugh. I open the stairwell door and walk slowly down the eight flights. Once I'm downstairs, I see Lexi pulling her foot backward up to her butt, stretching out her quads for the viewing pleasure of several male students lingering in the lobby, and she is just basking in the attention she's receiving. Me at that age literally could not get enough of it. You could have thrown my eighteen-year-old self on a stage in Madison Square Garden with a packed stadium, and that still wouldn't have satisfied my appetite for attention.

Lexi looks at me pitifully. "Took you long enough. Let's go." She does this little totally unnecessary jog in place. Her breasts bounce. Jeez, they look big. The guys are, of course, still staring.

"Are you wearing your chicken cutlets?" I say loud enough to embarrass her.

"No." She stops and checks her boobs to make sure they're still in place. "God, you're such a bitch, Alexis," Lexi huffs and walks off.

With Lexi out of sight, several of the guys are looking at me now. I must have something on my face, or they think I look ridiculous. One smiles at me, and then another and then another. I smile back the smallest of smiles. Nice—they must think I'm doable. Ah, young men: all penis and no brain.

It's a brisk fall day outside, so I power walk as I attempt to catch up with Lexi, trying to warm up a bit. She's probably pissed. Our small boobs have always been a sensitive issue for us. When the girls in school started growing breasts in the seventh grade, mine were still mosquito bites. I'd ask my mom all the time when they were going to grow, and she'd always tell me to be patient and that everyone develops at different rates. I thought they'd for sure grow, since my mom, aunts, grandma, and cousins were all well-endowed. Age sixteen hit, and I was barely a B cup. Age seventeen? No change, and by the time I went to college, I was wearing the chicken cutlets and heavily padded pushup bras regularly. I will tell you there is nothing more nerve-racking than making out with a guy and having to hide your chicken cutlets if he decides to hit second base. I had so many clever tricks. I'd slide them into my purse when he wasn't looking or chuck them under my bed quickly. One time I was making out with a boyfriend in his car and I only had my wristlet with me, which they clearly wouldn't fit in. When he took off his jacket, I slid them under the passenger's seat. I forgot them, and we ended up breaking up a few days later. I wonder if he ever found them.

"Hurry up, Alexis!" Lexi yells back at me.

I jog to catch up with her. "Let's just get this over with," I say, already out of breath. I'm definitely going to die today; at this point, it may be my only way out of this mess.

Fifteen minutes later, I'm gripping the handlebars of a treadmill, trying to hold on for dear life. My legs aren't keeping up. My lungs feel like they're collapsing. I may need CPR. My own sweat is blinding me.

"Run faster!" Lexi yells, swatting at my hands. "Don't hold

those and stand up straight. You're cheating." She sounds like a drill sergeant.

I try to stand up and run with my arms by my side (like a normal person), but I nearly trip and tumble off the machine. I grip the handlebars again and smack the speed button to a lower setting.

Lexi pries my hands away from the bars, cranking the speed back up.

I'm being berated and trained by my younger self. Is this hell? It doesn't get much worse. I should just let the treadmill throw me into the wall.

"That fat butt isn't going to run itself off." Lexi slaps my ass.

"Owww, stop! Wha—what is wrong with you?" I can barely get the words out; my breath is so ragged. I feel my heartbeat in my stomach. Is that normal? In my arm, too. Am I having a heart attack? I wouldn't fight it at this point. Just put me out of my misery.

"I need—water," I gasp.

Lexi grabs the water bottle sitting on the floor and squirts it at my face. "There's your water," she says.

I pull the cord from the treadmill, automatically stopping the machine. "That's it, I've had enough." My lungs scream for air.

"You've been here fifteen minutes. Stop being pathetic," Lexi scolds.

"In those fifteen minutes, you've yelled at me, called me names, slapped my ass, and squirted water in my face. Plus, I think I might be dying." I hold my chest and collapse into a chair.

"Oh, don't be such a drama queen. To get tough, you have to be tough," Lexi lectures. "If I can do this, you can do this."

"I don't want to be tough. I don't want to be fit. I want to be me. I want Andrew back. I want to be married. I want to have a family. I want to have a career. I want to be somebody. And I don't want to be here with you." My face quickly crumbles and tears roll down my cheeks, mingling with the rivers of sweat.

Lexi hands me the water bottle. "I don't want you here either. I'm just trying to help you—well, *me*—but you know what I mean."

"I just don't think I can do this anymore." I take the biggest drink of water I can possibly manage, nearly choking on it.

"Do what? The workout?"

"No, all of this. I want to go back to my time. I want my iPhone 10. I want to binge-watch 'The Office' on Netflix. I want to wear leggings as pants. I want brunch with Andrew on Sunday mornings. I want Wi-Fi everywhere I go. I want to express my feelings via emojis on Instagram. I want to wear my AirPods all the time so no one will talk to me. I want to listen to Billie Eilish when I'm sad and Lizzo when I feel like I can take on the world."

"Okay, I have no idea what any of that means," Lexi says.

"Exactly. You have no idea what my life is like."

"I may not know what's popular in your time or how much technology has advanced or who Andrew is, but I know what our life is like. Let's just finish the workout. I'll tone it down a notch for your old, brittle body, and I promise you'll feel better afterward." Lexi stands up and beckons me with her hand. There's a kindness in her face, a tinge of understanding.

"Fine," I say, wiping my face. I can't believe I just broke down, and I can't believe Lexi calmed me. Is she maturing?

Am I de-maturing? I take a deep breath. I have to be stronger. I have to work harder. I can't regress.

Lexi hands me a set of two twenty-pound dumbbells.

"What am I supposed to do with these?" I say, almost buckling under the weight.

"Squat."

"Uh, how many times?"

"Until I say stop."

Before long, my legs burn, my ass is on fire, my muscles are screaming—ones that I haven't used in a very, very long time. Lexi continues to correct my posture as I squat, but she's not rude this time—she's encouraging me.

"Nineteen . . . twenty. Okay, you're done," she says.

"Really? We can go?" I drop the weights on the ground.

"No, you're done with this set. Two more sets left, and then you'll do lunges."

Oh. My. God. Did I really do this to myself back then?

I want to cry. This was so much easier when I was her. My muscles were used to being trained. Now, they're used to sitting on the couch.

About an hour later, I'm surprised to be alive. Lexi pats me on the back as we exit the gym. "You did good," she says and smiles proudly.

My legs are like Jell-O, and I can barely lift them. I drag my feet across the pavement, scuffing up Lexi's tennis shoes. She doesn't seem to notice.

"Don't you feel better?"

"If better is worse, then yes, I do," I groan.

"That's the spirit! I can't believe Nikki didn't show. She was supposed to work out with us."

"Are you really that surprised? She said she was restarting her diet tomorrow, so maybe she won't work out until then."

Lexi shakes her head. "So, she really gets fat?"

"I never said that," I say quickly.

"Well, you alluded to it." Lexi looks at me and raises her eyebrows.

"You can't tell her, but yeah, between now and the middle of sophomore year, she packs on thirty-plus pounds."

Lexi laughs.

"Come on, it's not funny. She's our friend."

"Yeah, I know. But it is kind of funny. Does she lose the weight?" Lexi asks.

"Actually, yeah. Her jeans stopped fitting. She was in complete denial. You feel guilty about the whole 'Get Nikki Fat Plan' and come to her rescue and get her into the best shape of her life. Thanks to you, she learns self-control and how to follow through with a plan."

"Huh, that's funny," Lexi says.

"How so?"

"I taught her how to follow through with a plan, and by the sounds of it, I never followed through with anything." Lexi opens the door to the dormitory for us.

"That's not true. We follow through," I say.

"Name one thing we've followed through with."

"Well, ummm . . . we graduated college."

"I guess if you want to count that. But did we ever write that book? Did we travel the world? Did we study abroad? Did we open up our own business? Did we become a certified yoga instructor? Did we learn to speak another language?" Lexi questions, irritated.

"There's still time to do all that."

"How long have you been saying, 'There's still time to do all that'?"

She got me. "Since I was your age."

"Exactly." Lexi unlocks the door to our room. Once inside, she immediately grabs her shower caddy and towel and leaves without saying a word.

I collapse into her desk chair. Wait a minute. How the hell can she be mad at me for not accomplishing everything we've wanted to accomplish? She is responsible for achieving our goals too. Why is this falling on me? Because I'm older? I don't give a shit. It's her fault—she started it. She led me down a path of self-destruction, and now she's trying to pretend she's the better version of us. Are you kidding me? Since I've been here, all she's done is drink, party, eat, and sleep—with the exception of attending one class I *forced* her to go to.

I stomp down the hall to the bathroom to give her a piece of my mind, letting the door close gently behind me. The steam is thick once I approach the shower stalls; I can barely see through it, but it seems like she's using the last one on the left. At first, I think I hear her laughing—probably at me. But as I start forward to tell her to shove it, I realize she's crying.

THIRTEEN

I WALK BACK to the dorm room and close the door. That was odd. We don't cry, unless we're drunk. We're the type of person to bottle all of our emotions inside until we explode. Not the healthiest way to deal with problems, but it's what we do. So, why is Lexi crying? I didn't tell her anything new. I didn't tell her anything awful that happened to us. I take a seat in the desk chair and rest my head on my hands. I watch the minutes on the clock pass, until it hits me.

I just told her that we never accomplish any of our goals. We do nothing with our lives. That's got to be hard to hear. I mean, I've had time to process it and make excuses for it and say that there's still time to do it all (which there is). I'm only in my thirties. I have my whole life ahead of me, and so does she. Nothing's written in stone, right? She can still accomplish all those things. Isn't that the point of me being here, so *she* can fix our future?

Lexi slams the door behind her, her towel wrapped tightly around her body. She drops the shower caddy on the floor of her closet, her bloodshot eyes avoiding mine.

I smile at her. "You know it's all going to be okay, right?"

"No, I don't know that, and neither do you," she says coldly.

"Listen, the reason I'm here is so you can fix all this. Start over. Get some insight and a second chance."

"This is *your* problem, not mine. You need to fix yourself."

She sprays leave-in conditioner into her hair and runs her fingers through it.

She's too upset right now to argue with. She just needs to cool off. Lexi will come around—we always do.

"I'm going to shower," I say. "Can I have a towel and some clothes?"

She throws a washcloth, a pair of sweatpants and a T-shirt at me.

"How am I supposed to dry off with this?" I hold up the washcloth and roll my eyes.

"I'm sure you'll figure it out."

I groan, grabbing the shower caddy on my way out and slamming the door behind me.

The hot water soothes my already sore muscles. Somehow, I need to get through to her. I'm going about all this the wrong way. At eighteen, if it wasn't my idea, I wasn't interested. I need her to start thinking some of this is *her* idea—then she'll go along with it. Yeah, that's it.

After attempting to dry myself off with the washcloth, I finish up under the hand dryer and slip on the shirt and sweatpants Lexi loaned me. Glancing in the mirror, I find that "Juicy" is emblazoned on the butt of the pants, and the T-shirt reads "Bitch" across the chest.

Great. Thanks, Lexi.

When I return to the room, she's sitting at her computer, wearing shoes and a jacket. Lexi turns around and looks me up and down. "That top is perfect for you," she says with a laugh.

I ignore her insult as I toss the soaked washcloth in the hamper and return the shower caddy. "Are you going somewhere?" I sit on the floor and attempt to stretch out my legs, but I can barely reach my ankles.

"We're going somewhere," Lexi says, standing from her desk and grabbing a backpack from her closet.

I reach my left foot, but my knee comes up, and I end up just holding my toes with no actual stretching occurring.

"Get up. Let's go." She swings the backpack over her shoulder.

"Where?" I'm not getting up until I know what she has in mind. For all I know, she's trying to drag me to a party looking like this so she can embarrass me.

"I want you out of my life—"

"And *I* want out of your life," I interrupt.

She folds her arms in front of her chest. "So we're going to try things my way."

"I thought going to the gym was your way."

"No, that was just fixing some of the damage you've done." She's so rude.

I sit down on the bed. But maybe this is it—this is how I get her to come around. I listen to her ideas. I participate, and then if they don't work, I take over. Lead us on the right path. She still owes me, though. She said if I worked out, she'd do something for me, but perhaps I'll have to wait on that favor. I just need to get her on board, and this seems like the best way to do it.

"Fine. What do you want to try?" I let out a deep breath, knowing I'll probably regret this decision.

"We're going to the library." She opens the door.

My eyes grow wide. The library? Has she ever stepped foot in one of those? Does she even know where it is? Okay. The library is something I can get on board with.

"Let me change quick," I say.

"No time. Let's go." She immediately treks out of the room.

I look down at my T-shirt and sweatpants. It's now or never, I guess, so I stomp off after her.

FOURTEEN

I GET SEVERAL looks from students as I follow Lexi through the study area toward the stacks. I have no idea what she has in mind or if she's even serious. Maybe she wants to research time travel, space continuum, black holes... I don't know, something that'll explain what happened to us. If that's the case, then I'm rather impressed. I figured she'd have us doing something stupid or still be fighting with me over everything. We already looked up what we could find on the internet about time travel, but maybe she has something else in mind. That breakdown she had in the shower must have really gotten through to her.

"What are we doing here?" I ask.

Lexi turns back to me, putting a finger over her mouth. She's smiling. "Shhhh. This is a library." She starts to pick out books and movies from shelves. They all seem so random, and I'm convinced she's doing this to waste my time.

"Lexi, what are you doing?"

"Shhhh . . . I have a plan," she says over her shoulder as she stacks them in her arms.

We enter a small, empty study room, where Lexi drops the dozen or so books and movies on a table, fanning them out so I can see the titles. *A Wrinkle in Time, Groundhog Day, 12 Monkeys* . . . . I look at Lexi expectantly.

"Get it?" she asks, her face lit up.

"Not really."

"All of these are about time travel. If we try the things they did in these books and movies, maybe we can figure out a way to get you, uh, back to the future."

I shrug my shoulders. "Or you could just work on yourself instead . . . pretty sure that's the key."

"I said we're trying it my way."

"And if this," I gesture toward the table full of terrible ideas, "doesn't work, then what?"

She sighs. "Then we can try it your way, and I'll comply this time."

I tilt my head. "You won't fight me on going to class?"

She shakes her head.

"You'll stop partying and drinking so much?"

She nods.

I squint my eyes slightly, trying to read her. She's clearly excited about this idea, and she's put some thought into it. I've never seen her put thought into anything aside from picking out her party outfits and doing her hair and makeup.

"Fine," I say. *What do I have to lose?*

She claps her hands together joyfully.

I grab the videos of *Back to the Future I* and *II* from the table and hold them up. "Wait a minute! In these movies, they have a DeLorean to time travel in. What are we going to do, steal a car?" My forehead puckers.

"Fine. We'll eliminate those." She takes them from my hands and puts them in a stack on the table that I know she has no intention of actually putting back properly.

"Eliminate any others that are impossible to accomplish or will get us arrested if we attempt to do them," I add.

"Agreed."

"All right, you have yourself a deal." I extend my hand and shake hers, making another deal with the devil herself.

FIFTEEN

AFTER SPENDING MOST of the next day at the library, I come back to the dorm room, excited to change into sweats, pour myself a drink, and relax for the evening. Opening the door, I find Lexi lying on the floor, taking notes in front of a small TV while credits roll on the screen. A large bowl sits beside her containing remnants of popcorn kernels.

I drop my bag, kick off my shoes, and shut the door behind me. "Where's Nikki?" I ask.

Lexi sits up, looking at her notes and glancing briefly at me. "She went to dinner with Katie and Claire."

"You didn't go?"

"No, we have bigger fish to fry. I skipped all my classes today and watched *The Terminator*, *12 Monkeys*, *Groundhog Day*, *Time after Time*, *Donnie Darko*, *Bill & Ted's Excellent Adventure*, and *The Time Machine*. I took notes on all of them, so my part of the research is done," Lexi says proudly. "How's your research coming along?"

"Well, I'm halfway done reading *Replay*, which is really good, by the way."

"That's it? Come on, Alexis. I watched six movies today, and you can't even read four books? I gave you way less work." She folds her arms in front of her chest.

"Lexi, don't be dumb. I have to *read* them, which takes far longer than watching a film. Wait a minute—how the hell did I get stuck with all the reading?"

"I don't like reading." Lexi gets up and tosses a bag of popcorn in the microwave.

Oh yes, I forgot—I used to hate reading. But still. "That's not fair."

The kernels pop intermittently.

Lexi tilts her head. "Life's not fair."

"Touché," I say. Can't argue with that. "So what did you learn?" I sit on the floor, wincing as I try not to bend too much. My muscles are super sore from yesterday's workout. I practically moan in pain on the way down to the floor.

Lexi grabs the pad of paper and flips through the pages, scanning them quickly. When the microwave beeps, she removes the popcorn, pours it into the empty bowl on the ground, and pushes it toward me.

"Okay, here's what we have to do. For *The Terminator*, we have to be cyborgs or robots or whatever they are from the future, so actually, that's not going to work at all." Lexi crosses out some notes and scans the next bullet point down on her paper.

She paces the room back and forth while I snack on the popcorn and listen to her work all this out.

"Let's see. For *12 Monkeys*, there was some sort of deadly virus that kills everyone, and Bruce Willis's character was selected to go back in time to stop it. He ends up getting shot, though, and they don't find a cure or stop the virus, so this isn't all that helpful. Good movie, regardless. Would definitely recommend. And Bruce Willis is such a babe." Lexi swoons, then crosses out her notes on the movie.

"Okay. Nothing you've discovered is helpful whatsoever?" I deduce while snacking on a handful of popcorn.

"Hold tight, Alexis, and respect the research process," she says in a snarky voice.

I nod. I've never seen her this invested in anything. It's quite impressive but also entertaining because it's all total nonsense.

"Continuing on, *Groundhog Day*: the main character, Phil, is trapped in this time loop that no one else is aware of. He keeps repeating the same day. At first, Phil's a real dick, but then he becomes a nice guy, and he escapes the time loop. You're not technically stuck in a time loop, but you could still try being less of a dick and see if that helps." She smiles at me.

"Very funny, Lexi."

"Just a suggestion." She grabs some popcorn and tosses it in her mouth.

"What's next?" I ask.

"*The Time Machine*. The main dude is a scientist; he invents a time machine. With our math and science skills, that shit ain't happening. I'll just cross that one off." Lexi says, scratching it out with her pen. "There was also *Time After Time*. The guy had a time machine too, but Jack the Ripper uses it to escape the police and go to the year 1979. Wait, are you a serial killer?" She looks at me suspiciously.

"No, Lexi." I roll my eyes.

She scratches her pen against the paper again and shrugs. "You never know. I used to joke that if I wasn't famous by thirty-five, I'd turn into a serial killer and become notorious that way. Moving on."

"This doesn't seem too promising."

She ignores my comment. "All right, *Bill & Ted's Excellent Adventure*: they use a telephone booth to travel through time. There's one near the library on campus." Lexi looks to me with bright eyes.

"You want us to just stand in there?"

"There's no harm in trying."

"Well, I already used that phone booth when I first got here to call Andrew, and it did nothing. But if you really want to try, we can. Keep it on the list."

I've got to keep her interested in helping me get back to my time, so if I have to stand in a phone booth for a while, I will. Whatever it takes.

"Good. We'll try another phone booth, just to be safe." Lexi nods and highlights the text. "Last but not least—actually, it is the least, because it totally sucked: *Donnie Darko*. I still don't understand this movie. There's a bunny and a plane crash, and I have no idea what the hell happened. I watched that damn movie twice, too. All I have to say about this one is if getting you back to the future is as complicated and confusing as this movie, you're not going anywhere." Lexi forcefully crosses it off the list.

"Yeah, I've seen *Donnie Darko*. I didn't get it either."

"You saw it? Why the hell did I have to watch it, then . . . twice?" She tosses her pad of paper and pen on the floor, sits beside me, and stuffs her face with more popcorn.

"How long will it take you to read those books?" she asks. Several kernels pop out onto the floor. She picks them up and tosses them back in her mouth.

"I don't know. A couple weeks."

"Screw that. We don't have time for that nonsense. We're SparkNoting that shit," Lexi says, getting up to sit at her desktop computer. She powers it up and begins the process to connect to the internet. I haven't heard that annoying sound in years.

"I don't know how we survived waiting for internet connections. In my time, it's instant," I say.

"Yeah, right!" Lexi laughs.

"Fast as lightning, and it's on every cellphone. You're never not connected." I smile fondly.

"Seems a bit invasive. Kind of strange to always be connected," Lexi says just as sparknotes.com finally loads.

"I guess it kind of is."

She types vigorously. "I need my notepad and pen," she says without looking away from her screen.

I grab them and crawl to her because I find I can't actually stand. I hand them over and crawl back to my space on the floor.

She throws me a quick look. "If you worked out more, you wouldn't be so sore."

I don't say anything back. We don't need another fight between us, and she's actually trying to do something. But, of course, she would choose to SparkNotes these books rather than read them—always taking the easiest route.

This whole thing is such a dumb idea, anyway. Like following some fictional time travel book or movie is going to help me get back to the future. Let's face it: until Lexi makes a serious change and we somehow alter what's to come for us, I'm stuck here. But at least we're sort of getting along, and we haven't assaulted each other since yesterday, so that's progress.

Soon, she plops down next to me with her notes.

"Ready to present your findings?" I ask with a grin.

"Don't mock. But yes, yes, I am," she says confidently, sitting up a bit taller. She scans her notes. "*A Wrinkle in Time*: there's like these supernatural beings that transport these people through other dimensions and space and time. I think we'd need to pick up a Ouija board to give this one a try." She looks to me for approval.

"Fine. Add it to the list."

"Perfect." She smiles. "*Replay,* which you have yet to finish. Jeff, as you probably know, repeatedly dies and wakes up earlier in his life to relive it. Wait, did you die?" She eyes me cautiously.

"No, Lexi."

"Maybe that's the key to all of this." She raises an eyebrow and delivers a half smirk.

I roll my eyes. "You're not killing me. Keep going."

"Fine, fine, fine. Anyway, spoiler alert. He meets another woman that is also reliving her life over and over again, and eventually they fall in love and stop time traveling.

"What the hell, Lexi? I haven't finished reading it yet," I complain. She's the worst.

"What? I said spoiler alert."

"Yeah, and then less than a second later, you spoiled the ending for me."

"If anything, I saved you a couple of hours of time wasted on reading. You're welcome." She smiles.

"Time reading isn't wasted time."

"Yeah, okay," she says sarcastically. "Regardless, it won't work unless you have a time traveling lover, which you don't. Because you're super single." she adds and crosses it out on her paper. "Let's continue. *Outlander* is about this chick named Claire that travels to the past. From the sound of it, there's a whole hell of a lot of rape in the book. Not sure if that has anything to do with time travel. But in the end, she travels through time via a hot spring, I believe. Know of any hot springs?"

"No."

"Okay, then . . . we'll look into that one." She draws a question mark beside the *Outlander* entry on her notes.

"It doesn't sound like any of these are going to work." I groan and drop my head into my hands.

"Patience and positivity, please," Lexi says. She returns her focus to her notes. "*Slaughterhouse 5* has this guy named Billy, who is captured by an alien spaceship, which is what allows him to travel through time, I guess. The whole thing seems really complicated, and SparkNotes didn't do the best job of making sense of this one. He falls asleep in a hotel room and travels back in time at some point. So maybe we need to check out a hotel room?" Lexi looks to me again for approval.

"Do you have money for a hotel room?" I raise an eyebrow.

"Uh, no. Crossing it off."

This is all so stupid. But do I have any better ideas? Nope.

"What's next?" I ask. I've got to keep her happy and motivated. It's the only way to get her to do a complete one-eighty with her life.

Lexi reviews her notes, crossing out, circling, and highlighting. She writes up a list titled "Things to Do to Send Alexis's Big Butt Back to the Future." She clears her throat.

"Lexi," I warn with a grumble, eying the title on the page.

She gives a small smile and quickly scratches out "big butt."

"Okay, what we need are a hot spring, a phone booth, a bigger brain to build a time machine, robots, aliens, and a Ouija board." The corners of her lips spread widely in both directions.

"Ummm . . . that all sounds really dumb and super implausible."

Lexi frowns. "You said we'd try it my way."

"Only things we could *actually* do."

"Fine. I'll cross off aliens, robots, and a bigger brain. Can't we at least try the hot spring, phone booth, and Ouija board?" she begs. "On the internet I found a hot spring outside of Savage, Minnesota. That's less than five hours from here."

"And how are we supposed to get there?"

"Girl's trip! We'll get Nikki, Claire, and Katie to come. We can camp out for a night and do the Ouija board out in the woods. That's extra spooky, so it should work."

"Besides the fact that there's exactly zero connection between spookiness and time travel, how are you going to convince them to go with us? Why would they even want to?"

"Because they're my friends—and Mall of America is thirty minutes from the hot spring." Lexi is pleased with herself.

"Who the hell goes to malls anymore? Oh wait. This is 2002. Never mind."

Lexi cocks her head at me. "So . . . what do you say?"

"And what about the phone booth?"

I don't even know why I bring that up. I just need her to get all of this out of her system, so we can focus on really fixing things and getting me back.

"If the other stuff doesn't work, we'll do that when we get back. Pretty please?" She places her palms together and flutters her eyelashes, trying to be cutesy. But to me, there's nothing cute about her.

"Fine," I say reluctantly.

Her eyes light up, and she claps her hands together in excitement. I already know this is just going to be a big waste of time, but it's not like I have anything else going on.

The door opens and in walks Nikki, dressed in black sweatpants and a light jacket. Surveying our popcorn and movies, she asks, "What are you two doing?"

"Pack your bags. We're going on a road trip!" Lexi announces.

"Really? Where? When? Why? Okay, I'll go!" Nikki was always on board with anything and everything. She and I had the most fun together. A tinge of sadness comes over me when I remember we aren't even friends anymore. What happened to us?

Lexi starts pulling bags from her closet, tossing them on her bed. A duffel bag for her and another one for me. "Yes. Saturday. Minnesota . . ." She pauses. "It's for a class. But we'll stop at Mall of America for fun." She smiles at Nikki.

"Ooooh, yay! Claire and Katie too?" Nikki's voice is full of enthusiasm.

"Yes. Text Claire, and I'll let Katie know."

Nikki immediately pulls out her phone and starts tapping away.

"We leave first thing Saturday morning," Lexi declares like she's the captain steering a ship. But rather than setting sail on a wonderful voyage, this ship is more like the Titanic.

SIXTEEN

"**HOW MUCH LONGER?**" Claire moans.

"We're only halfway there," Lexi says, looking at her MapQuest printout.

Katie, Claire, and I have been cramped into the backseat of Nikki's Toyota Corolla for the past few hours, while Lexi has shotgun, because she called it on Friday—the day before we were actually leaving. We've already listened to Nikki's special road trip CD three times—consisting of all the 2002 greats: Christina Aguilera, Eminem, Nelly, Avril Lavigne, Vanessa Carlton, Sean Paul, and Missy Elliott—and now I'm about ready to chuck myself out of the speeding car.

Does MapQuest still even exist? I forgot how much of a struggle it was before technology took over our lives. I miss my iPhone, and I hate to say it, but I miss Siri, even though she got me lost many times and never understood what the hell I was saying. But she's far more reliable than Lexi with a map. And I miss Andrew most of all, who always knew where he was going with or without a map. Except on that beautiful spring day, the day we met. It was the only time he had ever gotten lost, and he ran smack-dab into me while he was out on a run. I call that fate. My Sony Discman had crashed to the ground, shattering into several pieces. At first, I was angry until I looked up and saw him, Andrew. He helped me to my feet, apologizing profusely and explaining that he had gotten turned around on his run and was lost. He ended up replacing my CD player that day and taking me to lunch, where we talked for hours. I loved him immediately—from the moment my ass hit the pavement.

"Where are we going again?" Katie asks without looking up from the book she has her nose in.

"I told you, a hot spring. It's for a class." Lexi smirks over her shoulder at me. She thinks she's so clever.

"What kind of class requires you to visit a hot spring nearly five hours away?" Katie questions Lexi, still reading.

"Geolography," Lexi says.

"Geology," I correct.

"Yeah, that's it." Lexi nods. "Turn here!"

"Where?" Nikki panics.

"Here!"

Nikki jerks the car into a ninety-degree turn at the last minute. I slide into Claire, who smashes into Katie, whose book pages crumple.

"Lexi! You need to tell me before the turn, not *at* it." Nikki breathes heavily and grips the steering wheel at ten and two.

"You have one job, Lexi!" Katie says, clearly annoyed. "Look at my book."

Lexi looks back at her. "You shouldn't read in the car anyway. It's bad for your eyes. Or is it your stomach?" She looks back at the map. "Okay, you're on this for a hundred miles."

Oof. It's a long stretch of road with nothing around but a smattering of cornfields, trees, and farms. That's the Midwest for you. Also, there's cows . . . lots and lots of cows.

"I'm so bored," Claire complains, looking at her cellphone, but of course, she doesn't have any apps.

"I spy some—" Nikki starts.

"No, Nikki," Claire cuts in. "We're not babies."

"Let's play two truths and a lie," I suggest.

Claire turns to me with eyes wide. "Ooooh, what's that?"

"You say three things about yourself—two are true and one's a lie. Then, other people have to guess which is the lie. I'll go first." I clear my throat. "I moved to Chicago after college. I've dated the same man on and off for the last twelve years, but seriously for the last seven. I went skydiving after high school and my parachute failed, so the instructor had to save me before I almost died."

"Oh my God! That same thing happened to Lexi. Did you guys skydive together? Were you tandem?" Nikki looks at me in the rearview mirror.

Lexi turns around and gives me a dirty look. "No, she didn't. That one is clearly a lie because that's my story."

I have to stop myself from laughing. I used to tell people that so they would think I was some sort of a badass who went through something as traumatic as almost dying. And here Lexi was, still telling that tall tale.

"She's right! That one is definitely a lie, and it never happened," I say, staring at Lexi the liar. "Your turn, sis," I add with a chuckle.

"I met Eminem backstage at a concert. I've been on MTV's spring break special twice. I used to compete in pageants." Lexi smiles, pleased with herself.

"Those are literally all lies," I say, shaking my head.

"That's not how the game is played," Claire says.

Lexi turns back in her seat. "Yes, it is, because two of those things are true."

I roll my eyes.

"Which two?" Claire asks.

"Eminem and pageants." Lexi shrugs her shoulders.

"You never met Eminem, and you sure as hell never competed in any pageants," I scoff.

"You don't know." She flicks her hand, dismissing me and the truth. "Your turn, Claire."

"Finally. Let's see, I scored a 30 on my ACT. I've never traveled outside of the country. I'm a virgin."

"Ha. Easy. You got a thirty on the ACT. That's the lie," Lexi says with a laugh.

Nikki shakes her head. "Yeah, there's no way you did that, Claire."

Katie raises an eyebrow but doesn't say anything, her nose still in the book. Claire sinks a little deeper in her seat, lowering her chin slightly. She looks sad, a little defeated, but I'm not sure why. I've never seen her like this, or perhaps I never noticed.

"So, which one was it?" I ask, bumping her shoulder with mine to pull her back out of the shell she disappeared into.

"She doesn't even have to say. It's obvious," Lexi says from the front seat. "Whooo! I love this song." She turns up the volume. "Dirrty" by Christina Aguilera plays loudly.

Nikki and Lexi flail their arms, dancing in the front seat, reciting the lyrics. Eventually, Claire joins in, like nothing had happened. Even Katie finally closes her book and starts to loosen up, singing along too and shimmying her shoulders.

The remainder of the car ride is filled with bad karaoke, Claire declaring she's bored over and over, several wrong turns (thanks to Lexi), and multiple rest stops because Nikki always has to pee. We finally pull into the parking lot just off the trail leading to the hot spring.

"Everyone's wearing their swimsuits under their clothes, right?" Lexi asks. "It's just a short hike away." She gets out of the car just as Nikki turns it off.

"What are we doing here again?" Katie opens her door, taking in the woods that surround us.

"Taking a dip. Hot springs are healing waters. They'll fix whatever is broken." Lexi raises her eyebrows at me.

We follow Lexi up the path: a dirty, uneven trail littered with loose rocks and overgrown tree roots. The path is surrounded by thick woods and fallen golden and crimson-colored leaves.

"Almost there," Lexi encourages, waving us to follow her.

Nikki trails behind, so I stop to help her, holding her hand as she steps over a fallen branch.

"Thanks," she says.

I catch Lexi looking at me with narrowed eyes. She turns away quickly and marches forward. She's so weird.

Just over the hill, we finally reach the hot spring.

On our way here, I had pictured something resembling the Blue Lagoon in Iceland, with steam rising from beautiful milky blue waters. But I was wrong—very wrong. The scene before us resembles a dirt-rimmed toilet bowl. The hot spring looks like a giant had gone out for a night of tequila and Taco Bell, then came back here and sprayed liquid diarrhea into this hole. But it got clogged and the water is ever bubbling up, trying to spill out over the rim onto the green grass surrounding it. This is our beautiful hot spring of salvation.

"Fucking disgusting!" Claire says.

"We drove all this way for this?" Katie says incredulously.

"It's not that bad," Lexi tries to convince herself and us. "It's called Boiling Springs because it looks like it's boiling in the middle. It's kind of magical." She points to the rapid bubbles exploding in the center of the spring.

Nikki sticks out her tongue. "It literally looks like boiling poop."

"You guys are so uptight." Lexi kicks off her shoes, slides down her pants, and pulls off her sweater, revealing a tiny black bikini. She ties up her long blonde hair in a bun on the top of her head. "Come on, let's go in," she says, dipping her toe in the simmering poop water.

Claire shudders, nearly gagging.

"The water's nice and warm," Lexi says, smiling back at us.

"Of course, it is. It's a pond of diarrhea," I say dryly.

I know I agreed to do it her way, but this can't be my way out of this mess. I mean, if it was, it'd be totally on brand. I had to black out to get back to 2002, and I guess I might just have to swim in shit to get back to my time.

The water creeps up her calves, her knees, her thighs, and all the way to her waist as she lowers herself into the hot spring. Lexi makes a refreshing sound. "Feels great," she says, inching in a little further.

"This can't be sanitary. You're going to get typhoid or E. coli," Katie says, stepping away from the spring.

The water reaches Lexi's chest, and she starts floating around the bubbling liquid, like a log in a toilet. She breathes in deeply, as if she's having some sort of out-of-body experience, and closes her eyes, allowing her arms to float to her sides. She glides her fingers through the water peacefully. She's putting on a show, and it's working: Nikki pulls off her pants and sweatshirt and steps into the spring.

"Gross, Nikki." Claire turns up her nose.

"She's right. It is warm." Nikki walks deeper into the water.

"Does it smell?" Katie asks, taking a tiny step closer.

Lexi breathes in deeply through her nose. "It's like lavender meets vanilla with a hint of lilac." She uses the soothing voice of a masseuse to convey her lie. It actually stinks like rotten eggs mixed with stale water, musty and pungent—and I can smell it from here.

Katie undresses and steps into the spring, avoiding the boiling center.

"There's no way I'm going in there. It's disgusting," Claire says.

"Haven't you ever had a mud bath at a spa before?" Nikki asks. "It's like the same thing."

Claire shakes her head. "I have, and it's not the same."

"Get your ass in here, or we're not going to the Mall of America!" Lexi yells.

"Fine!" Claire stomps her foot, removes her clothes, and wades into the water, cringing the entire time. She floats in a circle with the girls.

"These are supposed to be healing waters?" Nikki asks.

"That's right," Lexi says, still using her soothing voice. "Hot springs are filled with minerals that benefit your skin and help you relax."

"I'm not feeling any less anxious," Katie confesses.

Nikki glances over at Katie. "Anxious? Why are you anxious right now?"

Katie looks away for a moment and then back at the girls. "I'm always anxious. I have really bad anxiety."

"You do?" Lexi tilts her head.

"Yeah. I tell you guys all the time how anxious I am." Katie pulls her hands out of the water, looking at her wrinkled fingers.

"We thought that was about your studies," Claire says.

"It is, but it's also about everything else. It's . . . it's why I'm so Type A, because I need to feel in control over something, because I can't control how I feel about everything. Or at least that's what my doctor tells me." She shrugs, the tops of her shoulders coming out of the water for a brief second.

"Then we should probably stop giving you shit for studying all the time?" Lexi smiles, patting Katie on the back.

"Yeah, you should." Katie turns to Lexi, playfully splashing her with water.

Lexi splashes back. The four of them get into a splash war, laughing and giggling. I watch them, realizing this moment was different than all the moments I'd had with them. It was deeper, diving below the surface where our friendships had floated. I feel a change in me, but I don't know what it is exactly. It's subtle, but it's there. When they're done splashing around, they go back to floating in a circle again serenely.

"I'm sorry I didn't even know that about you, Katie," Lexi says after the splashing subsides, looking up through the trees at the gray sky.

"Me too," Nikki and Claire say in sync.

Katie smiles. "It's okay. You know now."

Lexi looks over at me and narrows her eyes. "It's your turn."

Damn it. I thought she'd forgotten about me.

"Yeah, get in with us." Nikki pats the water with the palms of her hands.

"It's really not as bad as it looks," says Claire.

"You promised." Lexi stares at me—or is it a glare? I really can't tell with her sometimes.

"I know. I know. I'm coming in."

I kick off my shoes and jeans and pull off my sweater. I take a deep breath before even putting my foot in the water—not because it looks like a toilet bowl, but because I'm scared it'll actually work. What if this is it? What if I wake up and I'm back in my time, and this is the last time I see any of them? I'm fine with not seeing Lexi, but not Katie, Nikki, or Claire.

We were just starting to become friends again, and I don't think I want to lose that yet.

"Come on!" Lexi calls out impatiently.

I step into the water; my foot immediately sinks into thick mud. I take another step and another until I'm nearly fully submerged. I join the circle floating around with the girls. Nothing happens—there's just warm brown water on my skin. It feels kind of nice, almost relaxing . . . that is, until I catch Lexi glaring at me, watching me like a predator would its prey. She's been so weird toward me since we got here.

"Well?" She raises an eyebrow.

"Well, what?"

"Do you feel anything?" Lexi asks.

"Not really. It just feels warm."

"It does, doesn't it? It feels amazing," Nikki says.

Lexi floats over to me, pushing me out of the circle into the corner away from the girls.

"What are you doing?"

"I'm helping." She puts her hands on top of my head, and in one fell swoop, she pushes me under water. Panic sets in immediately, and I suck in a gulp of water. I struggle for a few moments, my feet slipping on the muddy floor. Is she trying to kill me? My mouth opens again as I try to scream. Finally, I'm able to swat her arms off me. Resurfacing, I choke and push her backward, coughing up water out of my lungs.

Katie, Claire, and Nikki stare at us with concern, having missed what just happened.

"Are you all right?" Katie asks.

"Yeah, I just slipped on something," I lie. The girls go back to their peaceful floating.

"What the hell was that?" I whisper to Lexi.

"I was trying to get it to work."

"By killing me?"

"You really think I'd try to kill you? Come on, Alexis. I just thought you had to be completely submerged or something to get it to work. That's all." She shrugs nonchalantly and climbs out of the hot spring.

I stand there for a few moments, waiting until Lexi is far enough away from the hot spring before I get out. I don't need her trying to drown me again. I know me at eighteen, and I would never trust me.

SEVENTEEN

LEXI DROPS A few logs onto the fire, and the flames bounce and the coals crackle. Katie, Nikki, Claire, and I sit on stumps around the pit with blankets wrapped around us. The night is still and cold, like the inside of a closed refrigerator. Lexi takes her seat on her stump and pulls out a bag of marshmallows, graham crackers, and Hershey's chocolate bars. She stabs a marshmallow onto a stick and holds it over the fire.

"I thought we were staying in a hotel." Claire pulls the blanket tighter around her.

"We can't roast marshmallows in a hotel." Lexi's marshmallow catches fire, and she shakes it, trying to put it out, but it ends up melting right off the stick.

"Looks like you can't roast them here either," Nikki teases.

Lexi tries again, this time piercing three marshmallows and holding them a little higher over the fire, out of reach of the flames, and carefully turns them over. When they're browned on all sides, she pulls them away triumphantly.

"It appears I *can* roast a marshmallow here." Lexi smiles. "Who wants one?"

Nikki and Katie raise their hands. Lexi quickly puts the s'mores together and passes them out.

"Anyone else?" she asks.

Claire shakes her head.

"I'll have one," I say.

She holds the s'more in her hand, looks at me, and takes a big bite out of it, smiling as the melty marshmallow sticks to her chin.

What is her problem? First, she's giving me dirty looks on the hike, then she's trying to drown me, and now I can't have a s'more?

"These are so good," Nikki gushes, taking another bite.

Claire gets up, disappearing into the family-sized tent that's set up ten yards from the fire. Moments later, she comes back with a six-pack of Sparks. "Who wants one?"

I'm pretty sure they stopped making those because the insane amount of caffeine coupled with the alcohol content rendered them a health hazard. I almost share the information out loud before realizing it'd be another red flag that I don't belong.

"Me," I say instead.

As soon as Claire hands it over, I crack it open and take a long drink, my eyes closing for a moment. When I open them, I see Lexi is staring me down, and I almost choke. Is that a flicker of hatred I see?

"Cheers," Claire says after distributing the drinks.

We all tap our cans together, except Lexi, who pulls hers away from mine before I can make contact with it. She's so petty. The firewood crackles and pops, spitting up debris in the air.

"Did you get what you needed for your class?" Katie asks.

"Not exactly," Lexi says tonelessly, glaring at me again.

Huh—that must be what her deal is. She must want me gone more than I thought she did. She's just mad that her plan didn't work. We still have her other dumb ideas, and after that nonsense is over, we can get down to the real stuff.

"I still had fun." Katie gives an encouraging smile, which Lexi returns.

"Me too." Nikki nods.

"Same here," Claire says.

"Yeah," I agreed. "Thanks for including me." I smile at Lexi, but she scowls in return. After slamming the rest of her drink, she tosses the can in the fire and grabs the last Sparks can. The night is still and quiet, save for the crackling fire and the hoot of an owl in the distance.

"Don't worry, I've got two more six-packs," Claire says.

"Good. We'll need them for my next project." Lexi walks toward the tent like she's on a mission.

Oh great. It's Ouija board time. If this doesn't work, she'll probably kill me tonight. I best sleep with one eye open.

"What project?" Nikki asks, standing from her stump.

"Follow me." Lexi disappears into the tent.

By the time we pile into the tent, Lexi already has the Ouija board set up. Upward-facing flashlights in each corner of the tent make everything feel eerier than necessary.

"What the hell is this?" Katie asks, eyes wide.

"It's for a class," Lexi says, kneeling by the board.

"What kind of weird-ass classes are you taking?" Katie challenges but sits down anyway.

"Don't worry about it." Lexi flicks her hand and then places her fingers on the planchette. "Come on. Everyone puts your fingers on it."

"What's the point of this?" Nikki asks.

"We can find out things about the future." Lexi smirks at me.

"And this is for a class?" Katie asks.

"Save your questions for the board," Lexi says, motioning everyone to participate with a nod of her chin.

Despite our collective reluctance, we all scooch close and touch our fingertips to the plastic triangle. A portable propane tent heater set up in the corner of the tent hisses. Claire had borrowed it from a guy in the engineering class she's not actually enrolled in, along with most all of our camping supplies.

"Now, first we rotate the planchette in a circle three times, like this." Lexi guides it around in three circles on the board. "Then we ask it a question and dead people answer it or something like that."

"This totally freaks me out." Katie pulls her fingers away.

"Don't be a baby," Lexi says. "Put your hands back."

Shoulders up to her ears, Katie puts her fingers back on the planchette, worry marking her face.

"Do *not* move the planchette. Just let the other side handle that part." Lexi winks.

"Okay, I'll go first." Claire sits up a little bit taller. "Should I sleep with Jake?"

"No!" we all say in unison. The planchette also shoots over to "No"—very clearly not the work of the spirit world.

"You're supposed to let the spirits speak first," Claire pouts.

"Uh, they spoke through us," Lexi lies. "They were very clear."

"My turn. Will Lexi and I be friends in ten years?" Nikki asks, closing her eyes.

After a long pause, the planchette drifts over to "No." I look over at Lexi, who frowns, and I'm not sure if she moved it. Nikki opens her eyes and looks down at the board and then up at Lexi. She pushes out her lower lip, half pouting, half sad.

"It's just a silly game," Katie offers. "Will Claire and I be friends in ten years?"

The planchette doesn't move from "No."

"Well, damn!" Claire looks over at Katie, then Lexi, then Nikki.

"This game doesn't know what it's talking about, I'm sure," I say, trying to stem the wave of sadness settling over the tent.

"Will I marry Andrew?" I ask, trying to change the mood.

Again, the planchette doesn't move.

"This is just depressing." Katie shakes her head.

Claire's face lights up. "Ooh, will I marry a rich guy?"

The planchette slides over to "Yes" almost instantly. Claire claps her hands together. "See? Finally something good."

"That isn't good, Claire." Lexi twists up her face. "That's pathetic."

"Yeah, why are you so obsessed about finding some rich guy to take care of you?" Katie's voice doesn't have the snark that Lexi's did, but there's disappointment in it. "Don't you have goals of your own?"

Claire's face crumples. She doesn't say a word but crawls out of the tent.

"Where are you going?" Nikki calls out.

"To the bathroom." Claire's voice cracks at the end.

Lexi spreads her fingers a little on the planchette. "Fill in the space, girls. We've got more questions to ask."

Katie and Nikki realign their fingers, while I pull mine away. How could they not realize how upset Claire is?

"I've got to go to the bathroom too," I say as I leave the tent.

"Your bladder gets weak as you age," Lexi tells the girls, another snide remark about me.

I roll my eyes as I stand, looking around for Claire. Where did she go? I step into the enclosing darkness carefully. The night is quiet, aside from that nosey owl and a slight whimper coming from behind a large oak tree.

"Claire?" I whisper.

The whimper quiets for a moment and then comes back in full force, this time with sniffles. My eyes have adjusted to the dark, and I find Claire sitting on the ground behind a large tree, knees pulled into her chest and head down. The snap of a stick beneath my foot causes her to look up. She quickly wipes at her eyes.

I kneel beside her. "Are you okay?"

"Yeah, I'm fine." She brushes her face against her shoulder and sniffles again.

"You don't seem okay." I take a seat on the ground.

I know she's not. I never noticed it before, when I was eighteen, but I see it now: there's more to Claire than I realized.

"I'm fine, really," she says, trying to convince herself more than me, it seems.

"I don't think it's pathetic that you want to marry wealthy." If that's what she wants, who are we to tell her otherwise?

She's quiet for a moment and then says, "It *is* pathetic." Claire tries to hold back another sob, but it comes out sounding like she tried to swallow something too big and it got stuck in her throat.

"Then why is that your goal in life? Why is it all you talk about? I mean, that's what I've noticed since I've been here," I say, quickly covering up my mistake.

There's a long silence, and I fear Claire has shut down. I wouldn't blame her. She doesn't really know me, well, this version of me. I'm about to stand and leave her be, but her voice stops me.

"I just don't think I can do it alone," she says quietly, looking over at me. Her eyes burn with shame.

"Do what?"

"Succeed."

"Claire, are you freaking kidding me? You are one of the most beautiful girls I know—"

"Yeah, that's all I am," she interrupts. "I'm beautiful. I know. That's all I've ever been told. 'Claire, you're so pretty. Claire, you're so hot.'" She shakes her head. "No one has ever told me that I'm smart or driven or creative or anything that really *matters* in this world. Pretty only gets you so far. So, yeah, I don't think I can succeed on my own, and if pretty is all I am, then I'm going to use it to my advantage."

I had never heard Claire say anything like this before. She never confided in me, or maybe she did and I was really drunk, didn't remember, so she never brought it up again. All this time, I thought Claire was one of the most confident girls I had ever met, and it turns out she wasn't. She's just as self-conscious and insecure as the rest of us. If I didn't know this about one of my best friends, then I wasn't as good of a friend as I thought I was. In fact, I'd made fun of her superficiality when all along what was shallow was our friendship—thanks to me.

"Claire . . ." I say, "in the little bit of time I've gotten to know you, I can tell you're sweet and caring. You've accepted and welcomed me, and you've known me for only a few days. You are smart. I mean, you have to be. You got a thirty on your ACT! I got a twenty-eight, so you're definitely smarter than me. And if you were actually being graded in those classes you attend but aren't actually enrolled in, you'd probably get A's. From what I've heard from Lexi, you're creative and driven too." I smile at Claire and witness another tear roll down her cheek. "When you go after something, you always get it. Like all the camping gear. If it weren't for you, we would have frozen to death tonight. Don't sell yourself short. You're way more than just a pretty face. You're the whole package, and you don't even realize it."

She wipes the tear away and turns toward me with open arms, pulling me in for an embrace. I hug her back like I've never hugged her before. It's one of those embraces that's genuine and comforting—almost therapeutic.

"That's the nicest thing anyone has ever said to me," she sniffs into my shoulder.

"It's all true, Claire. You just have to know it's true too."

A tear unexpectedly emerges from my eye. I let it make its way down my cheek, linger at my jawline, and fall to my shoulder.

I'm exactly where I'm supposed to be.

"Thank you." She hugs me a little tighter.

I let go of her and look her in the eyes. I need to do more than just listen. I need to help. I can't just have this amazing chat end here. What if I end up going back to my time? Does anything change for Claire? Does she realize her potential? Does she remember our talk? Will she tell anyone else? I have to keep it going, make sure she believes she can do this, make sure she has a plan, and make sure she confides in the girls.

"Have you given any thought about what you want to do?" I ask.

She nods. "I have. My parents divorced when I was a teenager, and I always wondered if they could have tried harder, really fought for their relationship. I mean, I was a kid, but it seemed like one day they just gave up."

"I'm sorry, Claire. I had no idea."

"It's fine," she says, her voice stronger. "So, I'm thinking of becoming a therapist. The schooling is tough and long, and I don't know if I can do it, but I want to. I want to help people be better. I don't want to fix them, because fixing implies there's something broken. I don't believe people are broken. I just think they can be better." She smiles at me.

I place my hand on her shoulder and give it an encouraging squeeze. "You can do this, Claire, and you can do it all on your own. But know that I'll be there to help, and so will the girls. We'll figure out what classes you actually need to enroll in first."

She laughs. "Can we hold off on telling the girls until we get back in town? I don't really want to dampen the mood with my drama."

"Of course." It's not an easy thing to admit to, that you think you're inadequate, you're not who you want to be, and you're completely insecure in who you are. I've learned more about Claire in one night than I had in all the years I'd known her. How is that even possible? "Ready to go back?" I ask.

"I'm going to sit here for a few minutes."

I give her another hug before I get up and start toward the tent.

"Hey, Alexis."

I turn back toward her.

"What about you?" Claire asks.

"What about me?"

"What do you want to be?"

"I want to be better," I say, a smile breaking out on my face.

As I turn back toward the tent, I keep an eye on my feet for the first couple of steps around the tree. When I look up, I'm met with a pair of narrowed eyes that are practically glowing. Lexi stands in front of the fire with crossed arms and a scowl on her face, reserved only for me. Before I can ask what her problem is, she stomps off back toward the tent, quickly crawling inside of it.

EIGHTEEN

CLAIRE RETURNS TO the tent a few minutes after I arrive. Her face is bright and free of the worry, shame, and sadness it had before. She smiles while passing out cans of Sparks, which we happily open and start chugging.

All feels right again—aside from the death stare I'm receiving from Lexi. Her face is bright red, her jaw clenched. I know she was eavesdropping on my conversation with Claire, but I didn't say anything bad about her. If anything, I made her look good by telling Claire that Lexi had mentioned how driven and creative she is. Yes, I made that part up, but still.

Lexi puts her fingers back on the planchette. We follow her lead, although Katie hesitates at first, saying, "Ugh, we're playing again?"

"Yes. We're just getting started," Lexi snaps at her and then addresses the board. "Who's hotter, me or Alexis?"

Nikki giggles.

The planchette begins to move, spelling out L-E-X-I.

Lexi laughs. "These spirits really know what they're talking about."

I roll my eyes.

"That was rude," Claire says, defending me.

Lexi twists her nose up. "I was just having fun."

"At Alexis's expense."

"Oh, whatever," Lexi says dismissively. "Next question. Will Alexis ever get her life together?"

The planchette shoots over to "No." Lexi smirks at me.

"Is Alexis responsible for her own screwed-up life?" Lexi asks.

The planchette returns to the middle, but this time rather than shooting to an answer, there's a struggle. It starts moving toward "Yes," then toward "No," then toward "Yes," and then it goes flying off the board.

"Inconclusive." I smirk back at Lexi.

"You are responsible for it!" Lexi yells, her eyes burning into mine. She swiftly crawls out of the tent and stomps off.

"Ohh-kay." Nikki takes a sip of her Sparks, eyebrows raised. "Someone's had a little bit too much to drink."

"Yeah, what's her problem?" Claire asks.

The girls give me a sympathetic glance. Ugh—as much as I don't want to talk to Lexi, I know I have to be the bigger person and do it. I know how dramatic she can be, and I can see her marching so far out into the woods that she gets lost, and then we'd have to call for a search-and-rescue team to find her.

Yep, better to nip this in the bud now.

"I'm going to go talk to her," I say, crawling out of the tent.

"Here, take this." Claire holds out a flashlight, which I grab on my way out.

Outside, Lexi's not by the dying fire. I throw a couple more logs on to revive it. Embers fly into the air, swirling over the flames. Staggering out into the darkness, I shine a light in front of me, walking to the tree where Claire had hid. But Lexi's not there.

"Lexi," I call out.

No response—of course she's going to make this difficult. I trudge on. As I walk further and further into the woods, the hairs on the back of my neck rise. A thought crosses my mind instantly. What if she's luring me out here to murder me? She did joke about becoming a serial killer the other day. What if I'm Lexi's first victim? Would I even count since I'm technically her?

I tiptoe quietly, a little more cautious with my steps, shining my flashlight in all directions. I'm so far away I can't even see the fire anymore. A coyote howls in the distance. I assume it's a coyote. What other animals howl? A wolf. God, I hope it's not a wolf. I feel goosebumps cover my skin as I shiver.

"Lexi?" I call out again.

"What do you want?" she finally responds.

My flashlight finds her: she's leaning against a tree. Lexi steps away from it, folds her arms in front of her chest, and widens her stance.

I lower the flashlight out of her eyes. "I came out here to check on you."

"You really had me fooled," she says, raising her chin and narrowing her eyes.

"What?"

I can't possibly comprehend nor understand why or what she would think I'm fooling her about. I've been nothing but nice and cooperative since she started this little time travel research adventure.

"I know exactly what you're doing."

"Okay, what am I doing?"

She points a finger at me. "You acted like you really wanted to go back, but you're here trying to steal my friends and take over my life. I'm onto your game."

"I already had your life. Trust me, I don't want it back. I want *my* life back."

She snorts. "From what you've told me, there's nothing to go back to. So you're just going to traipse into mine and take it over."

"That's not at all what I'm doing."

"Then why the hell is Claire confiding in you? She's never confided in me. Why are my friends becoming better friends with you?"

"They were my friends first!"

"You're not even friends with them anymore! You had your chance."

"Can't you see this is *our* chance?" I can't believe this. She's jealous! How childish can she be? Can she not understand that we're the same person?

"No, I can't see that. When we get back to campus, I want you out of my life—for good, this time. You and I are done." She pushes her way past me, plodding off toward our campsite.

"Fine. Have it your way!" I call out after her. "I'm done fighting with you. You're going to get everything you fucking deserve!"

NINETEEN

THE NEXT DAY, we stop for lunch in Steven's Point. Lexi hasn't said a word to me the entire car ride. Any time she said something, she addressed it to everyone else but me, careful to use names so it was even more clear she wasn't talking to me. Although the day had been uncomfortable so far, the trip back hasn't been completely fruitless: Katie talked more about her anxiety, and Claire opened up to the girls about what she and I had discussed last night.

Now, after our Mall of America visit and three hours on the road, Lexi sits in the booth across from me, trying to pretend I'm not even there, but when I take a bite out of my McChicken sandwich, she scowls at me. When I shove a few French fries into my mouth, she cringes. It's the most she's reacted to me since our blow-up last night. Other than that, she's been pretending I don't exist. Technically, I don't, I think.

"This has been such a fun girl's weekend!" Claire says, dipping a French fry into her Oreo McFlurry.

The girls nod in agreement, sans Lexi. She dunks a Chicken McNugget into a tub of ranch and tosses the whole thing into her mouth.

Nikki is eating slowly, slower than I have ever seen her eat. She chews like she's counting the number of times she's chomping her teeth. It's odd, and this is the first time I've ever noticed it.

"Hey, I'm really glad you're going for it, Claire," I say. "I think you're going to make a fabulous therapist."

"Thank you," she says, dabbing her lips with a napkin. "And I hope so."

"Don't hope. You've got this," Katie encourages, patting Claire on the back.

"Thanks, guys. I don't think I'd even be trying to do this without you all."

I know for a fact that's true. It makes her words even more meaningful to me. If, at the end of this, nothing changes for myself, at least I'll know I helped someone.

I sip my Diet Coke, glancing over at Lexi. It's like I'm looking in a mirror, but the image I see is evil. It doesn't move like I move. It blinks when my eyes are open. It talks when my mouth is closed. A malevolent doppelgänger.

Nikki pulls out a journal and begins writing in it quickly—a little below the table so no one else notices. I catch her glance up a couple of times, almost as if she's checking to see if others see what she's doing. No one does but me. I can't help myself.

"What are you writing, Nikki?" I ask.

She nervously clears her throat. "Oh, nothing." She snaps her journal closed.

"Is that your diary?" Lexi teases.

Nikki swiftly stows it in her bag and goes back to eating her burger and fries.

"I write things down too," I say. "I love to keep track of things. Lists. Ideas. Plans." I take another bite of my sandwich.

Lexi rolls her eyes. She doesn't do any of that yet. But she will one day. She'll write to-do lists she'll never actually do, plans she'll never follow through on, and ideas that will remain just that—ideas, nothing more.

"And you know me. I have a list for anything and everything," Katie says with a laugh.

Nikki smiles.

"I can't really relate yet," Claire says. "The only lists I had before today were dating requirements. But I did come up with a bare-bones to-do list in the car for becoming a therapist." Claire is beaming.

I've never heard such enthusiasm in her voice—more than when she told me how she met that doctor a few months ago, well, seventeen years from now.

Nikki looks nervous to speak. "Well," she says at last, "I was writing down how I felt while eating."

"That's weird," Lexi says, turning up her nose. I kick her under the table, right in her shin. "Ouch!" She rubs her leg.

"Go on," I try to encourage Nikki, but I fear she's already closed back up, thanks to my dipshit younger self.

"Okay," she says, a bit uncertainly. "I write down how I feel before I eat, while I'm eating, and after I'm done eating, and I keep track of everything I eat." She shakes her head. "It's stupid really. But I've been doing it for like a week now."

"What made you start doing that?" Claire asks.

Nikki hesitates before speaking. "I actually started seeing a counselor to help with my relationship with food. She thinks I use it for comfort because my dad raised me by himself since I was a teenager, and he was hardly around. So apparently, I turn to food for comfort because I couldn't find it anywhere else. I don't know. It's dumb." She shrugs again and pushes her fries around.

I look at Lexi, whose mouth is hanging open slightly, and her eyes finally meet mine. She sees what I see: the "Get Nikki

Fat" plan. The making fun of her for always eating. *We're awful.* My God, I was a terrible friend. And I thought I had helped her lose the weight—when all along she was in therapy for an eating disorder.

I'm so disgusted with myself my skin starts to sweat. My stomach feels like it's been put in a blender. I feel queasy, like I might just throw up all over this table. I take a couple of small deep breaths, trying to compose myself. It's fine. That's why I'm here now. To fix all of this. I can be better than this. She can be better than this. My eyes shoot over to Lexi. She *has* to be better than this.

"That's not dumb at all," Katie responds to Nikki. "I have to do something similar for my anxiety. Track what makes me anxious. How I feel. It's a whole thing. But I think it helps."

"Thanks for telling us." My curdling stomach starts to calm as I smile at Nikki.

"You guys don't think it's weird?"

"Not at all," Claire says.

"Good, because I'm tired of hiding my food diary from you all." Nikki laughs.

"You don't ever have to hide anything from us," I say, and I mean it.

Nikki points the car toward the highway. We're less than an hour from home. Lexi looks at the clock every few minutes, like she's counting down until the moment I'm out of her life.

"Alexis and Lexi, you two still want to be dropped off downtown?" Nikki asks.

We had told the girls we wanted to be dropped off in downtown to go tanning, but really we're going to try Lexi's final stupid time travel idea on a phone booth in the downtown area. She said that because I'd already used the one near campus, it wouldn't work. At this point, I think she's just making stuff up.

"No," Lexi says, looking out the window.

"Yes," I say firmly.

"No." She turns back to look at me with squinty eyes.

"Yes," I say again, pressing my lips together. We're getting every one of her ideas out of the way—I don't want to hear Lexi say we didn't try everything. This ends tonight. And maybe, just maybe, I can convince her to try it my way after her last idea fails. But first I've got to get her to start talking to me again.

"Which is it?" Nikki furrows her brow.

"Fine. Drop us off." Lexi turns around in her seat and crosses her arms over her chest, staring out the passenger window dramatically.

"You two are so weird. I have a younger sister, and we never fight like this," Claire says with a laugh.

TWENTY

Downtown Oshkosh is really just a street lined with bars, tattoo parlors, and restaurants. It's nothing special and is basically deserted during the day, but it comes alive at night, when drunk and hungry college kids roam the streets.

"Where's this phone booth?" I ask.

Lexi looks pissed. "This way," she grumbles, walking down the street.

We pass the tattoo parlor I got that dumb tramp stamp at, and I make a point not to look at it. I don't need her getting any ideas. Rounding the corner, I see the dirty phone booth, covered in bumper stickers and graffiti. Lexi stops right in front, looking at it fondly, like it's her way out of this, or my way, for that matter.

She glances back at me and flicks her hand. "Get in. I don't have all day."

I glare at her. "What are you going to do if this really works? Is this how you want to see me for the last time?"

"I don't want to see you at all." She crosses her arms in front of her chest and taps her foot against the pavement. "Get in."

Of course I want this to work so I never have to see her again, but there's a small part of me that wants it to fail. One, to prove Lexi wrong, and two, so I can learn just a little bit more. I feel like I'm just getting started. Even though I've lived this life before, I've missed so much of it. It's like when

I'm reading a thriller and then there's the twist at the end that completely blows my mind—and I'm like what the hell did I miss? Where were the clues? So, sometimes you gotta go back to find them.

"I'm just supposed to stand in there?" I raise an eyebrow.

Lexi nods.

"For how long?"

"For as long as it takes. Hurry up; it'll be dark soon."

I let out a big puff of air, slide open the door of the phone booth, and step inside. It smells like a combination of dried piss and rotting garbage. I pinch my nose closed with my fingers.

"It's disgusting in here," I say, gagging.

"Don't be a baby. Just concentrate on going away." Lexi scowls at me through the dirty, smeared glass.

I close my eyes and focus on breathing through my mouth, not because I'm following Lexi's directions, but because the smell is so rancid. It's the only thing that's helping me not throw up.

I knew this wouldn't work—none of it. It was so dumb. Why did I even go along with it? Oh yes, so she'd be more cooperative and more willing to try things my way. But all it's done is made her more uncooperative. I should just leave and go live my life again as a thirty-something-year-old in 2002.

But I can't. Because of Andrew. Even in a different decade, I still feel a strong connection to him, like we're tethered together through space and time. I can still hear his voice. I can still feel his touch. And even through this rotting piss smell, if I concentrate hard enough, his scent is there—vanilla meets sandalwood. I have to get back to him and make things right. But in order to do that, I have to get through to Lexi.

I open my eyes and stare at her. She's looking down at her

wrist as if she's checking the time, but again, she's not even wearing a watch.

"I don't feel anything!" I yell.

"Give it time. You've only been in there for two minutes."

Lexi starts to pace back and forth, careful not to step on any of the sidewalk cracks. She can't keep this up for much longer. She knows this is just a waste of time. I smirk; I should be out of here and have her fully convinced that it's time for her to do things *my* way in about ten minutes.

Two hours later, I'm sitting cross-legged on the floor of the phone booth, ninety-nine percent sure I'm sitting in dried piss. Outside the booth, Lexi is leaning against the door so I can't get out (I've tried). She's held out longer than I thought she would. She bangs the back of her head against the door in frustration. It startles me.

"What are you doing?" I slam the palm of my hand against the door.

She turns around and looks at me. "None of this is working," she groans.

"Maybe it is." I scratch my chin.

"How?"

"Those things that Nikki, Katie, and Claire told us. I never knew about them."

"What do you mean?" She tilts her head, shifting her body into a more comfortable position so she can actually face me.

"I didn't know about Katie's anxiety. I didn't know about Nikki's eating disorder. I didn't know about Claire's insecurities, nor her aspirations. They never told me." I shake my head, ashamed I didn't know those things about my own friends. It's no wonder we all fell out of touch; we weren't as close as I thought we were.

"Why didn't they tell you any of that when you were friends with them?" Lexi asks.

"I don't know. Maybe because I never showed an interest. I never asked. Maybe because our friendships were shallow, just surface level: parties, drinking, shopping. Maybe because I only cared about myself."

I look up, meeting Lexi's eyes again. Her mouth is slightly open, and her eyes are wide, like she just discovered something for the first time.

"But they told us now," she says.

"Exactly. Things are changing. Can't you see that?" I search her eyes for understanding.

"Then why are you still here?"

"I don't know. Maybe it hasn't changed enough."

Lexi nods, considering it all.

"It's kind of strange," I say.

"What is?"

"I had seventeen more years I could have spent with them, and I had to come back to learn anything about them." I bite at my lower lip. "I wasn't a good friend."

"No, we weren't a good friend." Lexi agrees, finally letting up on the door.

Standing up and stepping out of the booth, I breathe in as much clean air as I can. Once I've snorted up all the fresh air, I ask Lexi earnestly, "Do you want me to leave now?"

She shakes her head.

"Then what now?"

"A deal's a deal. I'll try it your way." Lexi holds out her hand, and we shake on it.

TWENTY-ONE

"**I** LOOK LIKE a nun." Lexi pouts as she checks herself out in the full-length mirror. She turns side to side and then glances at me.

We're finally doing things my way—the right way. I walk up behind her and put my hands on her shoulders, my head craned around hers so I can see her full reflection in the mirror.

"No, you don't. Nuns wear veils," I say with a laugh.

A long-sleeve, black turtleneck covers her top half—everything but her face and hands. It's perfect. Her jeans are free from any holes. They're plain, a little high-waisted, almost like a nice pair of mom jeans. Her shoes are plain Adidas trainers. Her hair is free of any of those gaudy clip-in extensions, and her makeup is subtle. Just a nice flick of mascara, a tinted moisturizer, and some cherry Chapstick. She looks nothing like herself.

"I hate it."

I smile. "And that's how I know it's perfect."

Lexi plops down on her bed in a huff. "Shouldn't you have disappeared as soon as I put this stupid outfit on?"

"I think we need more of a change than just clothes, Lexi." I grab my bag and pull out a small notepad and a pen. A few days ago, I had created a list of things that needed to be done after Lexi's plans failed, which they had. "Back to the Future" is written on the front cover of the notepad. I flip the pad to the first page:

BACK TO THE FUTURE TO-DO LIST

1. Get Lexi to stop partying

2. ~~Get Lexi to stop dressing like a slut~~

3. DO NOT LET LEXI GET A LOWER BACK TATTOO!!!

4. ~~Put an end to the "Get Nikki Fat Plan"~~

5. ~~Get Lexi to go to class~~

6. Don't tell Lexi too much about the future

7. Never work out with Lexi again

8. ~~Figure out why I lost touch with my friends~~

9. ~~Get new clothes while I'm here~~

I think for a second and then add a couple more items.

10. Get Lexi to start working toward real goals

11. Get Lexi to go to all of her classes

Lexi sits up on the bed and looks at me as I check over my list, reading it carefully, crossing things off, and underlining things here and there.

"What's that?"

"Just a list of things you need to work on." I give her a small smile.

Lexi stands and walks over to her desk, pulling out a folded-up piece of paper.

"I have one of those for you too." She unfolds it and scans her list, slightly giggling as she reads it to herself.

"You already read me your list." I narrow my eyes.

"This is a new one." The corner of her lip perks up.

I walk over to Lexi, trying to get a look at it. "What? What's it say?"

"Don't worry. We'll try this list next after yours fails." She looks up at me with a coy smile.

I snatch the piece of paper from her hands and bring it up to my line of sight.

WHAT ALEXIS NEEDS TO DO TO GET OUT OF MY LIFE

Lose twenty pounds

Find a boyfriend

Take responsibility for her own mistakes

Stop stealing my friends

Be prettier

Remove stick from anus

I roll my eyes and toss the piece of paper back at her. "Those are just insults."

"It's constructive criticism." Lexi raises her chin but cracks a smile while tossing her list into the trash can.

I check mine over again before stowing it back in my bag.

Lexi makes a face. "Do you really think this is going to work?" There's no enthusiasm in her voice.

"It has to. We've already tried it your way."

She takes a deep breath. "Fine. What am I supposed to do today?"

"Well, you're going to go to all your classes and take notes. I will be checking them." I raise an eyebrow. "You're going to be nice, study after classes. No parties—and no drinking tonight."

She groans. "It sounds like I'm grounded."

"Sure, you could think of it that way."

"And what are you going to do today?" Lexi asks, challenging me a bit.

"I don't know. Just hang out. Do a little reading. Watch some television. Have some wine."

Lexi scowls. "This is bullshit! You just get to hang out, and I have to do all the work?"

"Hey!" I point my finger at her. "You dragged me to Mother Nature's toilet bowl and forced me to swim in it, wasted my time with a Ouija board that you were clearly manipulating the whole time, and made me sit in dry piss for two hours in that damn phone booth. I think this is the least you can do."

She tosses her book bag on her shoulder and crosses her arms. "Fine. But I'm not happy about any of this." Lexi marches with extra heavy steps to show how displeased she is with me.

"Have a good day at school, honey!" I wave my fingers at her as she slams the door closed behind her.

Hallelujah—she's finally out of my hair. I'm alone with just myself—and not my younger self. The only time I've been able to escape her in the past week was when I was showering or going to the bathroom, and even then, I could feel her presence. But not now. I'm alone. I'm free!

I spend the day doing exactly what I said I would. I read, I watch television, and around four p.m., I open a bottle of wine. I hear a key sliding into the lock to the door, and I tense up at first, thinking it's Lexi skipping out on her studies. But in walk Nikki and Claire, carrying stacks of books.

"Hey, what are you two up to?" I ask, swirling my glass of wine as I prop myself up on Lexi's bed.

Nikki places her books on her desk, and Claire drops to the floor to fan hers out—all psychology textbooks.

"Just got back from the library," Claire explains a bit breathlessly. "I met with an academic advisor today, and we got all my classes set up for next semester. It'll take me an extra semester to get my degree in psychology." She shrugs. "But that's fine. I picked these up to get a head start." Her face is flushed, perhaps from the excitement of starting down her own path.

"That's great," I say, drinking my wine.

Nikki pulls her backpack off her shoulders and sets it on the ground. "And I just picked up a couple of books on intuitive eating. I was reading about it online last night, and I think it'll help."

"Oh yeah, I've heard of that," I say and gesture to the wine. "Help yourself."

Nikki pours some into two red Solo cups, handing one to Claire, who takes a sip while casually flipping through one of her books.

"Where's Lexi?" Nikki asks as she climbs onto her bed.

"Library."

Claire and Nikki whip their heads in my direction.

"Really?"

I nod. "She's studying."

"Wow. That's . . . great," Claire says, almost as if she doesn't believe it.

"Honestly, you visiting has been so good for all of us," Nikki admits. "Like, Lexi is *studying*. I never ever thought that would happen." She laughs.

"Yeah, I'm taking school seriously too. Oh my God, you guys, what would my life have been if I hadn't started trying to do something with it now rather than waiting around for some rich guy to put a ring on my finger?" Claire giggles.

I know exactly what it would have been like. Unfulfilling and sad. But I feel like she's on the right path now. I've done such good work here. I truly am a fairy godmother of some sort. I've improved all of my friend's lives and Lexi's next on the list. She should be counting her lucky stars that I'm here to help.

The door swings open, and in stomps Lexi, dropping her book bag on the floor and collapsing dramatically next to Nikki on her bed.

"What are you wearing?" Claire scans Lexi's conservative outfit.

"Essentially a burka," Lexi complains.

"How was your day?" I sip my wine, peering at her over the rim of my glass.

"Terrible." Lexi rubs her head. "I went to all my classes, took notes, *and* studied."

"Sounds productive." I lean back into the pillows, crossing my legs at the knee.

"What did *you* do today?" Lexi squints at me.

I smile. "Oh, a little of this, a little of that."

"What's all this?" she asks, gesturing to Claire's books.

"Psychology books. A lot of intro-type stuff. I'm getting a head start." Claire is truly proud of herself. And she should be.

"That's great, Claire," Lexi says.

Good. She's being nice. I wasn't sure if she'd be able to pull it all off. But let's hope she can keep this up long enough to have some sort of an effect on our life.

This has to work. It just has to.

TWENTY-TWO

"I CAN'T DO this anymore!" Lexi cries as she slams the door behind her and throws her book bag on the ground—again. This is literally day two of her new regimen.

I look up at Lexi briefly and return my attention back to *The Lovely Bones*, which I'm reading with a glass of wine on her bed. She kicks her book bag, punctuating her frustration. She's literally a child. I'm starting to wonder how it was even possible that we graduated college. How did we survive anything?

She pulls at her shirt. "I hate turtlenecks. They're so itchy."

"No, they're not."

"My classes are so boring." She grabs a bottle of water from the fridge and sits down at her desk chair, facing me.

"They're *supposed* to be boring. They're core classes."

"My hand hurts from taking notes." Lexi wiggles her fingers and shakes out her hand dramatically.

When I don't rebut her last complaint, she goes on. It's the same thing every day.

"And I think I have eyestrain." She blinks rapidly, then opens her eyes as wide as possible, as if she's trying to stretch them.

I place my book flat on my stomach. "Are you done?"

She blows out a breath. "Why isn't this working? Why are you *still* here?" Lexi gulps from her water bottle.

"I don't know. You haven't changed enough, and you're

fighting it the whole way? Maybe that has something to do with it."

"Oh, so it's always *my* fault."

"Well, if the turtleneck fits." I smirk.

She mocks me, pretending to say what I just said in a sarcastic, whiney voice. She is doing the things I've asked her to do, begrudgingly, but she's doing them. I'm at a loss for what more can be done.

Nikki bursts into the room, carrying the original iPod and wearing headphones and workout wear. "Hey, guys!" she yells, not realizing how loud she is. "Lose Yourself" by Eminem blasts out of her headphones.

Lexi puts her hands over her ears.

"Oh, sorry." Nikki turns off her music and pulls the headphones from her ears. She wraps the cord around the iPod and sets it on her desk.

"Hey, where have you been?" Lexi asks.

"Went to the gym with Katie. Well, she did a yoga class while I was on the elliptical. Yoga's supposed to help with her anxiety, but I think it gives *me* anxiety. It's so boring, and there's *so* much breathing. No one breathes like that."

"I'm with you on the yoga thing. I like the bootcamp classes," Lexi says.

I don't comment. I don't even enjoy working out. I used to, obviously, but somewhere along the way, I decided elevating my heart rate for set periods of time just wasn't for me anymore. Maybe when I get back, I'll get back into it, join a CrossFit gym or something.

"You guys should come with us tomorrow," Nikki says, collecting her shower caddy and a towel from her closet. "Oh, never mind. I forgot—I'm leaving tomorrow for Thanksgiving break. What about you guys? When are you leaving?"

I look at Lexi, unsure. I completely forgot about Thanksgiving. This whole traveling-back-in-time thing has really messed with my sense of, well, time. I don't even know if Lexi would let me come home with her. How would she explain who I am and why I'm there to Dad and our older brother, Justin?

"We're leaving tomorrow too," Lexi says.

I nod in agreement, not sure if Lexi really means that or not.

"Cool. Well, I'm going to go shower." Nikki walks out of the room, closing the door behind her.

"Am I really coming home with you for Thanksgiving?" I sit up in the bed, closing the book.

"Yeah, what else would you do? Stay here alone? That's not cool," she says nonchalantly.

"What are you going to tell them?"

Lexi doesn't miss a beat. "That you're a grad student in one of my advanced communication courses. You know, to explain your soaring age and that you live out of state and couldn't make the trip home for Thanksgiving, so you came home with me."

"Wow, you thought of that fast."

"I thought of it when you were sitting in that phone booth." Lexi smiles. She gets up and grabs two granola bars, tossing one to me.

"You were never going to just kick me out of your life?" I ask, a bit surprised.

"At one point, yes. But you were right—I can't have another me just walking around." She sits back down in her chair.

"Thanks." I unwrap the granola bar and take a bite. "Are

Dad and Justin going to do the usual Pizza Hut thing for Thanksgiving?"

Lexi gives me a strange look. "No—Mom is making Thanksgiving lunch as usual, weirdo."

My mouth instantly drops open, and tears rush to the ridges of my eyes. I can feel my heart in my back, and I choke on the piece of granola bar in my mouth, coughing and spewing pieces of it everywhere. Lexi rushes over and pats me on the back until I regain control. She unscrews her water bottle and puts it to my mouth. I take a big gulp, washing down the food, fighting back the tears, and swallowing the pain.

"Geez, Alexis. Don't die on me now," Lexi says with a nervous laugh.

"Yeah" is all I can manage to croak out.

Lexi grabs two duffel bags out of her closet, setting one next to me and opening up the other one near her dresser.

"I'm going to pack. You can use that duffel bag for your stuff. Feel free to borrow some clothes. Justin is picking us up in the morning. Cool?"

"Yeah," I say, staring off in a trance, trying to wrap my head around what's about to happen.

I've been so caught up with everything else—friends, time travel, Lexi—that somehow, I managed to forget about the most important thing: my family.

Maybe this is it. Maybe this is why I'm here, and this is what's needed to get back to my time—closure.

TWENTY-THREE

"**A**RE YOU OKAY?" Lexi asks. We're waiting for Justin out in front of the dorms the next day. She can clearly sense that something's off, since I haven't said more than a few words since yesterday's revelation that we'd be going home.

I'm nervous and scared and worried and overwhelmed. I'm not sure I can do this or if I should even be doing this, but it's too late to say no now. "Yeah, I'm good."

I didn't rag on Lexi today about her clothes or her studies or anything. I have bigger things to worry about, like seeing my family and ensuring they don't find out who I really am.

My thoughts raced all night long, and I didn't sleep much. What if they realize I'm Lexi? What if I can't make it through the weekend? What if I get sent back to my time before I see my family? By this morning, after all the tossing and turning, I decided I'm going to get through this because I have to.

Justin pulls up in a blue Chevy Tahoe blaring "Without Me" by Eminem. The bass vibrates the vehicle as he pulls up to the curb. He's rapping to the music obnoxiously, but he stops when he sees us. Justin attends UW-La Crosse, so we're basically on the way home for him.

Lexi and I walk down to the vehicle, but I'm a step behind, nervous to see Justin, worried he'll know I'm his sister. Then again, Justin has always been pretty clueless, so maybe it won't be a problem at all.

He steps out of the vehicle and pops open the gate.

"Hey, this is Alexis," Lexi says. "Alexis, this is Justin, my older brother."

Oh, twenty-one-year-old Justin, with shaggy ash-brown hair, is nearly the same as he is in his thirties: six feet tall, average-sized, with a scruffy beard, dressed in jeans and a T-shirt. The hardships he endured seemed to have frozen him in time, like he never grew up.

I wave but try not to look at him, letting my hair fall in front of my face as he takes my bag from me. He sets it in the back.

"Nice to meet you, Alexis." He smiles and takes Lexi's bag from her, tossing it in with much less care than he did with mine.

"Don't just throw my stuff, jerk," Lexi scolds him, pushing his shoulder.

"Hey, you're lucky I even picked you up." Justin closes the rear gate.

Lexi hops in the front seat, turns back, and sticks her tongue out at him. "Mom would have killed you if you didn't."

He laughs. "Worth it."

I climb into the backseat while Justin gets into the driver's seat and closes his door. He glances at me in the rearview mirror; his eyes linger a moment too long. Shit—he definitely notices something is up. We look so much alike, and with our names, this is too fricking obvious, especially around our family.

Justin quickly turns the volume down after he starts up the car. "Sorry about that!" he says as he drives toward home.

Lexi shakes her head.

A few minutes into the trip, Justin breaks the silence.

"Alexis, what are you going to school for?" He glances in the rearview mirror at me.

Shit. He knows something. He's trying to put the pieces together.

"Um, communications. I'm actually a grad student," I answer.

"Oh, same major as Lexi, then?"

I nod. Damn it. I should have said a different major like science or math or something like that. We are far too similar. This is never going to work. How could we have been so dumb about this? We don't even have a plan.

"That's how we met actually. We're in the same communications class. I got into a graduate-level course for debate," Lexi says, trying to cover for me. She looks back at me and raises an eyebrow. I know what she's thinking—*you idiot*—and I don't blame her. I'm thinking the exact same thing.

"And where are you from?" Justin asks.

"Lake Geneva," I say.

Justin furrows his brow. "Lexi said you were from out of state?"

Fuck. I should just jump out of the car right now. "Yeah . . . uhhh, Lake Geneva, California," I lie. Hopefully he doesn't try to Yahoo it at home.

"Huh, never heard of it."

"It's a small town. Probably can't even find it on a map— or on the internet, for that matter."

Reel it in, Alexis. Less talking. One-word answers only!

But really, he needs to stop asking me questions. Justin never cared to get to know my friends. He thought they were annoying. So why is he talking to me? Shut up, Justin, shut up.

"What kind of music do you like?" He asks.

Before I can answer, Lexi interrupts, "Okay, enough with the third degree." She turns on the radio and cranks it up. "Let's listen to some tunes!" she yells over "Work it by Missy Elliott.

Oh thank God. I was about to rattle off a bunch of singers and bands, like Cardi B and Taylor Swift, which would have made no sense. How am I going to handle an entire weekend of this? What am I going to do when I see Mom again? I have to play it cool. I just have to be Lexi's older friend from school—no one's daughter or sister.

I take a couple of deep breaths and repeat those things to myself the whole car ride home.

TWENTY-FOUR

W E PULL INTO our parents' driveway a couple hours
later. Lexi did a wonderful job of keeping the tunes
playing the entire trip, so there was no lull for Justin to pry
into my life. After he parks, I get out of the vehicle and mean-
der to the back of the Tahoe slowly. Justin is quick to jump
out and open the gate. When I reach for my bag, he grabs it.

"I can get that for you, Alexis," he says, throwing it over his
shoulder.

"No, I can carry it."

"Not a problem." He nods and walks to the house.

"Why didn't you carry mine too?" Lexi yells, pulling her
duffel out of the back and slamming the gate closed.

"Carry your own bag, butt munch," he calls over his shoulder.

Why is he being so nice to me? Is he going to try to go
through my bag? Try to find some clues in there? It's basically
all of Lexi's stuff. That'll for sure be suspicious. *Why is all of
Lexi's stuff in your bag, Alexis?* Wait, I'm giving him too much
credit. Like he even knows what items his sister owns.

I take a deep breath and turn to look at the two-story
house. The red rose bushes surround the large front porch,
still vibrant even in November—my mother's touch. They
haven't been there in years. The shutters are a crisp shade
of white, and the siding is sky blue. Enormous oak trees sit
on both sides, giving it privacy from nearby neighbors. It's

exactly how I remember it, back when it wasn't a house—it was home.

I walk behind Lexi and Justin, dragging my feet, trying to avoid the inevitable. Justin swings open the front door and bellows, "Mom! Dad! We're home."

Bella, our five-year-old chocolate lab, comes running out of the house, wiggling her butt, more excited than ever to see us. She runs straight to me and jumps up. I catch her paws and do a little dance with her.

"Hi, Bella baby," I coo to her. "Who's a good girl?"

She immediately sits down. I put my finger on her wet nose and say, "You are."

She wiggles around some more and circles my legs, like we've never been apart. She's been gone for well over ten years, but it's like she knows me still. She knows my soul. I pat her on the head and tell her, "Go inside, Bella girl." She darts back in the house.

Lexi's eyes are huge. "She knows you," she says in disbelief.

"Of course she knows me. She's my Bella baby." Perhaps it's my scent. It is how dogs recognize everything in the world. I'm sure to Bella my scent is the same as Lexi's.

"Is she still alive?" Lexi asks.

It's a silly question. Of course, she's not still alive, but Lexi doesn't understand death. She's had no experience with it yet, so I don't fault her nor tease her.

I shake my head.

Lexi frowns and puts her arm around me, letting out a breath. "I'm sorry. I didn't even realize. This must be really hard on you."

"You have no idea." I squeeze my eyes closed and then reopen them, holding back the moisture that's been forming since I got in the car. Lexi walks me in, hand on my shoulder.

My heart swells as my eyes scan the house. It doesn't look like this anymore. From the front entrance, there's a set of carpeted stairs with a deep cherry wood banister directly in front of us going up to the second floor. The large open-concept living room is off to the left, and the dining room and kitchen are beyond it. The living room is extremely cozy, with numerous candles, décor pillows, and throw blankets throughout. A wraparound leather couch sits in the corner, a large screen television sits in another, and a stone brick fireplace stands between the two. Paintings and family portraits sprinkle the walls. The carpet is plush and so clean you wouldn't even know a dog lived here unless you saw it with your own eyes.

Justin comes down the stairs with a little bounce in his step. He looks at me with a grin and tells me that he put my bag in Lexi's room.

"Thanks," I say, avoiding his eyes.

Present-day Justin still lives at home and never married, let alone dated all that much. He finished school, and then just gave up on accomplishing much else. Now he works a job he's overqualified for and spends his weekends watching TV with Dad. I should try to get him on the right path while I'm here, whatever that is.

"Thanks for taking *my* bag up," Lexi says sarcastically.

"Anytime," Justin responds with a finger gun.

"Where's Mom and Dad?"

"They're in the backyard, doing yardwork."

Lexi walks up the stairs and stops halfway, turning back to me. "Are you coming?"

"Yeah, sorry." I try to shake off my unease and follow behind as we climb the stairs and head down the hall.

Our room is the last one on the left, right across from our parents'. I sneak a peek into the master bedroom: a king-sized bed filled with floral decorative pillows sits in the center of the room, flanked by two end tables, and a long dresser stretches along the wall. The room is so *tidy*.

I walk into our room: a teenager's paradise. The walls are covered in pictures of friends and posters of celebrities: Sarah Michelle Gellar, the cast of "Friends," Britney Spears, NYSNC, and a movie poster from *Legally Blonde*. A turquoise-clad full-size bed with decorative pillows sits along the far wall, a green-and-blue lava lamp on the nearby night-stand. A long wooden dresser, covered in bottles of perfume, a jewelry box, and knickknacks, sits in the corner. And of course, there's the four-foot-tall, jam-packed CD tower and a large 5-disc CD changer with detached speakers beside it. One of those tall fish bubbler lamps (that I haven't seen in years) stands beside the desk that's been turned into a makeshift vanity. It's exactly like I remember it, a hodgepodge of tackiness.

Lexi throws her bag on her bed and takes off her jacket, tossing it on the back of her desk chair. I do the same.

"Okay, let's go introduce you to the rest of the fam," she says with a wink, heading back through the door.

I swallow hard. Should I just tell her? No, I can't. It would ruin her far before it destroyed me. I nod, force a small smile, and reluctantly follow behind.

We walk down the stairs, and as we reach the landing, I hear the sliding glass door from the dining room open. Justin is sitting on the couch watching football, feet propped up on the coffee table, and a bag of Dad's special beef jerky in his lap.

"Oh, honey. I think the kids are here!"

Her voice is unmistakable to me—I'd know it anywhere.

I peek around the wall to look at her, trying to hold the blankest expression on my face, though it feels contorted and strained. I take a deep breath, attempting to relax, and set my eyes on Mom, who removes her gardening gloves and pushes her long ash-blonde hair from her face. She smiles wide, and her blue eyes light up when she sees Lexi. Lexi runs to her, giving her a hug.

"Mom, I missed you."

"I missed you too, sweetheart. How's my big college girl?" Mom rubs Lexi's back and holds her a little tighter before letting go.

"College is great. I love it there. I've made so many new friends." Lexi takes a step back.

"Hey, Mom." Justin gets up from the couch and gives her a hug.

Dad, a burly man with a big beard, walks in, with Bella following behind. He slides the door closed and turns to Lexi and Justin. Dressed in a pair of blue jeans and a flannel shirt, his usual attire, he greets his kids with hugs and pats on the back.

"You behaving, Lexi?" Dad asks.

"Always," Lexi says with a laugh.

"I'll take your word for it." He chuckles.

She turns to me. "Mom, Dad, this is my friend, Alexis. She's a grad student, but we're in the same advanced communications course. She's from California and couldn't make the trip home, so I invited her to join us. I hope that's okay."

I walk toward them, standing a step behind and to the right of Lexi.

"Of course, that's okay. Can't have you spending Thanksgiving alone. Hey there, Alexis." Dad extends his hand for a shake.

"Nice to meet you," I say to him.

"We're so happy you could join us, Alexis," Mom says.

"Beware, I'm a hugger," she adds as she leans in and wraps her arms around me, pulling me in for a warm embrace.

I fall apart in her arms but put myself back together before the hug ends. She steps back, holding onto my shoulders. "We're going to get to know each other really well this weekend."

"I hope so," I say back.

She gives my shoulder a squeeze and says, "Alexis, please make yourself at home. Whatever you'd like, feel free to help yourself."

"I will, Mo—" I catch myself, "Mrs. Spencer."

"Please, call me Alice," she insists.

"Yeah, and call me Jeff," Dad says.

"Okay, Alice and Jeff." I give a slight, awkward smile.

"Lexi, I didn't know you were taking a graduate-level communications course. I'm so proud of you." Mom is practically glowing.

Lexi's cheeks turn red, and I'm not sure if it's because she thinks she's been caught in a lie or she's blushing from them being proud of her. "Yeah, it's because of all the advanced writing and speech courses I took in high school," she quickly adds.

"Good work, kiddo," Dad says, patting her on the shoulder. "You get your brains from your mom." He smiles fondly at his wife.

I feel like a statue as I stand there taking in the scene before me, unable to move or speak, for fear I'll fall apart into a million pieces. My vision blurs slightly; the room feels like it's spinning.

"And your stubbornness from your dad," Mom teases. "All right, guys." She claps her hands together. "We'll have dinner at six and we're playing Scrabble afterwards." She rubs her hands together. "I'm undefeated in this house, Alexis." Mom smiles.

"Excuse me," I say, turning away from them and running back through the living room and up the stairs faster than the tears can run from my eyes. Closing the bathroom door behind me, I turn the faucet on and collapse to the floor, sobbing.

My body aches from holding all this in. Like there's a thousand needles pricking me all over. I pull my knees into my chest, rocking back and forth. I can't make it through this weekend. I just can't.

I hear a scratch at the door, and I open it slightly to find Bella looking at me quizzically. I call her in and pull her close, crying into her body. She rests her head on my shoulder and sits there, patiently absorbing my pain and returning it with comfort.

"I love you, Bella baby," I whisper. She snuggles even closer to me.

A knock on the door prompts Bella to turn her head toward it, but she stays close.

"Alexis? Are you okay?" Lexi asks.

I pull my head up. Bella's back is damp from my tears, so I dry her off as best I can while wiping at my own cheeks.

"Yeah, I'm fine." I force a couple of coughs, trying to pretend I was sick or something.

"Can I come in?"

"Yeah, just a sec." I stand up, splash water into my face, and quickly pat my skin dry with the hand towel. Looking at myself in the mirror, I wipe away the mascara and eyeliner that has built up underneath my eyes, fluff my hair, and pat my cheeks.

Lexi slides in after I unlock the door, which she closes behind her. She greets Bella and pats her on the head.

"What the hell was that?" Her eyes are full of concern and confusion.

"Nothing."

"That wasn't nothing. You ran off when my mom was talking to you, and I find you in the bathroom. And you've clearly been crying."

"It's nothing."

"Is there something you need to tell me? Is there something I should know?" She stares into my eyes, trying to read me.

"It's just . . . I had a big fight with Mom, and I hadn't talked to her or seen her in a long time, so it was a shock to see her, and it reminded me of how silly our fight was and how I've wasted so much time not talking to her, and I just miss her. Sorry."

"Oh. What was the fight about? I can't imagine not talking to Mom. It must have been bad." Lexi looks stunned.

"Honestly, I can't even remember why we were fighting. That's what's so dumb about the whole thing and why I feel so terrible about it."

She tapers her eyes slightly, but then relaxes them. "Well, you'll have the whole weekend to spend with her, and once we get you back to your present time, you two can make up." Lexi pats my shoulder.

I force a smile. "Yeah."

"Get yourself cleaned up. Justin wants to play pool."

"I forgot we used to have a pool table."

"Mom and Dad sold our pool table?" Lexi groans. "Why would they do that?"

"I don't know. Things change, Lexi."

Mom calls Lexi from downstairs.

"Coming, Mom!" she yells back. "You'll tell me more about these changes later, promise?" she asks as she opens the door, letting Bella out, and looks back at me for a response.

I smile again. "Promise."

She closes the door behind her, leaving me standing in front of the mirror. My reflection is there, but I only see through it. I close my eyes and take a deep breath. "Everything happens for a reason," I say.

I breathe deep.

"It will all work out in the end."

I inhale.

"Things go wrong, so you appreciate them when they're right."

I exhale.

"Everything is okay in the end. If it's not okay, then it's not the end."

I reopen my eyes, looking at myself in the mirror again. My reflection stares back. It's my only proof that I'm actually here.

TWENTY-FIVE

TIPTOEING DOWN THE stairs, I hope I can make it to the basement without running into Mom. Before I take the second set of stairs off of the kitchen to the basement, where the pool table is, Mom pops up from behind the counter with a couple of cans of corns in her hand. She gives me a warm smile.

"Hey, Alexis!" she calls out. "Are you feeling better? Lexi said you got a little sick."

"I'm okay, thanks. Just a bit queasy from the car ride," I lie. I can barely look at her.

"Come in here. I'll get you a 7 Up and heat you up some chicken noodle soup."

"Oh, no. It's fine. I don't want to be a bother."

"You're not a bother at all, and I won't take no for an answer. Now get up in one of these chairs." She points to the stools in front of the bar top counter.

I hesitate for a moment, but I know my mom, and I know she truly won't take no for an answer, so I take a seat at the counter and glance around the room, pretending to be interested in the various knickknacks and vases sitting on the windowsill and on top of cupboards—avoiding eye contact.

"Besides, you can keep me company while I prep dinner." She moseys around the kitchen.

"I can help with dinner," I offer instinctively.

I immediately regret my proposal. I can't be around her.

I have to keep my distance. Getting too close will only make things harder.

"Nonsense. You're not feeling well, but I'll take you up on that offer for Thanksgiving lunch tomorrow."

"It's a deal." I look up for a moment and smile at her.

A small silence follows as she stares into my eyes, but she breaks it with some small talk. She's always been good at talking to anyone and everyone. She's the type of person that you immediately feel close to after a short conversation. She just exudes genuine warmth.

"How's school been for you, Alexis?" Mom pulls out a can of soup and a pot. She lights the stove, opens the can, and empties the chicken noodle soup into the pot like she's done for me countless times before.

"It's been going really well, thanks."

"And you're a grad student?" She raises an eyebrow, and her eyes bounce around my face. She's studying me, trying to figure out my age.

"Yeah, I took some time off after undergrad. But it's been great getting to know Lexi. She's like a little sister to me," I lie. "And I help her with studying for our class." I plaster a smile on my face, hoping I sound sincere.

"I'm glad to hear. She's lucky to have you as a friend. Has she been keeping up with her studies?" She pours me a glass of 7 Up.

"Thank you," I say, accepting the glass. "Yeah, Lexi has been keeping up." I take a sip so I won't say anything more than that.

She nods and returns to the stove, stirring the soup with a wooden spoon. "Sometimes I worry about her," she says.

"Oh, really? Why?" I never knew of any concerns she had about me. Obviously she did when I was a child and a teen because every parent does, but beyond that, I guess I didn't know. But then again, parents always worry about their kids, right? Regardless of their age.

"She's kind of a free spirit."

"What do you mean?" Free spirit? Is that a fancy way of saying a screwup? Did Mom think I was a screwup?

"She puts a lot of faith in things just working out, you know, without any of the work or follow-through." Mom grabs a bowl from the cupboard and ladles the soup into it.

She knew my thought process was a problem and she didn't tell me? Why didn't she warn me that things don't just work out? Why didn't she say, "Hey Lexi, do something with your life and stop waiting for things to just happen—that's not how life works"? She should have told me, pushed me—heck, given me a heads-up of how cruel and unforgiving the world can be, on how life isn't fair, on how things just happen and there's really no reason or explanation for them.

She places the bowl and a spoon in front of me, pulling me from my thoughts. The steam rises from the soup, and I breathe it all in.

"Here you are, sweetheart. Do you want some crackers too?"

"No, this is fine. Thanks." I dip the spoon into the bowl, filling it with broth and noodles. I bring it to my mouth, blow gently, and sip it, careful not to burn my tongue.

"I don't know where she gets it from. Her father and I have worked hard all our lives. Nothing was ever handed to us, and we made sure never to spoil Lexi and Justin." She shrugs. "I'll leave the pot on the stove in case you want some more."

"Thank you," I say again, as if I could ever say it enough to her.

"I think I'm just being a worrier. Lexi's a smart girl. She'll find her way, I'm sure."

"Why don't you talk to Lexi about this?" I lift another spoon full of steaming hot broth and slurp it up.

"Lexi isn't the easiest person to talk to when it comes to planning for her future. If I told her what to do, she'd do the opposite anyway. She'll come around one day."

"You should at least try talking to her about it. She might end up surprising you."

"In time. I don't want to push her away by meddling too much. I've never been a meddler. I believe my kids should make their own mistakes. I'll always be there for them, but I won't live their life for them." She grabs a knife from the knife block and an onion from a basket beside the stove. After peeling the onion, she places it on the cutting board and chops it ever so gracefully.

My fingers find their way to my mouth, and I nibble on my nails. Stress. Anxiety. I'm not sure why I do it.

Mom pauses her chopping and glances over at me. "Lexi bites her nails too."

I pull my fingernails from my teeth and fiddle with them. "I've tried to stop," I say.

"Yeah, so has she. Can't seem to break the habit." She returns to her task at hand.

"Hey, Alexis! Are you coming down?" Lexi yells from the basement. I hear her thunder up the stairs.

"Just finishing up," I say. I tip back the bowl and drink the remainder of the broth.

Lexi stands at the top of the steps, tapping her foot impatiently. When I finish, I get up and put the bowl and spoon into their respective spots in the dishwasher.

"I've been trying to get Lexi to learn how to put dishes in the dishwasher for years," Mom says, smirking.

"I know," I mumble.

"Mom, I know how to load the dishwasher," Lexi says, throwing her hands on her hips.

"Could have fooled me." Mom scrapes the onions into a frying pan. They immediately sizzle as soon as they hit the hot oil.

"Mom, stop!" Lexi whines.

Mom waves her hand. "Oh, I'm just playing around, but it is nice to see Alexis knows how to clean up after herself."

"It took me years to learn." I smile.

"Come on, Alexis." Lexi beckons with her hand before disappearing back down the stairs.

I follow Lexi but stop before I go down to the basement.

Looking back at my Mom, I say, "Thanks for the soup and 7 Up."

She smiles and nods. "It's no problem. That's what moms are for."

TWENTY-SIX

I FIND JUSTIN and Lexi chalking the ends of their cue sticks in the basement. The balls are racked and ready to go. The pool table has a red felt finish, oak sides, and legs with gold embellishments. There's a dartboard on one wall, a card table with four chairs in the corner, and a few beanbag chairs along another wall. A popcorn machine, a mini fridge stocked with sodas and water, and a cotton candy machine sit on a buffet table. It was a nice touch that Mom had added a few summers before, and it made it the coolest place to hang out with friends during high school.

"What are we playing?" I ask.

Justin hands me a pre-chalked cue stick and grabs another one off the rack.

Lexi runs her finger across her neck. "Cutthroat."

"Be forewarned, Alexis, Lexi and I are pretty good," Justin says with a smile.

"I bet."

"You're the guest, so you go first." Justin tosses me the cue ball.

After winning the first game and the second game, I'm about ready to retire upstairs when Justin throws fifty dollars on the table.

"Winner takes all," he says, raising an eyebrow and the corner of his lip.

Lexi immediately puts her cue stick away. "I'm out. I'm broke, and I'm going to get changed for dinner."

"That's because you know you'll lose, loser," Justin says with a laugh. "What about you, Alexis?"

"Well, since I won the first two games, I may as well win this one too," I say, letting myself engage in some light trash talk.

"Ha. I play better with money." Justin racks the balls. "Ladies first." He gestures his hand to the table.

"I'll be back," Lexi says, trotting up the stairs.

I lean over the table and break. Two solids go into the corner pockets.

Justin frowns, but quickly turns it into a smile. "Impressive," he comments.

"Thanks. So, what are you going to school for?" I ask, though his life is no mystery to me. But I figure I'll use this time to find out why he doesn't end up doing a whole hell of a lot with his life.

His eyes brighten. "Accounting. I'd love to work as a finance manager someday."

I never knew he wanted to do that. He did get a degree in accounting but ended up working as a bookkeeper for a small business in town. I always said him working there was wasted potential.

"Well, then you should do that." I nod and shoot another solid into a side pocket.

"Thanks, I think I will. What about you, Alexis?"

"What about me?"

Justin leans against his cue stick. "What do you want to do with your life?"

I think for a moment before taking another shot. I hit the cue ball a little too hard, and the solid four ball just bounces all over. "Well, I'd love to do something with writing. Maybe copywriting or social media, and I'd like to actually be an employee of a company, not some contractor." I let out a huff. "I'd also like to get married and have two or three kids. And I'd like a house in the suburbs one day with a yard and a garden. I guess I'd have to learn how to take care of plants and children before all of that." I let out a laugh to extinguish my rambling.

Justin shoots and sinks a stripe. "Then you should do all of that." He smiles. "Sounds just like what I want. I mean the house, kids, marriage, and even a garden." He leans over the table and shoots again, missing this time.

I never knew that either. He never seemed to have any interest in dating. I wonder what changed. Why didn't he settle down with a wife and kids? Why didn't he get himself the house, the yard, the garden?

"You want kids?" I question as I sink two more balls.

"Yeah, I love kids." He grabs two Dr. Peppers from the mini fridge and hands one to me. "It's cool that I can talk to you about this stuff and it doesn't freak you out or anything. Girls my age aren't into talking about the future, or at least the ones I've dated." He opens the can and takes a drink, and I do the same.

"You'll meet someone who's interested in all of that, I'm sure," I say after my sip.

We finish the game less than ten minutes later, when I sink the eight ball, winning those fifty bucks.

"A deal's a deal," he says, slapping the fifty-dollar bill into my hand.

I hold the bill for a moment before extending my hand out. "No, I don't want your money, Justin. I had fun chatting with you," I say, and I mean it.

In all my life, he and I had never really had a conversation. It was just teasing, and then it was just small talk. It's good to know what he wants out of life, and hopefully, I can help my brother get it.

Justin hesitates but then takes the money back. "Thanks, and great—I needed that for new running shoes." He laughs.

We clean up the soda cans, water bottles, and popcorn kernels we spilled earlier on the buffet. I don't think he suspects that I'm his sister, but he's still acting strange toward me. I don't remember Justin even being this chatty with any of the friends I brought home.

"So you must have played before."

"Yeah, my parents had a pool table growing up, so I played a lot with my brother, J—" I catch myself. "Joshua-son." Shit.

Justin doesn't seem to notice the name I clearly made up. He puts the cues away and leans up against the pool table beside me. "That's cool." He glances over and then looks forward, staring at the wall.

He knows. He must. Why is he just standing here with me? The game is over. Doesn't he have things to do? Why does he keep looking at me? Can he see Lexi's face in mine? My face is different, but there's a hint of her still there.

"Yeah, I guess," I say stupidly. I don't know how to act around him. Do I make fun of him like I usually would? Should I be nice, since he's being nice to me?

"You know, it's cool that you came home with Lexi this weekend."

Oh God! He's definitely suspicious. I've never seen him act like this. Maybe I should just tell him. He might believe me. No, it's Justin we're talking about. He would never believe me. He would think Lexi and I were playing a prank on him and he'd tell Mom and Dad for sure. He was such a weasel at this age.

"Why's that?"

"I don't know. You're not like Lexi's other friends. You're different." He shrugs and repositions his weight, adjusting his lean against the table. "And you're different from the girls I know too." Justin looks over at me again with a raised eyebrow.

"Ohhh . . ." I manage to say. Where the hell is Lexi?

My eyes dart all over the place. My face reddens. I start to feel sweaty and clammy. I put my hands behind me on the edge of the pool table to hold myself up. They're so moist, they almost slip off.

He adjusts his hands again, touching mine for a brief second. When he realizes his mistake, he inches it over, leaving a centimeter of space between my hand and his. He glances at me, and our eyes lock for a moment. Before I can look away, he leans into me, his lips almost touching mine. I turn my head quickly.

WHAT IN THE ACTUAL FUCK?

"What the hell are you doing?" I yell.

He steps back as if I had hit him, stuttering, "Um, I don't . . . I—I like you. I thought you liked me. I thought that was obvious . . . ." He runs his hand through his hair.

"You have no idea how wrong that was!" I am absolutely disgusted. My brother tried to kiss me! I'm going to need a lifetime of therapy to deal with this.

I can see it now. The therapist would ask me what happened. I'd hesitate for a moment and then blurt out, "My brother tried to kiss me! His lips weren't centimeters from mine!" She would gasp and then bring in a second therapist, declaring, "I recommend double the therapy for this type of trauma."

"I'm sorry. I thought you were putting out signals or something," Justin says.

Signals? Does he even know what signals *are*? The only signal I was putting out was "I'm related to you."

Lexi bounds down the stairs but stops when she sees us. Standing ten feet away from Justin, with a look of absolute disgust and horror on my face, I'm practically spitting. Justin's cheeks are red, and his eyes dart from me to Lexi to his own feet.

"Uh, what's going on?" she asks.

"Nothing." Justin shrugs like nothing happened, trying to play it cool.

I point at him. "He tried to kiss me."

Justin's eyes bug out, and he stammers to get the words out. "I'm sorry! I thought—I-I don't know what I thought."

Lexi's eyes bounce from me to Justin—and she immediately bursts out laughing. "You tried to kiss Alexis?" she says in between deep fits of laughter.

"Well—"

"You have deep psychological issues, Justin." Tears crawl out of her eyes as her laughter goes silent, it's so deep.

"What? Why? What's wrong with that? Alexis is a beautiful girl. I know she's your friend, but still."

"I can't—I can't breathe—" she says, bending over, almost wheezing.

"Lexi, why is this funny? You don't think I could get a girl like Alexis?" Justin's clearly offended.

I want to crawl into a hole and die right now. Fill the hole in too; I'm done.

"Oh my God. Stop, Justin. It's too much," Lexi pleads, crossing her legs. "I'm going to pee my pants!"

"You're such a jerk," Justin says to Lexi. "What, are you afraid that Alexis won't want to be friends with you anymore if she starts dating me?" He crosses his arms in front of his chest.

Lexi just waddles toward the downstairs bathroom, laughing.

Justin looks at me for a moment and then looks at the ground.

"I'm going to have to go to therapy for this," she yells out as she slams the door.

"Kids, dinner's ready!" Mom calls from the top of the steps.

Justin stays still and looks over at me, a little nonplussed. "Well, I'll see you upstairs, I guess," he says, moving toward the stairs.

"Justin," I say. What am I doing?

I shouldn't say anything else to him. But I'm trying to be nice here, and I'm trying to help him too. He turns back, his eyes lighting up, and he's got a stupid grin on his face. Oh God, he thinks I'm interested. "Yeah?"

I fumble to find the words, and finally come out with, "Listen, you're a great guy, and if you weren't Lexi's brother," (or mine), "maybe we could see where this goes, but I'm Lexi's friend," (and your sister), "so let's just leave it at that." I pause, hoping I'm not leading him on. "But you're going to make some girl incredibly happy someday. And everything we talked about. The house, the job, the kids, the wife—you should *really* go for all of that. Never settle, okay?" *And don't go after your own sister.*

"Yeah, I understand," he says with a short nod. "Thanks, Alexis." He turns back around and runs up the stairs.

Lexi emerges from the bathroom, her face puffy and pink from all the laughing. "Hey, where's your boyfriend?" She pretends to look around the rec room.

I shudder. "Don't put that image in my head."

"That was beyond screwed up." She grins. "Did you let our brother down gently?"

"Please, never speak of this again," I say. I shudder as I walk up the stairs.

TWENTY-SEVEN

WHEN LEXI AND I walk into the dining room, the rest of the family is already seated around the table, which supports a smorgasbord of food: a pot of corn, a basket of homemade rolls, a plate of New York strip steaks cooked medium rare, a huge green salad, and a pan of twice-baked potatoes. Steam rises from the food, and the smell of fresh baked bread, melted butter, and tender meat melds together into one delicious aroma.

"Everything looks wonderful," I say as I sit next to Mom, who's at one head of the table while Dad sits at the other. Lexi takes a seat next to Justin and across from me.

"Thank you, Alexis. Eat up. There's plenty of food, and I have a special dessert in the fridge." Mom spoons corn onto her plate and passes the pot to me.

Justin and Dad each stick a fork in a steak and bring it to their plates. Blood drips from the hunks of meat, leaving a trail on the wood of the table.

"Bring the plate to the steak, not the steak to your plate. You're both making a mess," Mom scowls, wiping it up with a paper towel.

"Sorry, Mom," Justin says, biting into his steak.

"Sorry, Alice, but we're men. We eat like men," Dad says, ripping into his steak.

"No, you eat like animals."

Lexi, Mom, and I finish serving ourselves and begin eating while Justin and Dad reach for seconds.

"Mom, this is great," Justin says, biting into a roll.

"Yeah, thanks, Mom," Lexi says. "It's so much better than school cafeteria food."

Dad smiles at Mom. "It's wonderful." They both have a twinkle in their eye.

"Thank you, Alice," I say, jumping on the gratitude train. "I haven't had a home-cooked meal in years." I so desperately want to call her Mom it hurts.

Mom gives a sympathetic look while she cuts her steak into bite-sized pieces. "Well, that's a shame. But you'll have plenty of home-cooked meals this weekend."

"Justin, how's school?" Dad asks.

"It's good. Classes are good. I finally declared my major earlier this week: accounting," he says, A1 steak sauce coating his lips.

"That's my boy." Dad gives him a pat on the back.

Justin sits up a little taller, a little prouder, and wipes his mouth with a napkin.

"Lexi, how's Oshkosh?" Dad asks.

"It's amazing. They have a huge outdoor mall and tons of restaurants," Lexi says in between bites of food.

"My big city girl," he says, patting her on the shoulder.

Oshkosh is no city, but in comparison to the small town of Delavan, it's a city to them, and it was once one for me.

"Got your eye on any girls, Justin?" Dad gives him a little nudge.

"Jeff, stop," Mom says sternly. "Don't pressure him. He should focus on his studies, not chasing girls."

"Alice, he's a college boy. Of course, he's got girls on his mind. Don't you, son?" Dad nudges Justin again.

"Well, there is one girl." Justin looks in my direction, beaming.

Oh God—not again. I thought this was settled. I let him down gently, and that should have been the end of it. I quickly look away, my face beet-red, but not before Lexi notices. She chokes on her water as she tries to smother her laughter.

Dad pats Lexi on the back as she coughs. "You okay, honey?"

"Yeah, Dad." Lexi splutters, trying to clear her throat.

"What's so funny? Is there something funny about me liking a special girl?" Justin glares at his sister.

Lexi excuses herself and rushes to the bathroom. I let my face drop into my hands. How the hell am I going to deal with this? I'm stuck in 2002. My brother thinks he's in love with me. My parents don't recognize me as their own child, which I guess is for the best, considering I don't think Lexi and I could explain this. But still. Bella immediately knew who I was, and she's a dog. How can parents not know their own child? Maybe on some level they do. Maybe on some subconscious level, Justin knows too and that's why he feels a special connection to me. Actually, I hope that's not the case because that's even more screwed up. He could have some sort of Oedipus complex, but instead of Mom, it's me he's attracted to. That's gross. I hope that's not true either. I glance around the table, skipping over Justin. Mom and Dad both have confused looks on their face.

"What was all that about?" Mom looks at Justin.

He reaches for another potato. "I don't know. Lexi is butting into my love life."

Now I choke a little on a bite of steak—enough for Justin

to notice. From the corner of my eye, I see him smile at me. I raise my glass of water and take a big gulp.

This has got to stop.

Dad leans back in his chair, takes a deep breath, and pats his belly. It's how we know he's full and satisfied. Mom smiles at him, and he smiles back. Twenty-five years together and they have their own language. They can talk to one another and know exactly what the other is thinking without opening their mouths. It's truly special and something I've always wanted for myself. Andrew and I almost had it—or, at least, I thought we did.

My eye catches Justin winking at me. Shit, he's trying to develop the language with me too. I look away, looking around the table at all the leftover food.

"So who's the girl?" Dad asks Justin.

"Does Lexi know her or something?" Mom asks.

"Um, I'd rather not say," he mumbles.

Thank God! He's not telling them he has a crush on me. For all I know, Mom and Dad would probably push for it, thinking I'm a nice girl. Dad would think it's a great idea for Justin and me to go out, especially since I know he worries about Justin never having had a real girlfriend. Mom might say it's not a good idea, since I'm friends with Lexi, and she wouldn't want to see Lexi lose a friend over a failed relationship. In the end, Dad would probably tell Mom to stay out of it and let nature run its course, both of them not realizing that in the case of Justin and me, nature is biological (also sick and illegal in all fifty states).

"Since nothing is official—yet," Justin adds.

Oh shit—Lexi better get back here before I lose it. Of all the things I feared when I learned I was coming home for Thanksgiving, Justin crushing on me never crossed my mind.

Finally, a composed Lexi sits back down at the dining room. Bella follows behind and lies under the table between us. Lexi unfolds her napkin into her lap and picks up her fork, spiking pieces of steak and potatoes with it. "What did I miss?"

"Justin was telling us you've been meddling in his love life," Dad says, pushing his plate away.

Lexi laughs. "What love life?" she asks, her mouth full.

"See? That's what I'm talking about," Justin complains.

Lexi chews obnoxiously, mocking him.

"Now, now, kids. You two are family, so be nice to one another. You don't have to like each other all the time, but at the end of the day, you both should love and care about each other." Mom looks pointedly at Justin and then at Lexi.

"Some of us love each other an illegal amount," Lexi mumbles under her breath.

"What was that, honey?" Mom asks.

"I said, you're right. That's all that counts," she quickly corrects.

Mom nods and looks to Justin.

"Yeah, Mom. You're right," he says.

"Good. Now, who's ready for dessert?" Mom pushes her chair back and disappears into the kitchen. When she comes back, she's holding a glass cake pan filled to the brim with fluffy lemon cheesecake, with a graham cracker buttery crust and graham cracker crumbs sprinkled on top. Mom makes the best homemade cheesecakes. They're so light, so creamy, so fluffy, and so perfect, and they don't last long in this house.

Automatically, I get up to go to the cupboard and pull out a stack of small plates. I grab a serving spatula from a drawer and a handful of forks from the silverware drawer. I place a plate and a fork in front of each person and hand Mom the serving utensil. It's all muscle memory.

"Da—" I catch myself. "Jeff, Justin, would you like a glass of milk?" I ask.

They both look at each other, a bit surprised, and nod. I grab the gallon of milk from the fridge and pour two glasses, bring them to Dad and Justin, and take a seat.

It's then that I notice that Mom hasn't sat down yet—she's standing there, cheesecake pan in her hands, her mouth slightly agape. Lexi, eyes wide, mouths *What the fuck?* at me while Justin and Dad sip at their milk, always oblivious.

And then it hits me: how would I, Alexis, friend of Lexi, who has never been in this house before, know where the plates, the forks, and the glasses are? How would I know that Justin and Dad always have milk with their cheesecake? How would I know not to bother asking Mom, since she's never been a fan of milk?

"Thanks . . . Alexis?" Mom says.

I've got to fix this mess, explain it away, but how? Think. *Think.*

"Oh, it's no problem at all. I've got a photographic memory, so when you were making my chicken noodle soup earlier this evening, I got pretty familiar with where everything was," I say quickly.

I hope that's believable and enough of an explanation. Are they really going to buy that?

"Yeah, that's right," Mom says. She looks like she wants to believe me, but she knows something's up and she can't put her finger on it. Mom and I have a language of our own too, but she doesn't know that *I* know it.

Justin and Dad continue sipping on their milk. Dad was never one to notice things anyway—like when I used to sneak out of the house in high school. He'd walk into my room, say goodnight to my empty bed, and then retire to his room. When I agreed to come back home with Lexi, I was never worried about Dad or really Justin for that matter (well, aside from his creepy crush on me). It was Mom that I worried about. They don't have a clue, but on some deeper level, I feel like Mom knows. I'm not sure she would allow herself to even believe it. Even if she did consider it, she'd probably never say it out loud.

"Serve us up, Mom," Lexi says loudly, trying to dispel the weirdness.

Mom blinks a couple of times and sets the cheesecake down on the table. Everyone holds their plates out as she serves each of us first and then herself. I catch the lemony sweet scent as I take my first bite of the dessert. The citrus mixed with the buttery taste and the crumbly crust unleashes a lifetime of memories in my mind that I didn't realize I still had access to. By the time I finish my piece of cake, I've experienced my highest highs and my lowest lows, all while sitting at a table with my family, enjoying my mother's homemade cheesecake. The mind is a powerful thing, but it's the simplest things that can activate every square inch of it. Lost in my own thoughts, I catch Lexi waving her hand in front of my face.

"Hello? I asked if you wanted another piece," she says impatiently.

I snap out of it. "Yes, please."

Mom scoops another slice of memories onto my plate. "There you are."

"Thanks, Alice. It's so delicious. It's my favorite."

"You're welcome, sweetheart. You know it's Lexi's favorite too," she says.

"I know," I mumble, taking another bite.

TWENTY-EIGHT

"WHO'S READY FOR Scrabble?" Mom places the game in the center of the cleared kitchen table. We're now having wine spritzers, and I'm feeling a little more relaxed. Thank God, my parents' thinking on drinking was a bit old school. They believed once you were eighteen, you made your own decisions just as they had when they were that age. So, Lexi having a glass of wine or a wine spritzer at eighteen with Mom and Dad was fine—which means I get to enjoy it too. The alcohol warms my core, melting the tension in my shoulders away.

When Lexi, Justin, and I cleaned up after dinner, I caught Mom watching me, so I began flinging open random cupboards, pretending like I didn't know where things went. I also asked, "Where does this go?" at least ten times. I definitely overdid it when I asked where the forks went three times in a row.

While I cleaned, Mom asked me a lot of questions about my home life and about my family, so I had to come up with things on the fly. She seemed satisfied—and Justin seemed particularly interested in my answers. I swear to God, if he tries to make a move on me again, I'm going to punch him in the face.

Mom holds out the bag of letters. "Everyone pick a letter. Closest to the letter 'A' goes first."

The game is only for up to four players, but Mom pulled a

Scrabble stand from an older version we have and added it, so everyone could play. Justin had offered to be on my team, but I quickly declined.

Justin picks a "Z." "Dang it," he groans.

Dad picks "N." Lexi picks "K." Mom picks "A."

"Looks like I'm going first," Mom teases.

I reach into the bag and pull out a blank tile.

"Alexis, coming in hot," Justin says with a shit-eating grin on his face.

I drop the tile back into the bag and shudder, avoiding eye contact with him; Mom collects the rest of the tiles and gives them a good shake.

"You're first, Alexis," Mom says, passing the bag to me. "Pick seven tiles."

I reach my hand in and feel each tile, my fingers outlining the grooves to identify the letter. An "S"—I'll take it. I pull it out and put it on my stand. I reach back in, feeling around again.

"Hey!" Mom grabs the bag from me.

"What?"

"You can't feel the tiles before pulling them out. That's cheating." She looks disappointed, and I want to just die.

"I'm sorry, Mo—Alice." How many times have I done that already?

"Here, I'll hold the bag for you." Mom smirks. "You're just like Lexi. I have to hold the bag for her too."

I look to Lexi, who grins. I pull out six more tiles and place them on my stand.

"Sorry, Alexis—I didn't mean to be harsh. We just take Scrabble *very* seriously in this house," Mom says.

"No, we don't," says Dad, motioning to him, Justin, and Lexi. He points to Mom while chuckling. "But she does."

"Oh, Jeff! Don't be a sore loser. You haven't even lost . . . yet." Mom hands Dad the bag of tiles after Lexi picks her seven.

"You know, I'd come up with a clever comeback, but I'll save my energy for the game." Dad places his letters on his tile stand.

"Good idea. You're going to need it, honey." Mom smiles.

Dad passes the bag to Justin and then looks at his tiles with determination, beginning to rearrange them. He doesn't really like Scrabble—English, spelling, and grammar were never his strengths—but he plays it for Mom. She's the creative one with a love for the written word, while my Dad has always loved math and working with his hands. Justin took after Dad, and I took after Mom. Although I didn't discover my love for reading until I met Andrew. I think it was all the boring books they made me read in high school. Mom won every game of Scrabble since I could remember, but I'm the only one who ever came close to beating her. Dad tried, but he never played to win. In his mind, he'd already won, just being able to play at the same table with the woman he loved.

Mom quickly rearranges her tiles. Satisfied, she sits up a little bit taller and takes a sip of her wine spritzer.

"Alexis, you get to go first," she says.

I pick up five tiles and place them horizontally in the center of the board: LOVES.

"One, one, four, one, and one is eight, and a double word score is sixteen. Great job, Alexis." Mom writes down the score.

"That *is* a really good word," Justin smiles.

Lexi makes a gagging sound, and I roll my eyes, though my face is burning.

Mom lays down a "G" in front of my word: GLOVES. "Ten points." She writes down her score.

"Good job, Alice," Dad says.

"Oh, I'm just warming up," Mom rubs her hands together. She gets really into this game—always has.

Justin lays down "E" and "X" underneath the "S." "S-E-X," he says, chuckling, a little embarrassed.

Mom purses her lips together. Dad gives him a high five. Lexi rolls her eyes. I keep my eyes on the board and shudder.

"You know what they say," Lexi says. "If you can't do it, spell it!" Lexi laughs.

"Dad, tell her to stop!"

"What? Just making an observation."

Mom ignores their banter. "Ten, and the double letter score on 'S' is eleven." She writes down Justin's score. "Your turn, Jeff."

Dad places an "O" under the "G." "G. O. Go," he says.

No one says anything. Mom writes down three measly points and looks to Lexi, whose turn is up.

"What, was that a bad play?" Dad asks innocently.

"You're doing fine, Jeff." She reaches across the table and places her hand on Dad's. They exchange a look of love and appreciation for one another. It's pretty amazing how much we can say to the ones we love with just a look. Our bodies say more than our mouths ever could, so much more that if we don't stop and take it in, we miss most of it. I never realized that before. But I'm noticing things that I never really saw the first time around.

Justin's looking at me again. Damn it. Why is he always looking at me? Especially when I'm being profound and realizing shit? *I'm going to need another one of these*, I think, as I chug the remainder of my wine spritzer. Mom notices my empty glass, immediately grabs it, and goes to refill it. Setting the full glass back down on the table, she gives me a look that says, "I know you know me, and I think I know you." Or maybe that's just how I'm interpreting it.

Lexi sets down a couple letters, forming the word "GoGo." "Four and triple letter score is ten," she says with a smile, reaching into the bag to replenish her tiles.

"Good one, Lexi." Mom writes down her score.

"Not as good as mine," Justin chimes in. He finishes his drink and walks into the kitchen for a refill.

"Okay, Dad has three points, Lexi has ten points, Justin has eleven, I have ten, and Alexis is winning, with sixteen points," Mom says.

"Uh-oh, honey. Alexis is going to give you a run for your money," Dad jokes.

"She just might." Mom leans into me a bit and pats me on the back. "But we're just getting started."

I smile at her, and she smiles back. She straightens up, drinking her wine spritzer just as Justin comes back with two bottles of red wine and a liter of 7 Up. Dad gives him a look.

"This way we don't have to get up for refills," he says.

"That was completely unnecessary, son." Dad tops off his drink with a red wine.

"What?" Justin says. "It'll make the game go by faster."

"Ah, good point." Dad chuckles.

A couple of hours and wine bottles later, we finish the game.

Mom tallies up the final score while Lexi and I pack up the game. "All right, the final scores are Dad with 148, Justin with 176, Lexi with 342, me with 471, and Alexis with 475. We have a new winner in the house!" Mom claps. Her eyes light up, as if she's proud of me.

Justin, Dad, and Lexi all give a little clap too. Justin's clap is more enthusiastic than anyone else's.

I can't believe it—I finally beat Mom in Scrabble. That's never happened before. Lexi also looks surprised. I used to read the dictionary in preparation for Scrabble games so I'd have a better chance of beating Mom, but not because I really *wanted* to beat her. I just wanted her to be proud of me. But now, after finally winning, I think she was proud of me all along, and a game of Scrabble wasn't going to change that.

"Looks like we'll have to have a rematch at some point," Dad says.

"We absolutely will." Mom raises her glass. "To Alexis, and to family."

Justin, Dad, Lexi, and I all clink glasses and finish the rest of our spritzers. Justin grabs the empty glasses. "I'm heading to bed," he says after loading them into the dishwasher. "I've got the Turkey Trot in the morning."

"That's right. Are you going with Justin and Lexi, Alexis?" Mom asks.

"Oh, I don't know. I'm not much of a runner."

"I could stay back and walk with you," Justin offers.

Lexi giggles.

I keep my eyes on Mom. "Yeah, I'm definitely not going. I can help with Thanksgiving lunch instead."

"That would be wonderful." Mom smiles. Lexi and Justin disappear upstairs, but I stay downstairs to toss out the empty wine bottles and clear up whatever's left of our evening. Dad heads up to bed with an apple and a bowl of peanuts. It's how he ends every day.

Mom comes back from letting Bella out just as I finish wiping down the table. "Oh, you didn't have to do that," she says while I shake the rag over the garbage and rinse it in the sink, squeezing it out and hanging it up over the faucet.

"I know," I say as I wash my hands. "Thank you for such a great evening."

Mom stands there, regarding me. I can see her mind is racing a million thoughts a second. She knows I'm a stranger in this house, but in her heart, she feels as though she's always known me—doesn't she?

Bella catches my eye and trots over to me.

"Hi, Bella baby." I scratch her ears. Bella wiggles her butt excitedly.

Mom gives me an odd look. "That's what Lexi calls her."

I don't look up at her. "Yeah, I overheard her say it when we got here. I guess it stuck."

"You know," Mom says slowly, "you remind me *a lot* of Lexi."

"That's what our friends say. They think we were separated at birth—well, not at birth, since I'm older." I chuckle. I know I sound nervous.

"Yeah, maybe," she says stoically.

We stand there for a few moments longer. I try to avoid eye contact, fearing if she looks into my eyes, she'll know for sure that I'm her daughter. I'm being paranoid, but they always say the eyes are the windows to the soul. She shakes her head, almost imperceptibly. "All right, well, I'm going to go to bed. Extra blankets and pillows are in the linen closet upstairs if you need them," she says, turning to head upstairs.

"Thanks, Alice," I say.

"'Night, sweetheart," Mom calls back.

"Goodnight, Mom," I whisper.

TWENTY-NINE

THE NEXT MORNING, I wake up alone in Lexi's bed. I feel like I barely slept, thanks to a series of continuous nightmares involving my mother finding out who I really am, then disowning me. But worse than that was the nightmare I had of my wedding day: I'm walking down the aisle in a beautiful gown, escorted by my dad, but when he hands me off and my veil is lifted, I discover Justin is my groom. It was horrifying. I woke up in the middle of the night in a pool of sweat, trembling. Just thinking about it, I gag.

The clock reads 9:00 a.m. The smell of bacon permeates the house, causing me to jump out of bed. At Lexi's vanity, I quickly brush out my hair, wipe the sleep from my eyes, and pat my face. In the bathroom, I splash some water on my face and also brush my teeth with Lexi's toothbrush since I don't have one. Who cares? We're the same person anyway.

A couple of deep breaths, a little pep talk, and I'm on my way downstairs.

In the living room, Dad is sitting in his recliner with a cup of coffee and a plate of bacon and eggs. The Macy's Thanksgiving Parade plays on the television, and he switches between reading the comics section of the newspaper and peering at the screen. I tiptoe into the kitchen to find Mom at the stove, frying up more bacon.

"Good morning," I say.

She jumps a little, turning to me. "Oh, heavens, you scared me. Good morning, Alexis. Bacon and eggs?"

"Yes, please." I nod. "Anything I can help with?"

She looks around the kitchen and shakes her head. "All I need for you to do right now is take a seat and enjoy your breakfast."

"I can do that." I sit down at the bar counter as she sets a plate of scrambled eggs and chewy bacon in front of me. Chewy is best, don't @ me. Although Andrew loves it crispy or burnt, as I like to say.

"Orange juice?"

Before I can answer, Dad says from the living room, "I'll have some orange juice."

Mom shakes her head. "You know when I ask him to do something or help me out with something, he conveniently can't hear me," she whispers to me. "But all of a sudden he can hear my conversation with you in the next room?" A small smile creeps across her face.

"I heard that," Dad says.

"See what I'm talking about?"

"I heard that too."

"Jeff, can you take out the trash?" Mom says loudly. She cups her ear as if listening intently for an answer. A few seconds pass. "See? Nothing." She laughs.

Mom pours two glasses of orange juice, hands me one, and walks into the living room with the other.

"Here's your orange juice, honey," she says to Dad.

"Of course, I'll take out the trash. I'd do anything for you."

I hear them give each other a quick kiss. Mom returns to the kitchen with a smile that spreads from one ear to the other.

I dig into my breakfast, taking sips of orange juice in between bites.

"Let me know if you'd like more, Alexis," Mom says, cracking eggs into a bowl.

"Oh, this is plenty. Thanks for making breakfast."

She nods and smiles while she whisks up the eggs. "Justin and Lexi should be back from the Turkey Trot soon," she says. Mom busies herself around the kitchen, cooking up more breakfast foods and prepping for Thanksgiving lunch. She glances at me several times but doesn't say a word for a while.

Finally, she asks, "Would you like to go Black Friday shopping with Lexi and me later tonight?"

"Yeah." I nod. "I'd like that." I haven't gone Black Friday shopping in years—I actually hate the long lines, the crowds, and the general absence of humanity and courtesy from fellow shoppers. But if it means spending more time with Mom, I'll gladly go.

"Great. Lexi and I have a tradition of getting midnight breakfast at Perkins and then going to some of the good sales afterward. We always end up at Starbucks in the wee hours of the morning. Then we spend Friday watching holiday films, drinking hot cocoa, eating sweets, napping, and decorating for Christmas." Her face lights up with joy as she details their traditions. Well, *our* traditions.

"That sounds really nice," I say, speaking the truth as I poke my eggs around, taking bites here and there.

"It is. Christmas is my favorite holiday. As soon as Thanksgiving is over, I start decorating for it." She dumps the whisked-up eggs and milk into the frying pan. "But I fear Lexi's getting too old for some of our traditions." Mom scrapes the pan with a spatula.

"Oh, I don't think she ever could."

She gives me a strange look.

"I mean, because of the way she talks about it."

Mom half-smiles, surely not knowing what to make of the things I'm saying.

I'm talking too much. I've got to just keep my mouth shut until Sunday. I take my dishes to the sink and rinse them before putting them in the dishwasher.

"That's how I tell you two apart," Mom says.

"What?"

Tell us apart? What does she mean? Does she know we're the same person? Is this her way of questioning it or confirming it? What do I say if she point-blank asks me if I'm Lexi? I can't lie to her. I can't lie to my mom. I feel my face warm—I'm sure it's as red as a tomato right now.

"Last night, when I said you remind me of Lexi. Well, that's how I tell you two apart." She gestures to the dishwasher. "Lexi would never load the dishwasher."

I let out a weak laugh. "Oh, ha. I'm going to go shower and change. Thanks again for such an amazing breakfast." I head upstairs as quickly as I can. I need to get away from her. She's too close to figuring it all out, if she hasn't already.

"There's extra toiletries in the cabinet in the bathroom," Mom yells from the kitchen.

I close the bathroom door behind me and turn on the shower. Okay, she definitely doesn't know because she wouldn't explain where things are because she would know I already knew, right? Unless she's playing along, like I did when I helped put away the dishes last night. If that's the case, then I really am my mother's daughter.

As I step into the shower, the water coats my hair and slides down my body. I have to talk to Lexi. I don't know how much more of this I can take. I shouldn't be here. This isn't my life anymore. I knew this would be hard, but I thought I could detach myself from this reality, like I was playing some sort of game or watching a movie, but I can't. It's all too real.

Who am I, and how did I end up here? I allow the water to tap against the back of my head and cry. I cry for my past. I cry for Lexi. I cry for my Mom. I cry for the girl I was. I cry for the girl I am. I cry for the future. And I cry because there's not a goddamn thing I can do about any of it.

There's a knock at the bathroom door. "Hey, Alexis. It's Justin. I gotta get in the shower quick."

The tears instantly stop. I dry off faster than I ever have in my life and get dressed. Justin *would* walk in on me, thinking it would be some sort of a cute encounter between us and that I'd fall deeply in love with him. After wrapping my hair in a towel, I fling open the door to find him standing there, like he's waiting for me, not for the bathroom. His hair is pushed back, and his cheeks are flushed. I hope from his Turkey Trot and not from blushing.

"Hey," he says.

"Hi." I walk past him into Lexi's room, where Lexi's sitting at her desk. It was supposed to come off as sarcastic and rude, but I think he thinks it's flirty. *Please don't follow me.*

"I got you something." At the door, he hands me a turkey stuffed animal with a Santa Claus hat on it. Oh God—he's trying to be cutesy. "I won it. Second place overall." Justin smiles proudly. My stomach turns.

"Congrats." I close the door and toss the turkey onto the bed.

Lexi turns around in her chair. "Okay, that's hilarious. He must really like you."

"Please, help me make him stop, and please, help me with Mom. She's getting suspicious. I think she knows."

"Mom doesn't know anything, and I'll try to help with Justin. Probably won't be much help, though—I find the whole thing far too entertaining." She gives me a devilish smile.

I pick up the turkey and throw it at Lexi, but she bats it away, giggling like mad.

"You *have* to. It's messing with my head. How does he not have a clue?"

"He's never had a clue."

"*Please.*"

"Fine. I'll try to keep him away from you as much as possible," she says.

"And what about Mom?" I ask.

"Don't worry about Mom." Lexi shakes her head. "She doesn't know anything. You're just being paranoid because you probably feel guilty that you haven't talked to her in months, so you're acting weird and overanalyzing everything. Now, I'm going to shower downstairs because Justin will probably be in the upstairs shower for a while," she says, smirking, "because of you." She laughs as she heads through the door, closing it behind her.

Maybe she's right. Maybe I'm overanalyzing everything. Mom can't know. How could any rational person conclude that their daughter's friend is *their* daughter from the future? I just need to play it cool . . . super cool.

After I get dressed and through some makeup on, I head downstairs, where Dad is still sitting in his recliner chair and Mom's still in the kitchen, now basting a stuffed turkey. Cans of cranberry sauce and corn, a box of mashed potato mix, and a bag of fresh green beans litter the counter. Mom is already humming Christmas songs. I recognize "Up on the House-top" almost immediately and start to sing along to her hums without even realizing it.

She looks over at me. When our eyes meet, I realize I'm singing.

"Sorry," I say.

"Oh, that's all right. I love singing Christmas jingles." Mom beams at me.

"Me too," I smile. "Actually, that's my favorite Christmas song." Dang it. I shouldn't have said that.

"It's Lexi's favorite too." She closes the oven door.

Why couldn't I have said that "Rudolph" or "Frosty the Snowman" were my favorite? I just keep adding to the pile of coincidences. Maybe, on some level, I want her to know. Actually, I *know* I want her to know. But it would make things worse for Lexi.

"Hey Alexis, would you open all those cans for me?" Mom asks, her hands full.

"Absolutely." I pull out a can opener from a nearby drawer and start opening the cans. She watches me.

Dammit—I've done it again. This isn't my house anymore. *I'm not Lexi.* I repeat this to myself. I just have to make it another three days, then I can say my goodbyes and not have to worry so much about being found out.

"Would you like me to slice up the cranberries too?" I ask.

"Yes, that'd be great," Mom says. She starts putting together a green bean casserole as I slice the cylinder-shaped cranberries. "You know this is Lexi's first time home since she went off to college?"

"No, I didn't know that," I lie. I never wanted to go home because I didn't want to miss out on the parties and hanging out with friends at school. I regret that now. I should have come home more often and spent time with Mom and Dad.

"It's so nice to have her and Justin home together." She pauses. "Now that she's an adult and off on her own, I worry that she won't want to come home anymore," she confesses.

"I wouldn't worry about that, Alice. She was so excited to come home."

"Really?" She snaps the ends of a green bean off and looks at me.

I nod.

"I've just always fretted about how my relationship with my kids would change once they became adults. Jeff tells me not to worry about it. He says we'll always be their parents no matter how old they get. But sometimes I fear that she'll stop needing me at some point."

"Trust me, Alice. She'll never stop needing you."

Mom smiles at me and fills a pot, then places it on the stove. "Thank you, Lexi."

I freeze.

Her back is to me at the stove. She's sprinkling salt into the water. She can't see that I'm frozen with fear, with relief, with happiness, with sadness, with every emotion known to man. She called me "Lexi." Does she know?

My hands are shaking so badly, I can't slice the cranberries anymore. I take a couple of deep, silent breaths as sweat trickles down the back of my neck.

She knows. She has to know.

THIRTY

WE PART OUR hands and lift our heads after saying grace. The feast before us is epic. Mom and I spent all day preparing the meal. Justin and Lexi helped on and off, but they both said they were too tired from the Turkey Trot to commit to cooking the Thanksgiving meal, so they instead agreed to clean up afterward. They, along with Dad, spent the afternoon watching football. But for some reason, Justin changed into a nice pair of slacks, a white button-down, and a tie. That's not his usual Thanksgiving attire, and I fear he's going to try to shoot his shot again.

"Honey, this looks incredible," Dad says, carving into the turkey.

"Thank you. But don't just thank me—Alexis did a wonderful job helping me out today." She winks at me. I feel a bit relieved that I'm back to "Alexis" now. But there's a flicker of disappointment mixed in.

"Well, then. Hats off to the chefs," Dad says, tipping an imaginary hat.

"I love a woman who can cook," Justin says, dishing up his plate. Yup, called it. Great, another uncomfortable meal with Creepy McCreeperson.

"Gross!" Lexi shakes her head.

"What's wrong with that?" Justin turns his nose up at Lexi.

"There's nothing wrong with that, son. That's why I fell

in love with your mom." Dad smiles at Mom as he places a turkey slice on her plate. "Well, that and every other single thing about her."

Mom blushes.

"Will you two knock it off? I'm trying to eat over here," Lexi says.

Mom dismisses Lexi's comment as she stands to lean over the table and give Dad a peck on the cheek.

"Can you guys not do that over the food?" Lexi rolls her eyes.

"Without our love, you wouldn't have been born," Dad quips as he serves himself several slices of turkey.

"Don't threaten me with a good time," Lexi says, chuckling.

"So, you got second place, Justin?" Mom changes the subject.

"Yes, I did. I beat my score from last year too. Lexi got third." He tries to ruffle Lexi's hair.

She ducks him. "I wasn't even trying," she says, shoving a forkful of mashed potatoes into her mouth.

"It's not a competition, you two." Mom spreads butter on her roll.

"Actually, Mom, that's exactly what it is. Why else would they hand out awards?" Justin says.

Dad pats Justin on the back. "What did you win?"

"A fifty-dollar gift card to Blockbuster and a stuffed animal, and Lexi won a twenty-five-dollar gift card to Walmart," Justin says, digging into his creamed corn.

"Better use that Blockbuster one quick before they go out of business," I say with a smirk.

"Blockbuster is thriving—it's an American staple. I don't

ever see that changing. Heck, I'd bet money on it." Dad looks at Mom. "We should invest in some stocks. Right, Alice?"

Mom shakes her head. "No business talk at the table."

Dad was never known for his business or finance savvy, and I'm sure that's exactly why Mom shut the conversation down. Whenever Dad gets an idea in his head, it stays there until he's acted on it. Unfortunately, his intuition for the stock market has pretty much always sucked.

"And if Blockbuster went out of business, where would we get our movies from?" Justin asks with a laugh.

"Netflix," I say without thinking.

Justin looks at me, puzzled.

Lexi kicks me under the table and says quickly, "In our communications course, we're looking at sustainability for different business models based on comm theory and conflict resolution. Blockbuster was one of them, so that's why Alexis brought it up."

How the hell did she come up with that?

Dad and Justin just nod as Mom smiles at her, clearly proud that Lexi is retaining information from her classes, although what she just said was completely made up. I'm not even sure it makes sense.

"That's great. I'm proud of you both," Mom says, then changes the subject. "Lexi, are you still interested in doing our Black Friday tradition this year?"

Lexi looks at me, and I nod and smile with my eyes wide, trying to relay that she is and should be excited about it. After listening to Mom's worries earlier, I feel awful for all those times I didn't come home or acted uninterested or refused to do things she wanted to do. I was such a selfish brat.

"Of course, Mom," Lexi says, smiling brightly. Oh, good—she got it.

"That's wonderful. Alexis said she'd love to join as well." Mom beams.

"Great. Can't wait."

I can't tell if she's being sarcastic, but I assume she is.

"I'm really looking forward to it," I say with complete and utter sincerity.

Mom rubs my shoulder with a smile.

"Maybe I'll go this year too, Mom," Justin pipes up.

Oh, no! Vomit creeps up the back of my throat, but I quickly force it back down with a swallow. Not only would I have to deal with the troves of people that left their humanity at home for the day, but I'd also have to spend the whole time shooting down Justin's advances.

"We'd be happy to have you," Mom says.

Noooooooooooooooooo!

"No! Girls only." Lexi glares at her brother.

Whew! Thank you, Lexi.

"That's sexist," Justin taunts Lexi.

"No, it's not, you half-wit. You never wanted to go before, so why now?" She narrows her eyes at him.

"It just sounds like a fun time."

"You don't even like shopping," Lexi challenges.

"Justin, you're more than welcome to come. Isn't that right, Lexi?" Mom looks to her daughter.

"No, it's not right. It's not fair, Mom," Lexi pouts.

"Why isn't it fair?"

"Because Justin only wants to come because he likes Alexis!" Lexi nearly shouts.

I die a little inside. Why is this happening? Mom frowns and glances over at Justin. Lexi folds her arms across her chest.

Dad smiles. "Is that true?" he asks.

"No." Justin's voice is low, and he keeps his head down, too embarrassed to look up.

"Yes, it is," Lexi tattles. "He tried to kiss her last night. He gave her that stupid stuffed animal he won at the Turkey Trot, and Alexis turned him down at least twice, but he won't leave her alone."

Dad and Mom look at each other, then at Justin.

"Okay, it's a little true," Justin admits, shrinking a little smaller into his seat.

Kill me now. Honestly, this would be the perfect time to go back to the future. I've learned enough. I've heard enough. Lexi's as good as she'll ever be. I'll deal with my shitty life if I can just leave this table right now.

"Um, I think it's best that you stay home, Justin." Mom pats his arm.

"You know, son, your mom turned me down at first before we started dating. You just have to keep trying," Dad says, giving Justin a bit of unnecessary encouragement.

"Dad, don't tell him that. It sounds rape-y," Lexi says.

"Don't say 'rape-y' at the table, honey," Mom says.

"Then tell Justin to stop acting rape-y at the table."

Mom stands up suddenly, changing the subject again. "Okay, who wants pie?" Without waiting for an answer, she goes to grab the small plates.

Dad leans into Justin. "You know, I didn't mean go after a girl in a rape-y way."

"Dad, stop! I know," Justin pleads, casting a furtive, if apologetic, look at me.

"I'm just trying to help, son."

"I don't need help with girls."

"Yeah, you do," Lexi says with laugh.

Justin throws his napkin on the table, scoots his chair

back, and stands. "Shut up, Lexi." He turns to me. "Sorry I liked you."

Mom reenters the dining room just as Justin stomps off toward the living room. "Justin, where are you going?"

"To bed, Mom!" he yells from the stairs.

"But it's Thanksgiving," she says sadly. She tries to compose herself as she sits, but she's clearly upset. "Go talk to him, Jeff."

"Oh, he just needs to cool off. It's only 4 o'clock. He's not going to bed."

"Jeffff . . ." Mom groans.

Dad huffs and begins to stand, but I stand up quicker.

"Wait, I'll go talk to him," I say.

"You don't have to do that, Alexis," Mom says.

"It's fine, really." Making my way to the stairs, I look back at the dining room table and catch Mom's eye. She smiles at me and mouths *Thank you.*

Upstairs, I tap gently at Justin's door. "Justin. It's me, Alexis. Can I come in?"

A bit of silence precedes a very unsure "Sure" from him inside.

I open the door to find him lying on his full-size bed, tossing a football up in the air and then catching it over and over again. The blue walls are covered in posters of athletes, like Michael Jordan and Brett Favre, and half-naked girls. His trophies from track and field fill a bookshelf in one corner. Justin stops throwing his ball, sits up in his bed, and looks at me.

"Hey." I take a couple of steps into his room.

"Hey." He sets the football down beside him.

"Are you okay?" I ask.

"Yeah."

"Are you sure?"

"I'm just sick of Lexi busting my chops about girls and Dad worrying about me because I haven't really dated a girl, and I'm sorry I told you I liked you. I shouldn't have." He doesn't look at me.

I sit on his bed, but not too close—I don't want to give him any wrong ideas. "It's fine that you told me that," I say, wondering how I can resolve this once and for all.

Although this whole thing is awkward, I also never realized he was so sensitive, and I didn't know the things I used to say to him bothered him so much. I thought it was typical brother/sister banter.

"Thanks. I know I made it awkward for you, and I'm sorry for that," he says quietly.

"You know, Justin, if what Lexi says to you really bothers you, you should tell her."

"No. She'd just make fun of me and call me a wuss." He flicks his hand, brushing off the idea.

"Just try talking to her and try talking to your dad too. I think you might be surprised. They're your family, and although they may give you shit and tease you, at the end of the day, they love and care for you," I say, looking him in the eye.

"You sound just like my mom."

He's right; I do sound like Mom.

"She's the one I can always talk to about everything," he says.

My heart sinks. I didn't even realize he had no one else to confide in. "You should really open up to others, Justin. It'll help," I say.

He smiles and puts his hand on my knee. I immediately slide his hand off of it.

"Good talk." I pat the top of his head and stand up. "Now, come back down and have some pie with us."

He nods, stands, and follows behind as I lead us back to the dining room.

Mom smiles ear to ear as we sit down at the table. Her family is back together again.

She passes out slices of pumpkin pie, and we all eat and carry on with pleasant conversation for a couple hours. In the end, it's Justin and Dad who clean up all the dishes and food, because Mom declares that the girls must get a nap in before the annual Black Friday shopping extravaganza, as she puts it.

THIRTY-ONE

THE NEXT MORNING, Lexi, Mom, and I slowly wake up, stretching out our arms and legs and yawning as we shake the last bit of sleep from our bodies. We're spread out across the living room in various positions on the couch, loveseat, and recliner. Shopping bags are scattered all over the floor, as are several cups of coffee from Starbucks on the table. Our matching pajamas boast a candy cane pattern. Mom picked them up, along with three Santa hats, at one of the stores as a surprise.

The shopping extravaganza was everything I hoped it would be, culminating into an amazing whole in which the entire evening was spent being with Mom, laughing until it hurt and eating a big midnight breakfast. Even spending time with Lexi was now more of a joy than the chore it once was. She and I were partners in crime for the night, ensuring Mom got everything that was on her list of things to buy and that no one pushed us around or tried to take our items.

Lexi, Mom, and I look around the messy living room and then at each other and instantly start laughing.

"I had a wonderful time with you two," Mom says, still laughing.

"Us too, Mom," Lexi says.

"It's not over yet. We have the whole day of tradition still, right?" I ask.

"We do," Lexi and Mom say in unison.

Dad walks into the living room, wearing his striped pajamas. He surveys the living room and then looks at us all giggling like a bunch of schoolgirls.

"Looks like you three had a good time last night." He smirks.

"We did." Mom gets up off the couch and gives him a hug.

"Good." Dad wraps his arms around her, kissing her softly on the forehead.

"Remember, the living room is off-limits today. We have presents to wrap and a house to decorate." Mom looks over at us. "Right, girls?"

We nod our heads.

"Then I will carry on with my after-Thanksgiving tradition and take Justin out for the day. I'm thinking breakfast, movie, lunch, movie, dinner, movie," Dad jokes.

Justin emerges at the top of the stairs. "Sounds great to me," he yells down.

"Then let's do it!" Dad lets out a little laugh as he walks back up the stairs to his bedroom.

"All right, girls, pick out the movies and get the DVD player set up. I'll make some coffee and start on breakfast," Mom says, walking with a little pep in her step toward the kitchen.

"Did you ever get sick of doing this *every* Thanksgiving?" Lexi asks.

"No," I say. It is true—I never got a chance to get sick of it.

A couple hours later, we're all sitting in the living room helping Mom wrap the presents she got for Justin, Dad, and various friends. *Scrooged* with Bill Murray plays on the television screen as we snack on candy and sweets, continuing the gluttony that is Thanksgiving.

By the time we've finished, it's after six o'clock. The house is so adorned and festive that it looks like the Christmas section of a department store. The artificial tree is smothered with hundreds of lights and ornaments. Garland wraps around nearly everything. Tiny snowmen, Santas, and nutcracker figurines crowd almost every surface. To celebrate our Christmas accomplishments, Mom makes her homemade hot chocolate at the same time Dad and Justin arrive home.

"The place looks incredible," Dad says, taking in all of the new additions.

We all smile, proudly looking around at our creation.

"Mom, we saw *Harry Potter and the Chamber of Secrets, 8 Mile, Die Another Day,* and *I Spy,*" Justin says. His eyes are wide and glossy.

"How in the world could you even keep them all straight?" Mom asks as she ladles hot chocolate into five mugs.

"I didn't. I know there was one I didn't like, but I can't remember which one it was," Justin ponders, tapping his finger on his chin, playing *The Thinker.*

"We just ordered a few pizzas for dinner, so I hope you're both hungry," Mom says.

Dad pats his belly. "You know me. I can always eat."

Justin pats his too. "Me too, Ma."

A little later, we watch *Christmas Vacation,* my mom's favorite, while stuffing our faces with pizza. Everything is great, until I realize I haven't seen this movie since 2003.

That was the year my mom passed away.

After one of the most wonderful days of my adult life, it hits me all at once. Tears fall from my eyes, and I hope the reflection of the television doesn't catch them.

There's something wrong with Mom's heart, and there's nothing we can do to stop it. Her heart is a ticking time bomb, and one day it'll go off suddenly and unexpectedly, ripping her from this earth, this home, and from us. Lexi can't know—it would change the course of our lives, and it would destroy her, more so than it ends up doing. All I can do is say goodbye to her as a stranger, not as her daughter.

On Sunday, I'll have to let her go again. But at least this time I'll know that this goodbye is forever.

THIRTY-TWO

"D O YOU HAVE everything?" Lexi asks as I'm zipping up my duffel bag. Wearing jeans and a sweatshirt, Lexi pulls her long blonde extensions to the side in a low ponytail. She looks the same, but somehow, she's different.

I glance at my reflection in the mirror. I'm also wearing a hoodie and jeans. My blonde hair rests just above my shoulders. I look the same—but different, too. I packed up all the gifts that Mom had given me: the candy cane pajamas, a Starbucks holiday cup, a box of homemade desserts we made together, and a silver snowflake necklace.

Mom picked up the necklaces for all of us during our shopping trip. She said it was to serve as a reminder of our time together and how special it was to her. She included a little handwritten note in each of our boxes. I'm not sure what Lexi's said, and I haven't had the courage to open up mine yet. It'll be the last thing I ever receive from my mother, so I want to wait to read the words she wrote to me, to savor them. For all I know, they may say something as generic as "To Alexis, From Alice." After all, to her, I'm just her daughter's friend—nothing more, nothing less. I'm just a stranger that she had an unexplainable connection with over a holiday weekend that she'll never see again.

"Yeah, I've got everything," I say. I pull the necklace out of the box from my bag, leaving the card tucked away inside, and clasp it around my neck. I look over at Lexi, who also puts on her necklace.

"Look, we're matching." Lexi smiles.

"Yeah, kind of," I respond. "What did your note from Mom say?" My curiosity is getting the best of me.

"Something about me being special and her loving me," Lexi says nonchalantly.

"That's nice."

"Yeah, just typical Mom stuff." She throws her duffel bag over her shoulder.

"Let's go!" Justin yells from downstairs.

"We're coming!" Lexi yells back. Then she looks at me. "Are you going to be okay saying goodbye to Bella?"

I nod, walking behind her. Lexi squeezes my shoulder.

I take a deep breath and glance back once more at my old bedroom. How does one move on? How do the living keep living? One day, my mom was here, and the next, she was gone. How do I live all the other days without her? Maybe I don't have to go back. Maybe I can stay here and spend the next year close to her, soaking in every moment I have left with her. Maybe that's why I'm back: to have more time with Mom.

I swallow and breathe deeply. Trying to keep my composure, I follow Lexi down the hall. She keeps glancing back at me to make sure I'm okay. If only she knew what I was carrying inside of me. She'll carry it too someday.

Lexi walks downstairs as I hesitate a moment, looking down to watch Justin give Mom and Dad a hug before carrying out his bags. He's always been one for quick goodbyes, at least until Mom passed. Now, goodbyes last a lifetime for all of us.

Mom is smiling up at Lexi and me. Lexi gives her a big hug.

"Call me when you get home. Your dad and I are heading down to Chicago tonight for our little mini-anniversary getaway, so I want to make sure you're home and safe before we leave," Mom says.

Lexi nods. "Of course."

"The same goes for Justin. So remind him. You know how he is."

"Yeah, really dumb?"

Mom frowns. "That's not what I said."

Lexi lets out a laugh. "I know. I know."

She lets go of Mom and hugs Dad, telling him she'll see him soon. Bella runs inside from the front door. She gets a pet and a hug from Lexi before bolting up the stairs to me.

"Bye, Bella baby," I whisper into her ear. "Be a good girl." I squeeze her tight. She licks the side of my face. I smile and giggle, scratching her ears and giving her a pat on the head. I catch Lexi glancing up at me. Her eyes are wet. She nods at me, and I nod back.

I walk down the stairs and turn to Dad first, giving him a hug. "Thank you, Jeff, for letting me stay the weekend."

"It was so good meeting you," he says, returning the hug. "Make sure you keep Lexi in line."

I laugh. "I will."

Justin pops his head inside. "Dad, can you take a look at one of my tires?"

Dad nods and follows him outside.

"Here, let me take your bag, Alexis," Lexi says. "I'll put ours in the car."

I hand it to her, and she walks out the front door, leaving me alone with Mom. Bella follows behind Lexi.

I blow out a breath. "Thank you so much for having me, Alice."

"It was my pleasure," she says, leaning in for a hug.

She wraps her arms around me as I wrap mine around her. I breathe in the smell of Jovan musk and Pantene Pro-V, a smell that has lingered at the tip of my nose for all these years but is real in this moment. She holds me so tight, it feels as though my scars have faded away. I sniffle, and she does too, but I'm not sure why—she must be getting a cold. I could stand here in this embrace for a lifetime, making up for all the lost hugs. For all the times I needed her. For all the times I wanted to tell her something. For all the times I dialed home knowing no one was there just so I could hear her voice on the answering machine. For all the times I had to remind myself that she was really gone.

And for this time, for this time that she's here in front of me but doesn't know me. How can a mother not recognize her daughter?

She pulls back, leaving her hands on my shoulders. Mom examines my face, my eyes, my nose, my mouth, my hair. Her eyes are glassy. She takes a deep breath, pushing a few strands of hair from my face and straightening the snowflake necklace. "The necklace looks beautiful on you." She smiles.

"Thank you."

"Did you read the card?"

"Not yet."

Her eyes dim a little. She pulls me in for another hug and tells me that she had a wonderful time. She tells me to come back again soon and that I'm welcome anytime.

A tear rolls down my cheek. Another tear follows.

Mom takes a step back and immediately wipes my tears. "Oh, what's wrong, Lexi?"

She did it again. She called me Lexi.

"I'm just missing my family," I say, rubbing my eyes.

"I know, sweetheart. I know." She slides her hand to my shoulder and then lets it drop to my hand. Mom squeezes it, saying, "It'll all be okay in the end. If it's not, then it's not the end."

"Alexis, are you coming?" Lexi shouts from outside.

"Bye, Alice." I let go of my mother's hands and turn toward the door.

"Bye, Lexi," Mom says. She walks me out to the car and puts her arm behind Dad's back, leaning into him. Bella sits beside Mom.

"Bye, Mom. Bye, Dad. Bye, Bella," Justin and Lexi say in sync while I climb into the back seat.

Our parents wave goodbye.

Before I close the door, Mom yells. "Hey, Alexis!"

I look at her.

"Read the note," she says with a smile.

I smile back. A tear escapes her eye and rolls down her cheek. The same tear rolls down mine. I close the door.

"All right, let's hit the road." Justin puts the car in drive and starts to pull out into the road.

I lunge back, pulling at the bags, unzipping my duffel, and removing the jewelry box to retrieve the note from it. With shaking hands, I unfold it and read: *Lexi, A mother always knows. Love, Mom.*

I pull the note into my chest, holding on for dear life. I look back at Mom. She waves and mouths the words *I love you.*

I mouth back *I love you too.*

Tears stream down my face as she and Dad fade out of

sight. She knows. My mother *knows*. Even believing something as unbelievable as going back in time, she still knows.

She knows me. She knows her daughter, in all forms, at all ages.

THIRTY-THREE

"A RE YOU SURE you're okay?" Lexi asks as she unpacks her bag.

I've been lying on her bed for over an hour, tennis shoes and jacket still on, trapped inside my own mind, wondering what it is I'm doing here. What the hell is the point of all this? Was I sent here to say goodbye to my mother? And if that's the case, why am I still here?

Lexi waves her hand in front of my face. "Earth to Alexis!"

"Yeah," I say, blinking my eyes.

"Are you okay?"

"Yeah."

She stares at me a little longer. "I know that was hard for you."

"You have no idea," I mutter as I sit up, leaning against the wall.

She sits next to me, resting her head on my shoulder. "It's all going to be okay."

"How do you know that?" I push back, looking her in the eyes. Why did this happen to me? So I could experience the loss of my mom again? So I could spend days fighting with Lexi? What the hell was the point?

"Because it always is," she says with a calmness like she absolutely believes the words coming out of her mouth.

"No, it's not, Lexi. It's never okay." I throw my hands up. "Look at us. We've accomplished nothing. We've spent our lives feeling sorry for ourselves, and maybe we have a right to feel sorry for ourselves. We keep saying it's all going to be okay, but it never is. Don't you get that, Lexi? It's never okay!"

I pull my knees into my chest and put my head down on them. Lexi puts her arm on my shoulder, but I shrug it off. I just want to be by myself and that doesn't include the younger version of me.

"It doesn't have to be like this. Isn't that why you're here? So we can change *everything*?"

"Who the hell knows why I'm here?"

"It doesn't matter why you're here. It just matters that you're here. We can change. We can change it all," she says.

I lift my head, growing angry. "Yeah, well, some things you just can't change."

"Well, let's try," she pushes.

"I'm tired of trying. I'm tired of all of this. I'm done." I put my head down again.

"Listen, I know this weekend was tough for you. It was tough for me too. Let's just have a time-out from it all, and we'll start again tomorrow."

"You don't know what tough is."

"Why are you acting like this?" she asks.

"Like what? Like you?"

"You're a child, Alexis. You may be older, but you didn't grow up." Lexi stands to face me.

"And who's fault is that?" I narrow my eyes.

"Yours." She puts her hands on her hips. "Seriously. What is your problem? I bring you home to my family, and this is how you act?"

"You mean *my* family!" I shout.

Lexi shakes her head and starts unpacking her bag again—

this time with much more force. She opens and slams her dresser drawers and aggressively puts her shirts on hangers.

"You just don't get it. I need to go back. I can't live through this again," I say.

"Live through what?" She stops and turns toward me, holding onto a pair of jeans.

"Nothing, Lexi. Just hold up your end of the deal so I can get back."

She doesn't know what I've been through, and I'm not about to tell her. Time will tell her. That's its job, not mine. None of this is about me. This is about her. *She* can start again tomorrow, because I'm done. I'm done with the past. I'm done with the present, and I don't give a shit about the future.

Nikki flings the door open. Wearing bedazzled jeans, a super long skinny scarf, and a pair of Ugg boots, she strolls in and tosses her duffel bag on her bed.

"Hey, girlies," she says cheerfully.

We greet her while I wipe the wetness from my face before she notices.

"How was your weekend?" Nikki sits on her bed, pulling off her boots and leather jacket.

"Great, and yours?" Lexi says.

I don't say anything.

Nikki slides her cell phone from her pocket and presses some buttons, saying, "Fine. Oh, Claire wants to go to Alpha Sigma Sigma's toga party tonight. You two in?" Nikki looks up at us.

"Um, I think I'll skip it tonight." Lexi puts some folded clothes in a dresser drawer.

Nikki looks at her, shocked. "You're joking, right?"

"No, I've got class in the morning and some homework to

catch up on." She pulls out her makeup bag and places it on her dresser.

"Uh, where's Lexi, and what have you done with her?" Nikki asks, laughing.

Lexi waves her off.

"I'll go," I say.

"Oh, wait. Will the real Lexi please stand up?" Nikki points at me.

Lexi turns to me, giving me a *What the hell are you doing?* look.

"Yeah, it'll be fun. I really need to cut loose and blow off some steam," I say with a shrug.

I'm done with all of this. I'm done trying to figure out why I'm here. I'm done trying to get Lexi to be better. I'm done trying to get back to my time. I'm just going to do whatever the hell I want. Drink and party my way back to 2019. Nothing's worked anyway, so at this point, who cares?

"That's the spirit!" Nikki says, clapping her hands together.

"Don't you think we have more important stuff to focus on rather than going out and getting drunk?" Lexi whispers to me.

I look at her, stone-faced. "Nope."

Lexi presses her lips together and narrows her eyes. "Fine. Have it your way." She looks at Nikki. "I'll go too." She's trying to prove a point, but there's no point to prove.

Obviously, there's no point to any of this: trying or not trying, studying or partying, working hard or hardly working. It all ends the same. We all die, and nothing we do can or will ever stop that. I may as well enjoy the ride, because the destination is the same for all of us, regardless of the path we take, the work we do, or the people we become.

It all ends.
It all just fucking ends.

THIRTY-FOUR

CLAIRE, LEXI, KATIE, Nikki, and I make our way up some porch stairs that lead to a large two-story house. The place looks oddly familiar, but I can't be sure. I'm quite tipsy as it is, after several shots of vodka back in the dorms. Lexi quietly judged me, sipping on a Smirnoff Ice while Nikki, Claire, and I took shots. I did two for every one of theirs. Katie sipped a glass of wine—totally on-brand for her. Nikki and Claire accused Lexi of being pregnant for a good half hour before she took a shot of vodka herself.

I don't know why Lexi is trying to be a goody two-shoes now. She's not fooling anyone, especially me.

Loud music coming from inside the house shakes the windows. Hoots and hollers can be heard over the bass.

"Can we leave by eleven?" Katie asks.

"How about midnight?" Nikki negotiates.

"Deal," Katie agrees.

Nikki and Claire's teeth are chattering. Lexi is rubbing her arms to try to stay warm. The four of us are wearing matching bras and panties underneath our skimpy togas, while Katie wears jeans and a T-shirt underneath—clearly more practical, since it's a little below freezing outside. Thanks to the alcohol, I don't feel much of the cold air. I don't feel much of anything.

"Well, what are we waiting for? Let's just go in," Lexi says, heaving open the front door.

We scurry behind her into a crowded living room. In the far corner, a mass of people holding red Solo cups stand around, shooting the shit, while someone pumps the keg and another fills the cups. Three muscular guys wearing togas and sporting frosted tips sit on the couch, chatting and drinking. The music isn't nearly as loud as it sounded outside. "Gimme the Light" by Sean Paul starts up.

Past the living room crowd, everyone in the dining room watches a raucous game of beer pong. The stairs leading to the second floor absolutely crawl with toga-clad students. This place seems so familiar to me, but I doubt I'd know anyone.

"ALEXIS!" booms a deep male voice from the living room.

"Hey, party girl!" another one says.

The guys on the couch point at me, look at each other in near disbelief, and start chanting, "Shots! Shots! Shots! Shots! Shots! Shots! Everybody!" It's President Mark, Frosty, GQ model, and the tribal tattoo guy.

This is where I woke up. This is where I started in 2002.

Lexi gives me a look, wondering how I could possibly know them. I smile as the guys get up and rush me. They pick me up and carry me to a beer bong, chanting "Chug! Chug! Chug!" as the GQ model fills a funnel with a can of beer. Instinctively, I place the tube end in my mouth and take a knee.

The warm beer rushes into my mouth, slipping past my tonsils and settling deep in my gut. Some beer foam spills to the floor when I pull the tube from my mouth. The guys cheer, one yelling, "Three seconds flat!" I'm pulled to a stand, where they all give me a bear hug.

"Hey, Alexis! It's me, Mark—you know, president of

Alpha Sigma Sigma. Remember?" He's wearing a haphazardly wrapped toga.

"Hey, Mark." I feel my cheeks redden. Probably the alcohol. "I remember."

"Good. Let me know if you need anything," he says with a smile. He's obviously drunk. Then he leans down, whispering into my ear, "Come find me later."

I nod and smile back, acknowledging the poor decision I'll most likely make. It's not like things can get any worse, so I may as well enjoy my time.

"All right, I'm next in beer pong!" he yells as he pushes his way into the dining room.

Nikki slams her beer and shimmies onto the impromptu dance floor. Claire yells, "He's so cute!" into my ear as she high-fives me and starts dancing with Nikki. Katie sits on the couch and sips on a beer. The song "Hot in Herre" by Nelly starts up, and Nikki and Claire go wild, belting out the lyrics.

Lexi nudges me. "What the hell was that?"

"What was what?" I grab a cup from a stack and make my way over to the keg.

"How do you know them?" She gestures toward the frat boys.

I fill my cup and chug it, then fill it again.

"From around," I say nonchalantly, glancing around the party.

My eyes catch Mark's as he tosses a ping pong ball into a cup. He smiles at me and tosses his hair back. I wink. Who the hell winks? Apparently, I do. I really don't want to get into this with Lexi tonight. I just want to enjoy myself, but knowing her, she'll never drop it.

"That's bullshit. Tell me how you know them!" Lexi shouts.

I grab her arm and pull her aside into the mudroom. The drywall has yet to be painted, and the flooring is just plywood under the mountain of coats.

I slide the pocket door partially closed and turn toward her. "Listen, the day I appeared in 2002, I woke up here. I have no idea how I got here, but I woke up in a bedroom upstairs. The guys told me I had shown up the night before. They took me in, and we all partied, I guess. None of them knew who I was, and I didn't know who they were. That's all I know." I swig my beer.

Lexi's eyes light up. She grabs me by the shoulders and shakes me, causing me to spill my drink. "That's got to be it. There's something here that will help you get back."

"No, Lexi. There's nothing here, just alcohol, frat guys, and whatever's left of my dignity." My vision starts to blur. My eyelids feel extra heavy, and there's a thick glaze over my eyeballs, making everything just a tad hazy. I kind of like how the world looks this way. I take another drink.

"Why would you show up here? There's got to be something, a reason why you'd wake up here." Lexi rubs her right eyebrow as if she's deep in thought.

"It's all random. There's no reason to any of it. It just is what it is." I take a step toward the door to the living room.

"What's all random?" Lexi grabs my arm to stop me.

"Life. This. You. Me. All of it." I shrug her hand off.

"You're not making any sense!" The vein in the middle of her head tells me she's frustrated. But her cold, long stare tells me she's not giving up, even if I do.

"That's because none of it makes any sense. I've accepted that, and you should too, Lexi. We've tried, and I'm done. It's over." I turn away from her.

"Fucking Christ, Alexis! You're giving up. That's all you ever do," she says.

I walk back into the party, ignoring her. She's trying to get a rise out of me, and I'm not giving it up. She doesn't know me. She doesn't know my life, what I've been through, what I've lost.

In the living room, I grab an open bottle of vodka from the coffee table.

"Heyyyy." Some guy stands from the couch, scolding me.

"Heyyyy, yourself!" Mark yells from the dining room. "Alexis is with me, and she can have whatever she'd like."

"Sorry," the guy says, sitting back down.

I take a long swig. It goes down like water.

Nikki and Claire appear on either side of me.

"Slow down, girl," Katie says from the couch.

I pull the bottle from my lips and smile.

"Ooh, my turn," Nikki says. I hand her the bottle, and she takes a quick pull, making a disgusted face after. Claire does the same.

"This is disgusting." Claire coughs and scrunches up her face.

"It's alcohol. It's supposed to taste as bad as the decisions we make while drinking it." I grab the bottle from Claire, taking another swig. "Wooooooo!" I yell, throwing my hands up.

"Shots! Shots! Shots! Shots! Shots! Everybody!" everyone seems to chant, pumping their fists and jumping up and down. The music gets louder, the bass buzzing the entire room as we all dance.

Claire, Nikki, and I pass the bottle around, taking swigs intermittently, although their pulls are so quick, I don't even think they're drinking any. This is the best I've felt in a long time. Not a care in the world—I'm numb to it all. In this moment, I don't care why I'm here or that I'm even here. I don't care about Andrew or Lexi or anyone. None of it matters. I sway back and forth, letting the music move me and the alcohol guide me. I feel warm. My skin is flush and hot to the touch. I twirl, shake, and shimmy. Claire and Nikki follow along, dancing and passing the bottle round and round. None of it matters.

In this moment, I'm Alexis, and I'm okay. I don't need Andrew to be okay. I don't need Lexi to be okay. I don't need my mom to be okay. I'm Alexis, and I'm okay. I'm Alexis, and I'm free from the burden of reality and life. I can't tell if I'm still spinning or if the room is. Either way, I don't care. I hope it never stops spinning. It's all a beautiful blur.

"Alexis, what the hell are you doing?" Lexi grabs my arm, stopping me mid-spin.

The bottle of vodka slips from my hand, shattering on the hardwood floor.

"Having fun, bitch!" I say, but it comes out all slurry.

"You're making a fool of yourself. Look at you!" She gestures toward my body.

Claire and Nikki take a step back, their eyes wide. I look down—my toga is on the floor and I'm standing there in a black lacy bra with matching panties. If it weren't for the alcohol, I'd probably be embarrassed. But I'm not. I couldn't care less.

Throwing my hands in the air, I yell, "LINGERIE PARTY!"

"That's what I'm talking about!" Mark shouts from the dining room. He jogs into the living room, ripping off his toga, revealing a chiseled chest and a pair of Calvin Klein underwear. He scoops me up, lifting me up and down.

I pump my fist in the air, shouting along to the words to "Lose Yourself" by Eminem.

Seemingly everyone removes their togas, revealing boxers, bras, and underwear. They all cheer and drink more. Nikki and Claire join in too. Katie pulls off hers, revealing a white T-shirt and jeans. Lexi huffs and storms up the stairs. Nikki and Claire call after her, but she ignores them. They keep dancing anyway.

Mark sets me down. His six-foot stature towers over me. He pulls my chin up with his hand, our eyes meeting. My vision is blurred, and he kisses me, sloppily and drunkenly. I kiss him back in the same fashion. My hands scramble all over his body, running along the ridges of his abs, the curves of his shoulders, and the bulges of his biceps. He pulls me close, kissing me hard, breathing me in and out. His hands travel down my lower back, following the curve of my butt. He squeezes both hands and pulls me up into a sitting position, my legs wrapping around his waist. One hand supports my butt while the other explores my body, touching every inch of my back, shoulders, and legs.

Mark pulls away, stealing a quick breath before whispering in my ear, "Do you wanna go upstairs?"

I nod my head, unable to speak. His mouth returns to mine, moving with my lips as he carries me up the stairs. I hear Claire and Nikki ask me what I'm doing. I hear a girl call me a slut. I hear a guy tell Mark he's the man. I even hear Katie roll her eyes.

Mark enters the bedroom, flicks on the lights, and tosses me onto the yellow-tinted bed sheets. While he closes the door, I glance around the room—it's the same room I woke up in.

Mark pounces on me, kissing me all over and telling me

how beautiful I am and how bad he wants me. I push against his shoulders, stopping him to catch my breath.

"Did we sleep together that night that I was here last time?" I ask. It's hard to get the words out.

"No. Why?" He's panting.

"Why didn't we?"

"I don't know. We wanted to, but you were really drunk, and I was really drunk, and you kept going on and on about some guy named Andrew," he explains.

"Oh." I try to remember that night but can't.

"Are you still with him?" He runs his hand along my face, attempting to keep the romance going.

"Who? Andrew?" I ask, still struggling to recall the memories from the night I showed up in this decade. But they're simply not there.

"Yeah." He leans in, kissing my neck.

"No. Uh, yes. Kind of. I don't know . . . it's complicated." I feel confusion creep into my brain.

"I know how that goes." He places his lips on mine. His kisses are sloppy, nothing like Andrew's. Andrew's are smooth, controlled, and passionate.

The door flies open, slamming against the wall and startling us. Lexi, fuming, has her hands on her hips, her eyes full of shame and anger.

"Alexis, let's go!" she yells.

"Who's that?" Mark asks.

"Me," I say at the same time Lexi says, "Her sister."

Mark shifts off of me and stands up on the other side of the bed, looking confused and bewildered.

I sit up slightly, glaring at Lexi. "Get out!" I yell.

She grabs one of my legs and tries pulling me off the bed. I kick and scream as I slide toward her.

"You're coming home with me!" she snaps. "You're not ruining both of our lives!"

Ruining both of our lives? She's the one who ruined mine. What in the hell is she talking about?

She pulls me off the bed, and I hit the floor with a thump. I stand up immediately and charge at Lexi, tackling her into the hall. We thrash, pulling each other's hair, swinging, and blocking.

"Girl fight!" I hear some guy yell.

All eyes are on us as we scream and throw our fists.

Katie charges up the stairs. "Knock it off, you two!" she says firmly. Nikki and Claire appear behind her, and the three of them pull Lexi and me off each other. Nikki holds back Lexi while Katie and Claire pin my arms behind me.

"You're such an embarrassment!" Lexi yells.

"If I am, then you are!" I yell back.

"Yeah, real mature," Lexi says. "You know what? Fuck you, Alexis! Fuck you for showing up here. Fuck you for messing up your own life. Fuck you for blaming me. Fuck you for never taking any responsibility. Just fuck you!"

"Fuck me? Fuck you!" I yell back.

Lexi breaks free and stands up, straightening the bedsheet wrapped around her. When she speaks next, her voice is calm. "You're not going to ruin our life. I'm not going to let you." She narrows her eyes at me.

"You're too late. Our life is already ruined."

"No, we can still fix this." Despite her firm voice, there's a plea in her eyes.

"There's nothing to fix. It's done. You'd be better off putting us both out of our misery by ending your life now," I spit out at her.

Katie gasps.

Nikki's mouth drop opens.

Claire crumples up her face.

Lexi clenches her jaw. "I'm so ashamed you're the person I become."

Katie, Nikki, and Claire look at us and then at each other in complete confusion. None of what we said makes any sense to them, but it makes perfect sense to us. The party has returned to its outrageous decibel level. But the five of us stand at the top of the stairs, staring at one another in total silence.

"Screw it," Lexi says, taking off down the stairs. "I'm going to get that goddamn tattoo you hate so much!" she yells over her shoulder.

"The hell you are!" I take off after her.

"You guys, stop it!" Katie calls out.

I nearly fall down the stairs, holding onto the railing for dear life as I take the stairs two at a time. Lexi runs out the front door. She looks back, taunting me. I grab my sheet from the living room floor and wrap it around me before following her outside. My feet aren't doing what I think my brain is telling them to. There's clearly a disconnect, because I trip and fall down the porch steps, scraping up my knee. It bleeds, but I don't feel anything.

"Are you okay, Alexis?" Katie yells from inside. She's grabbing our purses while Nikki and Claire try to rewrap their toga bedsheets.

I think I nod, but I'm not sure what my body is doing. I get back to my feet and they move forward at a stumble first, then a trot, then a slow jog.

Lexi has half of a block on me, but I feel like I'm gaining on her. It could be my blurred vision playing tricks on me. Like I'm looking at her through the reflection of a side mirror on a car—*objects in mirror may appear closer than they actually are.* I blink repeatedly and open my eyes as wide as possible. It doesn't help. Everything is still distorted.

"Get back here!" I call out.

Lexi looks back at me. "No! You want to blame me for ruining your life? I'm going to ruin it even harder." Her pace quickens.

I try to jog faster. What's faster than a jog? What's that fucking word again? Oh yes, run. I try to run, but my body isn't moving the way my mind tells it to. Lexi looks back at me again. I can't tell if she's taunting me, making sure I'm still behind her, or checking to see if I'm gaining on her.

"Lexi, stop!" I yell, but it comes out gaspy and breathy and slurry. Are those even words?

"No. You know what? I think I'll get a tattoo that says 'Alexis, get your fucking life together' right across my forehead," she yells behind her. "But I'll get it done backward so you can read it in the fucking mirror!"

I think I quicken my pace. A surge of anger flows through me. She would do something that dumb just to get back at me.

"Or maybe the tattoo will say 'I, Alexis, am the problem'!" Lexi calls out.

She looks back over her shoulder, smirking at me while she steps off the curb.

The next thing I hear is the squeal of rubber shedding its outer layers as it scrapes against concrete, going from thirty-five miles per hour down to zero in a matter of seconds. Lexi's body slams against the hood of the vehicle, spinning up into the windshield, shattering it. She goes limp when she rolls off the car onto the pavement.

I scream, but I'm not sure if anything above a gasp comes

out of me. I see Nikki, Claire, and Katie run toward the scene, shrieking.

I arrive to see the horror: the bone sticking outside of the skin, the blood pooling around her on the ground, the scraped arms and face that have peeled so horribly it's as if the wounds have appeared and begun to scab all in the same moment. The world goes silent as the shock hits.

I drop to my knees beside Lexi. Her eyes are closed. She's not moving.

What have I done?

THIRTY-FIVE

KATIE PACES IN the hospital waiting room. I stay seated on the floor, my back against the wall. Nikki half-sits in a chair, her leg bouncing nervously. Claire gets back from the vending machine with an armload of bottled water. She hands one to each of us and then sits next to Nikki. The waiting room is empty, save for us.

"What were you two even fighting about?" Katie gives me an accusatory look. I could tell she was thinking over the entire night.

I don't know what to say. But I don't even have the energy to lie. We don't know about Lexi's condition, other than the fact that she's alive and is now in emergency surgery for her leg. The hospital also tried to get ahold of our parents, who aren't answering their home phone because they're down in Chicago celebrating their wedding anniversary. Without cellphones and not knowing which hotel they're staying at, there's no way to get ahold of them. They were able to get ahold of Justin. He has exams this week but said he'd get things moved around and come down as soon as possible.

"Alexis!" Katie says.

"What?" I blink and glance up at her. The lights are too bright in this room.

"What were you two fighting about? How did this happen?"

"I don't know. Just typical dumb sister stuff." I bring the

water to my lips and chug half of it, staring forward at nothing.

"It doesn't make any sense." Katie tries to block my view with her earnest face. "You two were talking about tattoos and ruining each other's lives and *becoming* one another."

Nikki shakes her head and steadies her bouncing leg. "Katie's right. Now that I think of it, *a lot* of things you two say to each other make no sense."

I can feel Nikki's eyes on me too. Both want answers. But I don't have any. I take another drink of my water.

"Well?" Katie puts her hands on her hips.

"Well, what?" I close my eyes. I think my head lulls to the side for a moment. I really can't do this right now. Everything is foggy, and my body feels weak. I'd leave right now, but I'm pretty sure I'd fall over if I tried to stand up.

"You guys, just drop it. It's not the time to be pointing fingers," Claire says.

Katie stares at me a moment longer, then seems to give up and plops into a chair.

A while later—maybe hours, I'm not sure—I feel a tap on my shoulder.

"Alexis, wake up," Claire says.

I open my eyes to see a doctor in scrubs approaching Katie and Nikki. My eyes go immediately to his face. I've seen the face of a doctor bearing bad news before: a mix of guilt and anger for not being able to save your loved one and sadness for having to be there to convey the message. Claire helps me to my feet.

"I'm Doctor Welch," he's saying as we join the huddle. His face is calm, his eyes kind. "Lexi's out of surgery, and she's okay, but she's sedated. She suffered a concussion, couple of fractured ribs, a broken leg—her tibia, to be exact—and some cuts and bruising. I'd advise you all to go home and get some sleep tonight because you won't be able to see her until tomorrow. But she's going to be okay. She'll have some recovery ahead of her, of course, so she'll need friends like you to help her through it."

"And she's going to be okay?" Katie confirms.

The doctor nods.

"How long will she be in here for?" Nikki asks.

"About a week. Okay, go home and get some sleep," he says, eyeing our togas.

He stops for a moment when he looks at me. "You should see a nurse before you go," he says, gesturing to my legs. I look down at them. My knees look like chewed-up bubble gum, scraped and bloody.

"I will. Thanks, Doctor Welch," I say as he turns and walks away.

We all glance at each other, a look of relief on each of our faces. Now that I know Lexi is okay, I can leave. I've only made things worse since I've been here, and we've tried everything to get me back. Maybe this is my life now.

"You said your parents are out of town until Thursday?" Claire asks.

It takes me a moment to realize she's talking to me. "Yeah," I say, nodding.

"And there's no way to get ahold of them?" Katie looks at me.

"I don't know what hotel they're staying at, so no."

"Okay, then we'll make sure we take care of Lexi until Justin or your parents get here," Nikki says. "I'll bring some of her stuff tomorrow morning."

"Yeah, I'll let her professors know what happened first

thing tomorrow. I can get her set up with one of the tutors from the study center so she doesn't fall behind," Katie says.

They all gather their stuff and start to walk toward the exit.

Claire turns back to me. "Are you coming?"

Nikki and Katie stop too, looking back at me.

"You guys go ahead. I'm going to stay so I can be here when she wakes up tomorrow and get my injuries checked out." This might be my way out of this mess. I can just leave and start fresh somewhere else. None of them will ever see me again.

Katie, Claire, and Nikki look at one another and then to me. Claire walks over to pull me in for a hug. "This isn't your fault," she whispers, patting my back.

I don't say a word.

Because I know it is.

THIRTY-SIX

"HEY, WAKE UP." Someone shakes my shoulder.

I slowly open my eyes. Nikki, in jeans and a sweater, crouches down, holding a tote bag.

I look around, trying to understand where I am. The carpet is thin and scratchy. There are chairs spread out with several people sitting in them. I'm in the waiting room of the hospital. I must have passed out—I can't even skip town right.

Sitting up, I rub my eyes. "What time is it?"

Nikki looks at a clock on the wall. "After ten." She sets the tote bag beside me. "I brought you a change of clothes and some other stuff."

"Thanks, Nikki." I'm still dressed in a fucking bedsheet, so the change of clothing is extra appreciated. Sliding my tongue against the front of my grainy teeth makes me grateful for the toothbrush and toothpaste I see sticking out of the bag. "Are you just getting here?"

"No, I've been here since eight. I didn't see you over in this corner when I walked in. Otherwise, I would have woken you up then."

My eyes focus better now that I've wiped the sleep from them. "Did you see Lexi?"

Nikki helps me stand. "Yeah."

"How is she?"

"She looks a little rough, but she's tough."

I lower my chin. "I should probably go see her."

I can tell she feels bad when she says, "No. She doesn't want to see you."

"What? She can't just not see me."

"I tried to tell her that, but she's adamant. She even told her nurse not to let you into her room." Nikki looks at me sadly.

My shoulders fall. What am I supposed to do now? I mean, I had wavered on leaving, but it looks like Lexi made that decision for me. I don't blame her. But I can't go without saying goodbye. We can't just leave things like this. I'm seeing a bit clearer than I was last night, and my cynicism seems to have evaporated with the alcohol.

"What are you going to do?" Nikki asks.

I look around the waiting room. Some of the patients glance over at me. I'm not surprised at that. I'm sure I look like a mess. Plus, I'm dressed in a dirty bedsheet. Others pay no mind to me, reading old issues of magazines left out on the tables. I consider my options. I won't let Lexi leave it like this. I know she's mad at me, but it's not just my fault. She was the one fighting with me too (I think?). I'm trying to recall all the moments from last night. Some are clear as day, others are blank spots in my brain. She's the one who came into Mark's bedroom and pulled me off the bed. She started it—but I'm going to finish it.

I look at Nikki. "I'm going to stay here until she lets me see her."

She looks confused. "You sure?"

"Positive."

"Okay, I'll let Katie and Claire know. We're trying to take turns while Lexi's here so she has some company. She's got a tutor coming as well, I think tomorrow, if she's up for it. But

I'll see you later. Good luck." Nikki smiles, patting me on the shoulder.

I don't care how long it takes. I'll stay here until she agrees to see me.

THIRTY-SEVEN

IT'S BEEN TWO days already, and my patience is beginning
to wear thin. I've filled my days walking the halls of the
hospital, reading books that the girls brought for me, and
watching television in the waiting room, which is always set
to bad daytime soap operas. I've had enough. I'm going to see
her whether she likes it or not.

I walk down the hall, watching for her nurse to leave her
room. I know she's due for a quick lunch break; I overheard
her tell the receptionist as much fifteen minutes earlier.
When the nurse leaves the room, I know this is my chance.

"Alexis," a voice calls out behind me.

I turn to find a woman with blonde hair on the top and
black hair on the bottom. Instantly, I recognize her. "Veronica."

She closes the distance between us, stopping in front of
me. "Yeah, I haven't seen you in a while. How are you doing?"
Her face is kind, and her words are sincere.

"I've been better." I look down at her hand and notice it's
wrapped in bandages. "What happened?"

Veronica holds up her injury. "Hazard of the job. Shot
glass shattered while I was cleaning it. Hurts like hell."

"Damn, I'm really sorry to hear that. I hope it heals fast." I
slightly tilt my head.

"What are you here for?" she asks.

"My sister was hit by a car," I say. "She's fine," I quickly add.

She gasps. "Wow. I'm so sorry. I hope that's not the person you were trying to make hit rock bottom."

I force a strained laugh.

"Well, I hope she gets better soon," Veronica says with a nod. "It was good running into you." She pats me on the shoulder and winces. "Forgot about my wound for a second there." Veronica chuckles and turns on her foot.

"Hey, Veronica," I say.

"Yeah." She turns back.

"What was that you said about helping people back at Kelly's Bar?" My brow furrows.

"You can't help someone who won't help themselves," she says with a smile and walks off.

I glance up at the large clock on the wall and realize I don't have much time to sneak into Lexi's room before her nurse returns.

At the door, I don't knock—I slowly push it open, peeking my head in. Lexi is sitting up in her bed with a couple of books on her lap. She looks much better than I thought she would. Her hair is combed, and it looks as though she's applied some makeup to cover up her scrapes and bruises. Why does she have makeup on while she's recovering in a hospital? My eyes scan the room—the answer to that question is right next to Lexi.

Sitting beside her with a book in his lap is a young, good-looking man with short brown hair. Even though he's sitting, I know he's over six feet tall. Even though he's wearing a hoodie and jeans, I know his body is slightly muscular. Even though we haven't been introduced, I know he's AJ. And even though we haven't met, I know he's my future, my everything.

He's Andrew James.

I'm in disbelief seeing him, right in front of me, right

where we started, right where my life truly began. It was this day that changed it all for the better. It was this day that he seamlessly entered my life, like he was always there. But wait. No, that's not right. It wasn't this day. Andrew and I met in the spring while we were both out on a run. We didn't meet like this. How is this happening? How is he here?

"Hi," I say sheepishly.

I'm a little thankful he's here, though, because I know she won't scream at me or throw a fit or tell me I have to leave. She'll play it cool, act like everything's fine.

Lexi glances at me. A scowl replaces her blank expression, but she quickly wipes it away. "AJ, this is my older sister, Alexis." Lexi forces herself to be polite.

"Hey." He looks at me, getting up from his chair to reach his hand out to shake mine. "Nice to meet you. I'm AJ, Lexi's tutor."

I shake his hand, and I never want to let it go. I want to tell him how sorry I am, how much I've missed him, how much I love him. But he doesn't know me, and he's just met Lexi, a love story that has just begun. I gaze at him, knowing everything that he and I will become. We are a house burned down before we can call it a home, and that's my fault. I was the one setting all the fires, and he was the one putting them out—until the day the fire got too hot, too powerful, too overwhelming. And although he tried to put it out again, there I was, feeding it. It was always me. I was too busy building walls to notice he was already on my side from the very first day we met—this day.

Lexi is glowing, even though she was hit by a car a few days ago and even though she's enraged with me. She doesn't know it yet, but that glow is from Andrew. And no matter how sad she gets, no matter what life throws at her, no matter how much is taken away from her, that glow is going to be there for as long as he is.

Andrew offers me his seat, but I decline. I watch as they exchange those first glances, first smiles—all those little firsts that come along with first love, first real love. Lexi's eyes flicker. Andrew's eyes light up. Her mouth curves into a smile. His mouth follows suit. They're falling for each other and, God, it's so amazing and terrible to watch. To know I end up destroying this in the end. To know that I fuck it all up. To know that we never had a chance. I can't believe how long he stayed with me, how patient he was with me. He clearly loved me more than I will ever know.

And I can't believe I let him slip away.

But still. How is he here? This isn't how we met. My brain races with thoughts, trying to put it all together. If Lexi broke her leg, there's no way she'd be able to go running in the spring, so she wouldn't/couldn't meet Andrew that way. My being here changed that, and yet, he still enters our life. It's fate. Destiny. Whatever you want to call it. We were meant to be.

I have to pull myself away from those thoughts before I break down and cry. Did I ruin us? Did I change what he had? *Stop. Focus on Lexi.* I have to get Lexi to start talking to me, so when Andrew leaves, she'll keep talking and not just throw me out or call for security.

"What are you two working on?" I ask, making small talk.

"Math," Lexi says.

"Yeah, some advanced algebra. Maybe you two can work on this together after I leave. You know, help her run through a couple of problems." Andrew smiles at Lexi.

"I don't think I'll be much help," I say, chuckling.

"You can't be as bad at math as Lexi is here," he teases affectionately.

"Oh, you have no idea."

"Lexi, I've got to get going to class," Andrew says. "Same time tomorrow?"

"Absolutely." Lexi beams.

She holds out her hand to shake his like it's a deal, but instinctively he leans in for a half hug. I can see it on his face: he's not sure why he did that, he just met her after all, but it just felt right. That hug should have been awkward and out of place, maybe even inappropriate, but oddly, it wasn't. It felt like those are the arms she's supposed to be wrapped in for the rest of her life.

Andrew smiles at Lexi and nods a goodbye at me. He packs up his bag and says bye to us once more before leaving.

I sit in the chair, still warm from Andrew, his residual heat radiating up into my body. The feelings that his presence evokes within me are being met by an actual molecular force. It makes me almost drop to the floor with vertigo as the tidal waves of emotions crash the balance of liquid in my ears.

Lexi's face turns sour as soon as the door closes, scorn and judgment all over it. "How'd you get past my nurse?" she asks accusingly.

"We need to talk."

"We don't *need* to do anything. Look what you did to me!" She motions to her damaged body. I can't see the extent of her injuries; a blanket covers her broken leg, and the hospital gown covers her fractured ribs.

"This wasn't *all* my fault."

She rolls her eyes. "Typical Alexis."

"What's that supposed to mean?" I lean back in the chair, folding my arms in front of my chest—a shield to repel whatever retort comes my way that could possibly bruise my fragile sensibilities.

"It means you never take responsibility for your actions. Nothing is *ever* your fault, Alexis. There's always some magical reason why you aren't to blame," she huffs, grabbing a book from the nightstand and opening it. It's *1984* by George Orwell, and I know Andrew gave it to her, his first gift. Well, second after replacing my Discman. But wait, that didn't happen now. So, it is her first gift from him. She flips the page of her book, ignoring me.

"He seems nice," I say to Lexi, knowing that should get her talking again. I remember the way I felt about Andrew in the beginning. He was all I thought and talked about.

She smiles. "Yeah, about that. I know you want to end up with Andrew and whatnot, but I'm not sure that's going to happen." Lexi resituates herself in her bed.

"What? Why?" I ask, almost in a panic. Does she know that AJ is Andrew? Did I ever tell her he used to go by AJ before he graduated college? Is she going to resist him to prove a point? Is she going to screw this up for me just to enact some twisted sort of revenge? Shit. Shit. Shit. This can't be happening. She can't ruin our relationship.

"Because AJ is perfect, and I couldn't imagine some other guy being any more perfect for me than him. So, I'm sorry to say, but Andrew's out."

I smile inside. Thank God. "I mean, it's your life too, Lexi. I can't tell you what decisions to make, especially once I leave," I say fake-wistfully. "So AJ's coming back tomorrow to tutor you?" I already know the answer, but I have to keep the conversation going.

"Yep. Every day this week." Her cheeks turn red, and she smiles happily.

"You seem to really like him."

"He's sweet. I mean, I only just met him, but sometimes you just know, you know?" She looks over at me.

"Yeah, I know." After a pause, I ask, "Is Justin coming to see you?"

"No, we chatted on the phone for a while last night, which was odd but also kinda nice. Not nice, like you and him nice," she says with a small chuckle. "But I don't think I've ever really had a real conversation with him. I told him not to worry about making the drive, since Mom and Dad will be here tomorrow."

"That's nice," I say because I don't know what else to say.

We sit in silence for a while, and she goes back to reading Andrew's book. My body is tense, expecting her to kick me out at any moment, but she doesn't, and I'm surprised by it. I think I would have kicked her out if the roles were reversed.

Lexi reaches for a button beside her bed and pushes it without taking her eyes off her book. A few minutes later, her nurse walks in with a smile. She glances at me for a moment, a peculiar look on her face. She realizes that I slipped in, but she doesn't say a word about it.

"What can I get for you, Lexi?" she asks.

"Two breakfasts, please."

The nurse takes a quick look around and says, "I'm only supposed to get you one, but I'll sneak you a second one—just this once." She smiles warmly at both of us and leaves the room.

"You still mad at me?" I ask cautiously.

"Not mad. Just disappointed."

I watch her as she reads, not saying another word back.

The nurse enters the room with two trays full of breakfast foods and the quintessential hospital Jell-O, setting them down on the table. "Before you eat, I want to check how the healing is coming along on your leg," she says.

Lexi nods, closes her book, and sets it aside. "Do I still get to keep the leg?"

The nurse flicks her hand and laughs. "You're too much." I move out of the way, accidentally bumping into the table. The glass of orange juice spills all over my jeans.

"Shoot," I say, pressing a handful of napkins to my pants and quickly wiping up the floor.

Lexi points to her bag off to the side of her bed. "There's an extra pair of Soffe shorts in my bag, and what's mine is technically yours." She raises an eyebrow.

"Go ahead and change behind the curtain; I'll clean the rest of this up," the nurse says.

I slip behind the room curtain with shorts in hand and quickly change. Before coming back out, something on my leg catches my eye, something that wasn't there before. A scar two feet in length runs up the front of my lower leg.

I gasp, and my hands shoot to my mouth. Tears stream down my face as realization sets in. Veronica was right. You can't help people who won't help themselves. But I'm the people.

I was wrong. I was wrong about everything.

THIRTY-EIGHT

I SLIDE THE room curtain back open as the nurse pulls up Lexi's blanket, revealing her leg. They look over at me as horror, shock, and shame spread over my face. My eyes scan the wound that's nearly two feet in length, running up the front of her lower leg. Her flesh is pulled closed with thread and staples.

"It's not that bad. Jeez," Lexi says, turning up her nose at me.

"You can look away or leave the room if you're uncomfortable," the nurse says, giving me a sympathetic glance.

Lexi doesn't realize what I'm seeing, what I know. She doesn't notice the new scar that has appeared on my leg, identical to her wound. She sits there nonchalantly while the nurse inspects the injury. "It looks like it's healing nicely." The nurse covers her leg again with a blanket. "I'll be back to check in on you in a little while," she adds as she leaves the room, carrying a handful of orange juice-soaked napkins.

I retake my seat while tears stream down my face. How could I have been so wrong?

"What the hell is wrong with you?" Lexi questions.

"Me," I say, looking at her, like, *really* looking at her.

Lexi shakes her head, confused.

I stand and point to the scar on my leg. She looks at it and then up at me.

Her eyes narrow. "You knew this was going to happen to me, and you didn't warn me?"

I shake my head. "This just appeared. This was never supposed to happen to you. I caused this."

Her eyes relax, but she's clearly still confused. "What does that mean then?"

"It means I'm the one ruining our life."

I run my finger around the new (well, old) thick scar and try to put it all together. It's there in my head, and I think I understand, but I have to make Lexi understand too. I half-sit, half-stand on her bed facing her, looking into her eyes—my eyes.

"It was never about *you*, Lexi. It was about *me*. You were right. It was never about fixing you. It was about fixing me."

She's quiet for a moment, searching my face. "You're telling me if you would have listened to me from the beginning and worked on yourself, we wouldn't have had to do all that dumb shit, like swimming in that diarrhea hot spring?" Lexi raises an eyebrow, and her lip perks up into a slight smirk.

I let out a laugh. "Exactly. *I'm* the one who needs to change."

Lexi puts her hand on mine. "I agree." She smiles.

I smile back.

"But I will say, I do feel changed," she adds.

I don't know if she means it or just said it to make me feel better, but I appreciate it. I place my hand on hers. I can no longer blame her for my present state. She's not the problem—I am. I've spent my whole life not taking responsibility for my actions. And although there were bad things that happened to me that I didn't have control over, like losing my mom, they were my obligation to handle. We can't stop bad things from happening to us, but we can learn how to pick up the pieces, put them back together in a new shape, and carry on.

"I'm so sorry, Lexi," I say, starting to cry. "I'm so sorry I put you through all of this. You are exactly who you are supposed to be at this point in our life. I'm not."

A tear slides down Lexi's cheek.

"You know the favor I never cashed in on? The one I almost died in the gym for?" I chuckle through my tears.

She laughs and nods.

"I know what I want."

Lexi tilts her head, tears streaming down her face. Tears stream down mine.

I smile. "I want you to live your life the way you want to live it."

Lexi sits up in her bed and wiggles slightly toward me. She opens her arms and pulls me in for a warm embrace. I hug her so hard that the pain I've held on to for so long starts to slip away. We cry for the past, the present, and the future. I close my eyes tightly, realizing why this all took me so long to figure out. The hardest things to admit are the things we have to admit to ourselves. I know now that I am the problem, but I also know I am the solution. There's still time for me to change, still time for me to make things better. I hug Lexi a little tighter, but as I hold her, I let go of the pain. I let go of the past. I let go of everything that's ever held me back, including myself.

"I love you, Lexi," I whisper.

Her shoulders shake as she cries with me. "I love you too, Alexis."

THIRTY-NINE

I PULL AWAY from our embrace, my eyes reopen, but the same pair of eyes aren't staring back at me. They're brown, like milk chocolate.

"Is that a yes?" Andrew asks.

"What?"

What happened? Where the hell am I?

I glance around at my surroundings, recognizing the kitchen from my apartment with Andrew in Chicago. He's dressed in a nice suit, looking down at me, smiling. His arms are wrapped around my shoulders as I'm nuzzled into him where I perfectly fit, like he and I are pieces in the same puzzle. He takes a step back. The Tiffany blue box sit opens in his hand, revealing a cushion-cut diamond ring.

"Is that a yes?" he asks, searching my eyes.

My eyes go wide. "What? Yes, yes, yes!" I cry.

He slides the ring onto my finger. It's perfect. Lifting my chin, he kisses me like no one else ever has—passionately. His lips interlock with mine like they were made for one another. His hands run through my hair as mine travel across his shoulders, down his arms, and around his waist. He tells me he loves me in between breaths. I tell him the same. I lay my head on his chest and I breathe, I breathe all of him in. He's everything I've ever lost, safely returned home.

When he pulls away, he's smiling. His eyes fill with joy and love and everything good in this world. He brushes a piece of hair from my face and pulls me into him again. We stand there in silence, holding on to one another.

I'm not sure what exactly happened. I'm not sure if it was all a dream or if it was real. But it doesn't matter either way, I suppose.

Because it was real to me.

"I have dinner reservations for seven, by the way," Andrew says. He kisses me on the forehead.

I smile. "I'll go get changed."

I can't stop looking at my ring. I can't believe it—I'm engaged to Andrew. Standing in front of the vanity mirror, I look the same, but I'm different. I apply some mascara, powder my face, and put on a tinted lip gloss.

My phone vibrates in the back pocket of my jeans. I have a phone again! I pull it out and glance at the notification.

A text from Justin reads, *Michelle and I will be in town next weekend. Are you and Andrew down for dinner?*

Who's Michelle? I don't know a Michelle. I immediately open Facebook, but before I search it, I notice the time on my phone. It's only 4:30 p.m. I pop out into the living room and ask Andrew, "You said dinner's at seven?"

"No, I said it's *for* seven." He looks up at me, confused. "Dinner's at 6:00 p.m."

"For seven . . . people?"

"Yeah. You don't think I'd invite your best friends to celebrate our engagement?" He smirks. "Katie and Jon, Nikki and Tyler, and Claire."

"Oh—yeah. Okay. Of course." I try to contain the shock and excitement on my face. "And Justin texted me. He wants to know if we want to have dinner next weekend with him and Michelle."

"Tell him, of course. I'm really looking forward to their

wedding in Mexico. It'll be nice to get away from the office for a week. Plus, we can see how stressful a destination wedding might be for our own nuptials," Andrew jokes. "Now, hurry and get ready!"

But wait? What about Alexis? Me? My friends all met her, so did Justin, and Andrew. Didn't they ever ask about my older sister? Wonder what happened to her?

"Hey, Andrew."

"Yeah, babe," he says with a grin.

"Did you ever meet my older sister?" I move my lips side to side, hoping this doesn't make him think I've lost my mind.

His face goes blank, and then he cracks a smile. "You're teasing, aren't you? Unless you're counting Michelle as your older sister?" His brow furrows.

I force a giggle. "No, I was just kidding."

"That champagne we had earlier must have gone straight to your head. Hurry and get ready. Can't be late to our own engagement dinner." Andrew beams.

Andrew doesn't remember, so the memory of me in 2002 is just one that Lexi and I share. It's our own special bond.

I nod, walking back to the master bathroom. Oh my God! Everything's different. Lexi must have changed it for us, even though she didn't have to. Or maybe I did. Or we did. Yes, that's it. We did. I changed. She changed. We changed together for the better. It's all different now. But Mom . . .

The ache in my heart is instant, and I know she's not here with me. She's gone. But the pain is different. It's not the anger and resentment I felt before. It's acceptance, a new normal that I've come to acknowledge. It still hurts, but it's a different type of hurt, like I've grieved it, not suppressed it. Like it destroyed me at one point, but I learned to pick up the pieces and put them back together.

What about everyone and everything else? I pull up the Facebook app and type in Nikki's name. I scroll through her pictures. She has a daughter. She's an elementary school teacher, married to a man named Tyler, who's a school principal. My eyes swim with tears as I scroll through her photos. I'm in so many of them, the maid of honor at her wedding, all of us on vacation, her daughter's christening. As I look at each photo, the memories of actually being at those places in time pop into my head, like magic.

I type in Katie's name and read her bio first. ER doctor. No kids. Married to a banker named Jon, who works at the same place as Andrew. They're best friends. We must have set them up. I'm in a lot of her pictures too: a bridesmaid in her wedding, double dinner dates with Andrew and Jon, and vacations. The memories flood my brain, and I try not to let my tears ruin my mascara.

After finding Claire's profile, I see she's still as beautiful as ever. I smile so wide when I see her occupation: therapist and author. The banner at the top of her page is an advertisement for her latest book: *Get A Plan, Not a Man.* Oh, Claire! Forget my makeup—I cry tears of joy for her.

I start to go get ready, but I sit down and go to my own Facebook profile instead. My bio says I'm a copywriter for an advertising firm in Chicago. The memories of my career journey populate my mind instantly, and I know Lexi would have loved that for us.

I take that coveted helfie photo and upload it to the app with the caption, "You have to learn to love yourself before you can truly love anyone else. I love you, Andrew James."

"Almost ready?" Andrew calls out from the living room.

"Yeah, just getting dressed." I grab a navy blue, A-line dress, and a pair of nude heels from the closet. I take off my shirt and jeans, revealing a black bra and matching panties. I still have the breast implants, after all, Lexi wanted those too. But my nose, it's unchanged. Before I slip the dress over my head, I look back at the vanity mirror and notice my lower back—it's free of any ink. The tramp stamp is gone, completely gone! I take a few steps backwards, trying to make sure what I'm seeing is real. I pull and rub at the skin. There's nothing there. I can't help but smile.

Taking one more look at my clean lower back, I let the dress slide down my body. At my dresser, I pick up a bottle of perfume, spritzing a couple of sprays on my neck, chest, and wrist. I set it back down beside a photo frame I don't recognize, with a photo I do. I hold it up. It's the picture of Lexi, Katie, Nikki, and Claire at a party—the one that used to be in the box marked "College" in the second bedroom closet. We're all standing in a row leaning into one another.

I trace the photo with my finger and stop when I get to Lexi. I smile back at her smiling in the photo and silently thank her for everything.

Andrew wraps his arms around my waist and rests his chin on my shoulder. He kisses my neck, and I giggle. I set the photo frame back on the dresser.

"Whatcha doing?" he asks.

I turn to face Andrew, and I kiss him. He keeps his arms wrapped around me, and as our eyes lock, his grin widens.

"Just reminiscing," I say with a smile.

A LETTER FROM
JENEVA ROSE

Dear Reader,
  First and foremost, I want to thank you for reading *The Girl I Was*. With so many incredible books out in the world, I'm so grateful you've chosen mine. You may have read this book because you previously read my debut, *The ~~Perfect~~ Marriage*, which is a twisty thriller and nothing like this. Believe it or not, *The Girl I Was* is the first book I ever wrote. And I thought it would never see the light of day, because it was one I wrote for myself—for a couple of reasons.

To prove that I could actually write a book. I had tried several times before and never made it past the first eighty pages.

To work through my own grief.

This book is a work of fiction (obviously—there's time travel in it, LOL), but there is some truth to it. And that truth is that I too, like Alexis/Lexi's character, lost my mother unexpectedly while away at college my freshman year. I still remember getting that phone call in class . . . the one that split my life into two parts: life with Mom and life without.

When I set out to write this book, I knew I wanted to include that aspect of my life in my main character so I too could work through it. I cried writing the scenes at Thanksgiving, but I cried the hardest when I wrote the ending because I so badly wanted to save Alexis's mother. But I knew this wasn't a book about changing the past. It's a book about learning to deal with the hand we're dealt, regardless of how bad it is. It's a book about learning to love every version of ourselves, also regardless of how bad it is.

If you too have lost a loved one or have regrets in life or find yourself looking back more often than you're looking ahead or even looking around, I hope this book has helped in some way (even if it just provided an afternoon of entertainment).

Thank you so much for reading! If you've enjoyed *The Girl I Was*, I'd be forever grateful if you could take the time to leave a review.

I also love connecting with readers, so feel free to get in touch with me.

Best,
Jeneva Rose

www.jenevarose.com
Facebook: /jenevaroseauthor
Instagram: @jenevaroseauthor
Tiktok: @jenevaroseauthor
Twitter: @jenevarosebooks

ACKNOWLEDGMENTS

Frst, I want to thank my agent Sandy Lu for believing in this book and doing everything possible to help me get it out into the world.

Thank you to my husband, Drew, for your endless support.

Thank you to my first readers. I'm pretty sure most all of you read the very first version of this book, which I apologize for. So, this is less of a thank you and more of an "I'm sorry." Sorry/thank you to Andrea Willetts, James Nerge, Austin Nerge, Caitlin Wahrer, Mary Weider, Stephanie Diedrich, Austin Nerge, Emily Lehman, Hannah Willetts, Bri Becker, Erin Valusek, Kent Willetts, Jessie Mitchell, Cristina Frost, and Megan Smith. If you were an early reader, and I missed including your name, sorry/thank you to you as well.

Special thank you to Kate Pello Mooney for that one night, back in Ithaca, NY. I was so upset about parting ways with my previous agent and all the rejections I had faced. I told you how badly I just wanted to be published. You encouraged me to take a different route, to submit directly to smaller publishers. I took your advice, and less than a week later, I had an offer of publication for *The ~~Perfect~~ Marriage*. It ended up being life-changing. Thank you, Kate, for your friendship and your support.

Thank you to Hannah Strouth for literally going out of your way to provide incredible feedback to me (a complete stranger). It was one of the nicest things anyone has ever done for me in this industry, and I am forever grateful. *The Girl I Was* is a better book because of you.

Thank you to my cover designer, Lesley Worrell, who created an absolutely gorgeous cover.

Thank you to my editors, Parisa Zolfaghari and Jenna Rohrbacher. Just when I thought this book was as good as it was ever going to get, you two made it even better.

Thank you to my mom, who encouraged me to write and pursue my dreams of becoming an author from a very young age. She even had me practice my signature for "all the books I'd sign one day," as she put it. You didn't live long enough to see my dreams come true, but I feel you in every word I write.

Finally, as always, thank you to my readers. I say it all the time, and I mean it every time.

READER'S GUIDE

The Girl I Was

JENEVA ROSE

READER'S GUIDE

*If you were able to go back in time
and speak to a younger version of yourself...*

- What would you say to them?
- Would you get along?
- There are several pop culture references throughout this book; what are you most nostalgic about from your youth?
- If you had the opportunity to change something from your past, would you?
- What changes do you think Lexi made to have such a positive effect on her future?
- How did you feel about Lexi and Alexis? And did your feelings about them change as the story progressed?
- If you could go back in time and meet a younger version of yourself, what age would you pick and why?

READER'S GUIDE

BOOK DISCUSSION ACTIVITY

T AKE THE TIME to reflect on all the previous versions of
yourself and thank them. Even if you're not proud of
what they did or how they handled life at the time, that version of you served a purpose.

Here's mine:

*Thank you to my eighteen-year-old self for trying, for
doing what you could to deal with sudden loss and
nearly unbearable grief.*

Thank you to my nineteen-year-old self for failing.

*Thank you to my twenty-one-year-old self for
deciding to go back to school and finish your degree.*

*Thank you to my twenty-four-year-old self for
breaking down the walls your previous versions had
built up and saying yes to a date with your future
husband, Drew.*

*Thank you to my twenty-six-year-old self for writing
the first draft of this book. It wasn't easy, but
somehow you did it.*

Thank you to my twenty-nine-year-old self for not giving up.

And thank you to my thirty-year-old self for taking the time to learn what makes you happy.

JENEVA ROSE is the bestselling author of the psychological thriller, *The ~~Perfect~~ Marriage*, which has been optioned for film and translated into eight languages. Originally from Wisconsin, she now lives in Chicago with her husband and her stubborn English bulldog. *The Girl I Was* is her first women's fiction novel.

www.jenevarose.com

Tiktok —@jenevaroseauthor

Instagram —@jenevaroseauthor

Facebook —/jenevaroseauthor

Twitter —@jenevarosebooks

Made in the USA
Middletown, DE
22 June 2023

33234168R00175